DIRTY LITTLE MIDLIFE DISASTER

A MOTORCYCLE HOTTIE ROMANTIC COMEDY

LILIAN MONROE

1

TRINA

THERE'S a cat in my living room.

Pressing the heels of my palms to my eyes doesn't make the furry little creature disappear, even when the last remnants of sleep dissipate from my mind, which means... Yep. There's definitely a cat in the living room.

"Why is there a cat in the living room?"

My mother looks up from the newspaper stretched over the dining room table in our temporary open-plan rental home, a cup of coffee held aloft in her hand. Her pixie-cut hair is mostly silver, sticking up in all directions in her particular brand of *just-got-out-of-bed* chic. Purple-rimmed reading glasses are perched on the tip of her nose, giving her owl-like eyes when she meets my gaze. My mother blinks, then tilts her head, brows tugging together. Then, she smiles. "Oh, you mean Mr. Fuzzles?"

Patience, thy name is Trina. "Yes, Mom, Mr. Fuzzles. Why is he in the house?"

"He showed up last night when you were out." She waves a hand, eyes returning to the newspaper. "I'm bringing him to the vet this morning."

I pause, waiting for her to go on. When she doesn't, I clear my throat. "And after the vet? Where are you taking him then?"

Small, soft arms wrap around my waist. "Can we keep him? Please, Mom?" Toby, my nine-year-old, looks up at me with wide, hazel eyes. "He's too skinny. He was meowing so loud at the back door and Nana said we could feed him. So we brought him in and gave him tuna. He ate it *all*. The whole can. And a lot of water too. So we went to the store and got cat food and he ate all of *that* too. Then he wouldn't leave. I think he likes us."

I resist the urge to pinch the bridge of my nose. "You fed him, Toby, so of course he likes you. He's a cat." My hand slides over the silk of my son's hair as he squeezes my waist again, blinking those big, green-brown eyes at me. I can already feel my conviction slipping, so I glance at the cat again.

More of a kitten, really. He's in a laundry basket with an old towel on the bottom, curled up in a teeny tiny ball, little eyes closed as his paws knead a fold in the fabric. Black fur covers most of his body, apart from the tips of his paws and a diamond-shaped patch on his forehead. He really is quite skinny.

Toby leans his head against my arm. "Please, Mom? Me and Katie will take care of him."

"Katie and I," I correct absentmindedly, hand still sifting through Toby's hair. I glance at my mother, who slurps her coffee. My eyes narrow. "Did you tell the kids they could keep the cat?"

"Hmm?" My mother looks up from the paper, as if she has no idea what I'm talking about. As if we haven't been discussing the cat for the past five minutes.

I lower my chin. "Mom."

"Why don't you get some coffee, Katrina? There's a full pot. And tell me about your evening! You didn't get home until nearly midnight. I'm guessing you had fun?"

"It was okay," I say, admitting defeat about the cat. I extricate myself from Toby's hold and head for the coffee machine. I'll lay down the law after I've gotten some caffeine in me, when the last remnants of the three or four drinks I had last night are cleared from my body. I should have known better than to stay out late.

"I noticed you took a cab home," my mother says, eyes still on the newspaper as I take a seat across from her. "I'll need the car to take Mr. Fuzzles to the vet."

"I had a couple of drinks last night," I explain. "Didn't feel safe to drive. I'll go grab the car as soon as I'm dressed."

Mom nods just as my seven-year-old, Katie, comes barreling into the room. She sprints toward me, then skids to a stop on the hardwood floors, hands clasped at her heart. "Can we keep him? *Please*, Mom? Please?" She blinks at me, her eyes greener than Toby's but no less potent. "I'll feed Mr. Fuzzles every day and take him out for walks."

"Cats don't go out for walks, Katie." Toby rolls his eyes. "You'll have to scoop his litter box. That's where he'll pee and poo."

A tiny wrinkle appears in my daughter's nose, but she smooths it out a second later. "I'll scoop his litter box," Katie says solemnly, as if she's vowing to throw herself on a sword, lashes still batting at me. "Please, Mom?"

The last thing I need right now is a new cat. My mother and I just moved to Heart's Cove a few weeks ago, and I'm in the midst of starting my life over after finding out my perfect husband wasn't so perfect after all. A pet just screams more bills and responsibilities.

For a woman with an impending divorce, no job, and a

dire need for a bit of stability, bills and responsibilities are already plentiful. I don't want to add any more.

"Mr. Fuzzles might have an owner already," I say, stalling for time.

"No collar," my mother helpfully cuts in. "But we'll check for a microchip when we take him to the vet."

My phone dings. Shamelessly avoiding my kids' hopeful stares, I glance at the screen and, reading the email notification on it, surprisingly, feel...nothing. It's from my lawyer. Looks like my divorce is no longer impending. Kevin finally signed the papers.

I should feel heartbroken, right? Or at least relieved? I should feel...*something.*

All I feel right now is annoyance about the damn cat. What the hell is *that* about?

I turn my phone over, and Toby drifts closer, glancing at my face every few seconds. He wants to keep the cat. No—he's *desperate* to keep the cat. Katie is practically vibrating next to me, and my mother just flicks through the newspaper without a care in the world, but her head is tilted toward me. She's listening.

Ever since I found out my soon-to-be—wait, no—my *now*-ex-husband had been having an affair, my life has been one long downward spiral. First, my marriage fell apart. Then, the divorce became a scary, life-changing reality. I had to move in with my mother at the tender, young age of forty-two. Finally, my sister Candice's house burned down, so I moved from one family emergency to another. Moving to Heart's Cove was supposed to be a fresh start, but I'm still waiting for it to get easier.

Now I'm here, with no marriage and no home and no job...

And a cat.

Katie jumps from foot to foot, brows arching high over her green-gold eyes. "Mom?"

Look, I don't dislike cats. I just don't need anything else on my plate. I don't like surprises. Not right now. Not after the last surprise was finding out my dear husband had a long-time mistress. What I need right now is stability. Routine. Beautiful, safe *boredom*.

"I'll think about it," I squeeze out through gritted teeth, already regretting the words when they pass my lips.

My daughter squeals and throws her arms around my neck. I barely have enough time to put my cup of coffee down without sloshing it all over myself before Toby appears on the other side of me, cheek pressed against mine as he hugs me close. I'm smothered by my children, and I know no matter what happens, I've already lost. We're keeping the cat.

"I'm getting dressed and picking up the car," I announce when my kids fall away from me and run to the kitten's box at the sound of a tiny mewl.

Before I can say anything about diseases, worms, and stray pets, Toby's reaching into the box and nuzzling the little bundle of black fur under his chin. Katie reaches over with a delicate hand, running one finger down the kitten's body. An adorable purr starts vibrating from the cat.

I glance at my mother, who peers at me above her purple glasses, then shrugs. She folds the newspaper and chucks my cheek. "From the moment that kitten appeared at the back door, we were never going to win this battle. Better to just accept it, Trina."

Sighing, I glance once more at the kids and go back upstairs to get dressed.

.   .   .

THE TAXI DROPS me off outside the Cedar Grove, a small bar nestled on one end of a strip mall next to a pharmacy and a barber shop on the road that connects Heart's Cove to the nearest airport. It's just outside the city limits. Close enough to be convenient, but far enough that I didn't run into anyone I knew last night. Like my sister Candice and her gang of merry besties.

I pay the driver and get out, eyes drifting to the car I left here last night. It's a rusty heap of junk, if I'm honest, but I'm on a tight budget until I can find a job in Heart's Cove. I'll get a payout from the divorce—my ex-husband was a successful artist who got big while we were married—but that money will have to be budgeted carefully. My kids need me to be smart right now, and buying a new vehicle just doesn't seem like a priority. Even if the car looks like it just rolled out of a junkyard.

I glance at the Cedar Grove.

My cheeks heat.

I came here last night hoping to see the handsome, sexy stranger named Mac who promised me a ride on his motorcycle a few weeks ago. I saw a Harley in the parking lot, and —like the desperate, divorced, forty-two-year-old biddy that I am—I couldn't wait to throw myself at him last night.

But Mac wasn't there. The motorcycle in the lot belonged to someone else.

Maybe it was a blessing in disguise. I was just lonely enough last night to do something stupid.

I had a glass of terrible white wine at the bar, until one grouchy old white-haired man in a Harley Davidson tee took pity on me and asked me to a game of pool. He had the remnants of a Scottish accent that'd been smoothed by decades away from home, and he called me doll in a way that was sweet and cheeky all at once.

So, I played pool.

The whole time, Mac's name was on the tip of my tongue. All I had to do was ask about him. Hamish, my old, Harley-loving pool partner, probably could have given me Mac's phone number. Mac did tell me all I had to do was go to the Grove and ask for him. When I found out Hamish owned the Cedar Grove, Mac's name nearly came flying out of my mouth, but I clamped my lips shut until the feeling passed.

I mean, desperate much?

Maybe I was too much of a chicken to say his name out loud, or maybe I was just having too much fun playing pool with an old Scottish biker-dude with a fondness for pet names, but I decided I didn't need to meet Mac again. I didn't need to meet *any* men. All I wanted was to have an evening away from it all. Away from the mess that is my life.

By the end of the first game (which I lost quite spectacularly, by the way) I switched to gin and tonic. When I ordered my fourth drink, I knew I'd be coming back to pick up my car in the morning.

And here I am.

The Cedar Grove is dark, with the big timber doors closed tight. It's barely eight o'clock in the morning, and I doubt it's open. Not that I'd be going in for a tipple at this hour. Shaking my head, I walk to my car. Last night was fun, but I'm not going to make a habit of it. I have kids to take care of. A mother who needs me.

And a kitten, apparently.

Unlocking the car doors with my fob, I frown when I close the distance with the final few steps. A long sigh slips through my lips as I tip my head toward the sky. Wonderful. Just—just *wonderful*.

The front tire on the driver's side is flat. I bend over and—

7

don't ask me why—I poke it, then straighten up again and reach for my phone. I can't drive on that thing.

Looks like my mother's vet visit will have to wait, and my children will be possibly infected with whatever worms and parasites Mr. Fuzzles has for another few hours.

"Everything all right?" a familiar, broad-accented voice calls out. Hamish exits the barber shop next to the Grove, his grey beard looking neat and trimmed as he strides toward me. He's wearing dark jeans, a leather vest over a ratty old black tee, and motorcycle boots. He looks cool, in a friendly-old-biker kind of way.

"Flat tire," I call out, pointing to the offending wheel. "Must have run over a nail or something." Or the wheels on this piece of trash car just decided they were ready to be retired. Or the universe decided I needed another problem on my plate.

Hey, congrats on your divorce! Here's another bill.

"I'll call my son. He'll be right over with a jack." Hamish already has his phone in his hand.

"That's okay, Hamish, I have insurance. I can call them and get a tow truck, or something."

Hamish just waves me away and speaks into his phone. "Son. Pretty lady here with a flat tire. Mm-hmm. At the Grove. Good." He hangs up and looks at me. "He'll be here in five minutes."

"Really, that's not necessary, Hamish, I—"

"We'll change your tire in no time. You got a spare?"

"Um..." I bite my lip and glance at the trunk. "Maybe?"

Hamish harrumphs. "Firstly we need to get you a spare, then maybe a more reliable car in general. Then we need to give you lessons on how to play pool."

A surprised laugh falls from my lips. "I wasn't that bad!"

He just levels me with a stare, which makes me laugh harder.

"I wasn't! I was keeping up with you. I nearly won that third game."

"Doll, I was lettin' you win that one. Then you went ahead and blew it anyway by potting the black." He hooks his thumbs into his jeans and jerks his chin to the trunk. "Unlock that, will you?"

I click it open as Hamish leans over it, pulling on a little tag I'd never even noticed at the bottom of the trunk. We both peer down at an empty space where a spare tire should be. I bite my lip. Hamish huffs.

"I should just call a tow truck, Hamish, really."

This time, Hamish just completely ignores me and glances at the road, presumably the direction from which his son will be arriving.

Sighing, I pull out my phone and call my mother. "Yeah, Mom? My car has a flat."

"Oh no! How did that happen?" A cute little meow sounds over the phone, and I wonder if she, too, is in love with Mr. Fuzzles and just used my children to convince me to keep him. I wouldn't put it past her.

"I'm not sure how it happened, but I'll be gone a little while before I can get it fixed. Can you ask Candice to take you to the vet?" The sound of an engine draws my attention to the road, where a massive pickup truck is turning into the lot. "I have to go."

"All right, honey. Call me if you need anything. *Who's a cute little kitty—*" She clicks off just as the truck pulls into a nearby parking space, and my stomach falls right down to splatter at my feet.

Because Hamish's son, the man who's come to save me from this flat tire?

Yeah. He's sexy, smoldering Mac, and he's looking at me like he wants to eat me right up.

2

TRINA

"We meet again." Mac flashes me a million-dollar smile as he shuts the door with his hip, his eyes on me as he heads for the truck bed.

"Hi, Mac." I mentally high-five myself for managing to speak. That's how low the bar is right now.

My mouth waters as I watch him move. His dark-chocolate hair is still mussed with sleep, but in a sexy, grown-man sort of way. He still has that two-day stubble lining his jaw, dark brown interspersed with silver.

His eyes are pale brown, almost gold, and they sparkle at my words. "And you remembered my name too." The corner of his lush lips tips up. "Here I was thinking you'd forgotten all about me."

"You've met Trina?" Hamish asks.

"Briefly." Mac's eyes crinkle at the corners, his eyes alight with a brighter smile than the tilt of his lips...and I start blushing. Hard. Oh no.

"She never told me her name, though." He angles his head as the sun catches on the masculine planes of his face.

"Trina." His lips shape my name, tasting it, and something warm glides down my center, settling low between my thighs.

This is bad. Very, *very* bad.

I glance away, gluing my eyes to the flat tire on my car. "Thanks for coming to my rescue. You really didn't have to."

"He most certainly *did* have to," Hamish cuts in, grabbing a jack from the truck bed as Mac hauls a spare tire out.

Mac grins at his father. "Dad says jump; I say how high."

I give them a faltering smile, hoping I don't look as out of sorts as I feel.

Then begins a show that I didn't think I'd get to see at eight o'clock on a Thursday morning. The two men set up the jack and start lifting the car, and my eyes seem to want to linger on the way Mac moves. His tee clings to his broad shoulders as he cranks the jack. A little strip of skin along his lower back is exposed when he leans over. His hair, dark brown and tousled, glints red and gold in the morning sun.

And his hands—oh, his hands. I have to look away after a while because watching those hands work feels positively indecent. The long, dexterous fingers. The hard, masculine tendons. The deft movements. The muscles along his forearms clenching and releasing as he works. With one last look at his bulging biceps, I tear my gaze away and study a crack in the pavement.

It takes a few long moments for my pulse to slow.

They're just *hands*, for crying out loud. Why does my body feel hot and flushed at the sight of them?

I should buy a new vibrator. Sort myself out before this gets out of hand—*Gah! Stop thinking about hands!*

When a machine starts whirring and the men remove the lug nuts from my tire, I work up the courage to look again. My heart stutters at the sight of Mac's strong thighs spread wide, the spare tire held in front of him as he fits it into the wheel well with a grunt.

I'm not a pervert. I swear, I'm not. There's just something about the way this man moves that makes my blood turn to honey.

Pulling a rag out of the back of his truck, Mac wipes his hands and lifts those amber eyes to mine. "All done. Should get you to the mechanic in one piece." His eyes crinkle at the corners as his lips tip up again, a deep crease bracketing one side of his mouth. I want to trace that crease with my tongue.

Blinking, I try to clear the image from my mind. What the hell is wrong with me?

"Thank you," I manage to respond. "I'll look up the nearest mechanic." I reach into my purse for my phone, but Mac makes a noise to get my attention.

"It's Remy's place. I'll go with you. My bike is there." Mac chucks the rag into the cab of the truck and nods to his father. "See you tonight?"

Hamish waves a hand as he turns and walks toward the Grove.

"Thank you!" I call out after him.

Hamish pauses and turns, then points a finger at me. "I was serious about those pool lessons, girl. You were a disgrace." Then he turns back around and marches toward the bar.

I grin, turn, then trip over my own feet, because Mac isn't in his truck—he's standing with one foot against the passenger side door of my own car. When I swallow, my throat is thick. "You... You're riding with me?"

Is it just me, or did Mac's eyes heat when I said that? He arches a brow and leans a hand against the roof of the car, stretching his long body to its full height. "That okay?"

"I— Yeah, of course. You... I don't— Yeah. Uh-huh."

Ohmigod. Stop. Talking.

Mac's eyes glimmer. "You sure?"

This time, I just clamp my mouth shut and nod. Then I make my way to the driver's side and get in.

Mac folds his long body and slides in next to me, and the air in the car turns stifling. He's just so...*big.* The top of his messy hair brushes the roof of the car. His thick, tree-trunk legs are spread wide, knees touching the edge of the glove box before he pushes the seat back and gives himself a couple inches of room. I watch those hands work to pull the seatbelt across his body, and I have to close my eyes for a moment just to compose myself.

There's something wrong with me.

There has to be.

Why else would the sight of someone's hands send me off the deep end?

Mac gives me directions after I turn the key in the ignition, and I do my best to keep my eyes on the road. My attention is on him, though. On the way he leans an elbow against the door, cupping his face between his thumb and forefinger. How he slouches down just a bit and his shirt rides up at the side. How the fingers of his other hand drum over his thigh to a rhythm only he can hear.

All this I see with my peripheral vision and a few brief, stolen glances. If I look directly at him, I might spontaneously combust.

Maybe if I turn the radio on, it'll give me something else to listen to. "You can choose the station," I tell Mac after I turn the volume knob to an appropriate level. "I usually just leave it on classic rock."

"A woman after my own heart," Mac says in that deep, sensual voice of his, and my panties grow damp.

Not knowing what else to do, I start chanting a mantra in my head: *Get a grip, Trina. Get a grip, Trina. Get a grip, Trina.*

I squeeze the steering wheel tighter. This is getting out of control.

He's just a man in black jeans and a tight tee. He's got a deep, smooth voice and a body I'd like to lick, and so what? I just separated from my husband six months ago! I am officially divorced as of *this morning.* I have children. I have responsibilities which now include a cat. The last thing I need is some romance with a badass motorcycle man who looks good when he's changing a tire.

"Pull in here. I can see Remy through the garage doors." Mac points to the mechanic in front of us and directs me to a parking space off to the side.

Is it wrong that I'm enjoying him telling me what to do?

My brain seems to have remained in the box with our new kitten this morning, and everything between my ears is scrambled mush. I park the car, thankfully without crashing and embarrassing myself, then let out a long breath.

"You okay?" Mac has one hand on the door, but his eyes are on me. "It's just a flat tire, Trina. Remy is a good friend of mine. He'll give you a discount." He tilts his head, gaze intent. "I'll ask him to service the car and make sure there's nothing else the matter with it. Everything will be okay."

Gah. He's being sweet. I don't know if I can handle Sweet Mac. Sexy Mac is nearly too much for me, but I can put him in a box reserved for sex and lock him away, because I do not have sex with strange men.

Repeat after me: *Katrina Viceroy does not have sex with strange men.*

Period.

End of story.

15

For him to look at me with soft eyes and tell me he'll take care of me? Nope. Too much.

I'm supposed to be focused on my children, my mother, and myself (and the cat). I'm supposed to be calling my lawyer and making sure everything is squared away. I'm supposed to be preparing for Kevin's visit in two weeks. I'm supposed to be doing anything but sitting in a car with a man who makes me want to strip naked and get in the back seat of this old beater.

Not to mention the reason I look so frazzled isn't the damn flat tire, it's the mountain of muscle and male sex sitting to my right. But can I tell *him* that?

Ha. Exactly.

I try to give him a reassuring smile, but my lips freeze when Mac moves his hand toward me. His touch is feather-light, barely brushing my skin as he tucks a strand of hair behind my ear. His finger runs along my temple, smoothing down the shell of my ear in a slow, deliberate movement.

I feel that touch somewhere much, much lower.

When I swallow, Mac's gaze brushes my throat, my collarbone, before sliding toward the garage, where Remy is angling toward us.

"I'm fine," I hear myself say, then I scramble out of the car.

MAC'S HANDS are near me again. He's currently clicking the clasp on a helmet under my chin, his eyes intent on his work. He's still dressed in his badass black outfit, except now he has an equally badass leather jacket and a helmet of his own.

I'm not into bad boys. Never have been. Kevin was soft, and sweet, and artistic. He took me on a picnic to the park for our first date. He spent his days painting and talking about textures and movement and shape. Our house wasn't a house, it was a "sculptural piece." If someone told him to ride a motorcycle, he'd probably just ask to paint it instead.

I liked that about my ex-husband. I liked that he wasn't macho, that he didn't need to prove his masculinity to feel like a man. I liked that he was talented and brilliant and unapologetically creative. I liked, most of all, that he was a caring father and a loving husband.

Then I found out he was cheating on me, and I wondered if I was blind, or just stupid.

But there's something about the confidence of Mac's movements that reaches deep into my gut and pushes my past aside. He changed my tire like he could do it in his sleep. He sat in my car like he owned it. He tucked a strand of hair behind my ear like touching me meant the world.

Now I'm standing next to a big, gleaming motorcycle with a helmet on my head, wondering how the hell *this* happened.

All I know is Remy and Mac greeted each other like old friends. They talked shop, took a look at my car, and Remy promised to take care of it. He gave me a quote that was basically just the cost of a new tire, then Mac put his hand on my elbow and asked me where I needed to go.

In a daze, I said home to Heart's Cove, and he told me he'd take me there.

"All set." Mac's lips do that hot, tilty, half-smile thing, his eyes full of humor. His fingers linger at my chin before dropping down to his sides.

I knock the side of my helmet with my knuckles. "Feels solid."

His grin widens, then he jerks a stubble-lined jaw to his machine. "Let's go." He swings a leg over the bike and lifts it off its kickstand, then turns to wink at me. "Get on. You'll love it, I promise."

Why is my heart thundering? All I can hear is the

whining of a machine in the mechanic's shop and the insistent thumping of my pulse in my ears. With a deep breath, I walk my heeled boots to the bike and swing a leg over. There's not much space between Mac and me. Not much space at all.

He turns his head to the side. "Hold my waist tight. We're going to go fast. Don't want you to fall off." When I hesitate, I catch that crease in his cheek appearing then disappearing. "You can grab onto my jacket. If you don't want to wrap yourself around me yet."

Um, *yet*? Excuse me? What does that mean?

But Mac revs the bike and I do as he says, shimmying closer as my hands find their way to his waist. My fingers curl into the soft, black leather of his jacket as my chest presses close enough to feel the breadth and solidness of his body. I close my eyes as the bike roars to life, and I realize that maybe I do like bad boys. Maybe I like motorcycles. Maybe I like feeling the vibrations of a powerful machine beneath me while my hands wrap around the sexiest man I've ever met.

"Hold on tight. You won't hurt me if you squeeze hard." He leans back a bit, as if he's looking for more contact between us. I curl my fingers into his jacket and hear him let out a low, masculine noise at the back of his throat.

For some reason, that noise nearly undoes me. I close my eyes and keep my grip tight, breathing in the scent of leather and Mac.

Then we take off, and my breath takes off with us. My grip on Mac's waist tightens as he accelerates, and I think I hear him groan. It's not until we're on the freeway on the way back to Heart's Cove that I realize how hard my arms are squeezing him and how tight my thighs are plastered to the outside of his.

Every inch of me is pressed tight to every inch of him.

From neck to navel, all I feel is Mac. His strong, muscular back encased in leather. His ass against the insides of my thighs. His ribs under my arms. It feels...good. Great. Amazing.

Too good. My breasts are pressed up against a strange man's back and all I can think about is how much I want more.

I haven't been this close to a man besides Kevin in over thirteen years. I haven't been this close to *Kevin* in years, either.

But when I try to loosen my grip, he speeds up and I have no choice but to hold on.

And it's magic.

The wind, the freedom, the feeling of flying. It takes my breath away. It makes my heart soar. I stop thinking about how hot the feel of his body next to mine makes me and about how wrong it is for me to enjoy it.

The heat of Mac's body is a blaze at my front, protecting me from the chill of the wind whipping past us. For a few glorious minutes I don't even mind that I'm plastered to his back, because it feels too good not to be. I rest my chin on his shoulder and watch the world rush past us.

Mac moves the bike like it's an extension of his body. He's totally in control. Totally confident. Totally freaking *hot*.

It's not until we cross the Heart's Cove town limits and slow down that I realize just how tight I'm holding him. I unclasp my hands from his jacket and Mac lets out a low chuckle.

"How was that?"

"Incredible," I breathe.

There's a smile in his voice when he responds, as if he's pleased with me. "Where to, gorgeous?"

Those three words should *not* make my insides clench the way they just did.

"Um…" Do I really want to drive up to my house on the back of Mac's motorcycle? I can just imagine the inquisition my mother would launch. "The Four Cups Café is fine. My sister owns it. She'll get me the rest of the way."

My sister, Candice, owns the café along with three of her friends. It's become crazy-popular in town, and I'm not surprised that Mac knows exactly how to get there.

But when we pull up outside, I *am* surprised to see him turn off the bike and set it on its kickstand. I attempt a graceful dismount and mostly succeed, even if I do have to lean heavily on his broad shoulders and teeter a little bit on the curb. Mac follows with a much more practiced movement, his hands immediately reaching to steady my hips.

How is he so *warm*? His hands feel so damn good against my jeans, fingers holding me tight as I try to catch my balance. Then his hands leave my hips and reach for the clasp at my chin, but my body hasn't caught up. I can still feel the imprint of his fingers on my hips, the heat of his body against mine.

I'm dizzy. Overwhelmed. Totally loving every minute of this and knowing I'm not supposed to.

When the helmet comes off, I run my fingers through my hair and bite my lip at the messy, flattened rat's nest I feel. I must look like a mess.

Another low noise escapes the back of Mac's throat. I feel it in my bones. When he speaks, his voice is deep and dark and sinful. "You keep biting your lip like that and I'm going to have to tug it free myself. And I might use my own teeth to do it."

I freeze, my bottom lip releasing. Then my eyes climb up

to Mac's and I see a look that is so far from sweet it's not even funny. I didn't know eyes could hold so much heat. My mouth goes dry and my lips part, and Mac lets out a short huff as he shakes his head.

"Next time you have a date playing pool with my dad, you call me first, all right?" He reaches into his back pocket and pulls out his wallet, then slides a hand into his jacket's breast pocket for a pen. I watch those wicked, beautiful hands write a phone number on the back of a receipt with neat, tight handwriting. Then he hands it to me, his eyes lingering on mine while I take the paper.

"Trina?" Mac says, arching his brows.

"Yeah?"

"You'll call me?"

"Um, yeah," I answer, because what else am I going to say?

Mac rewards me with a curl of his lips. "Good girl."

Heat gushes through me at those two little, not-so-innocent words.

Now, I'm not a girl. I'm very much a woman. And I've never had a man say *good girl* to me in a way that makes everything inside me clench...until today. When Mac says it, it feels like a reward. Like he's been waiting for me to agree to call him his whole life, and I just made his day. Like he'd like to say *good girl* to me again...and again...and again.

He sticks the spare helmet in one of the cases attached to his bike, gives me a little salute and a wink, then gets on the motorcycle and drives away.

I just stand there, hearing the words "good girl" playing in my head on repeat, feeling the imprint of his back against my chest and the brush of his fingers against my skin, wishing he'd made good on his promise to bite my lower lip himself.

Then the café door bangs open and my mother stands in the doorway. "Trina. Who in the world was *that*?" Her eyes are wide as she glances at Mac's disappearing shape, then swings her gaze to me.

Her eyes are full of mischief, and all I can do is groan.

Looks like I'm not escaping a Lottie Inquisition after all.

3

CANDICE

My sister looks flushed. My mother looks delighted. They walk to the display counter together and Trina gives me a pleading look.

"Coffee?" I ask.

"Please." She glances at her kids, who are sitting at one of the tables. There's a half-eaten muffin between them. Toby is playing a game on a tablet while Katie quietly works her way through a coloring book. Trina shifts her gaze to our mother. "Where's the cat?"

"At the house, in the spare bedroom, with a litter box, a scratching post, food, and water. The vet said he's healthy, and we gave him his first round of shots. No microchip, didn't match any of the missing posters, likely a stray. But enough about the cat. Who was that *man*?"

I fight a smile just as the café door opens and my own man strides through. Blake is a movie star in the outside world, but in Heart's Cove, he's just Blake. He gives me a broad smile before glancing at my sister's face, then changing course to hook an arm around my mother's shoulders. "Lottie, you're looking lovely this morning. Did you change your hair?"

"Oh, stop it." She swats at Blake's chest. "You know I haven't."

He winks at me, then gently directs my mother toward the kids' table...and away from Trina.

My sister lets out a long sigh and leans against the counter. "I think I just fell in love with Blake for that."

I laugh. "He's surprisingly perceptive."

She looks back at me. "How's the house design going?"

"The architects are taking their time responding to our comments," I answer. "They have this ultra-modern vision, but both Blake and I want something a bit more subtle. I think it'll take a while to get the plans approved." I glance at my sister. "But I heard back from the construction manager at my house, and it looks like they'll have the last of the fire and smoke damage fixed up within three weeks. You'll be able to move in before the start of the school year."

Trina accepts the coffee that Sven, our barista, hands her over the counter and takes a deep breath as she cups it close to her face. She shakes her head. "Are you sure you're okay with Mom and me moving into your house? You want to stay in the rental you're in with Blake and Allie?"

I shrug. "It makes sense, doesn't it?"

My house caught fire three months ago. The damage was localized, but I still had to move to a rental with my teenage daughter, Allie. That was right around the time I met Blake... and right around the time he decided he wanted to stay in town. Now we're living in a small, two-bedroom rental while the design of the new house on the coast gets finalized. Blake bought the property and told me he was staying, and he'd wait however long it took for me to realize we belonged together.

Swoon.

Thankfully, I came to my senses pretty quickly. I keep thinking Blake is going to wake up and realize he's happier in his swanky Beverly Hills mansion, but he keeps waking up and telling me that Heart's Cove feels like the only home he's ever had.

It's the fastest relationship I've ever been in, but it feels like I've known him my whole life. It feels right.

So Trina, her kids, and our mother will move into my old house when the repairs are done. I'm ready to move on, and I know my sister needs some stability right now. I'm happy to give it to her.

"Have you heard from the lawyer?" I ask.

Trina sips her coffee and nods. "This morning. Kevin signed."

I arch my brows. "It's all done? After all his talk about never signing divorce papers?"

Trina leans a hip against the counter and plays with the edge of her cup with her thumb. "I thought he was going to take his time. Drag it out. He kept complaining about giving me any money even though we had two kids together and he was the main breadwinner ever since his paintings took off."

"But you supported him with two jobs for the first four years of your relationship." I frown. "His paintings didn't even sell until a couple of years ago. *You* were the one who introduced him to the gallery manager who gave him his first big show."

Trina grimaces. "I don't know if that's exactly how Kevin remembers it. He's made a few speeches about bootstraps."

I roll my eyes. "He would never have been successful without you. You did his bookkeeping for years. You bought all his supplies until he could support himself. That asshole *owes* you."

"That's what my lawyer says," Trina replies. "That's probably why Kevin decided to sign the papers. I haven't asked for anything excessive. Just child support and a fair settlement. He gets to keep the house, the cars, everything. And he was all too willing to sign off on me moving here with the kids. It's like he *wanted* us out of his hair, which I guess worked out for me."

My brows lower and I glance over at Blake. We don't have kids together, but I can't imagine him doing that. Cheating on me. Kicking me out of the house...or letting me leave without even trying to fix it.

But Kevin isn't Blake, and maybe this is for the best.

My sister lets out a heavy sigh. "It's fine. I'm glad it's done. I don't want to turn bitter. Honestly, with the kids and the move and starting at a new school and everything, I'm glad he signed the papers. I just want this to be over."

"Oh, Trina." I reach across the counter and squeeze her hand.

Her eyes drift to our mother, who's still safely on the other side of the café and unable to lay into the thousand and one questions I'm sure she has for Trina. Which reminds me—

"What's up with the motorcycle man?"

She jumps. "Huh?"

"Katrina." I cross my arms and pop a brow.

"What?" is her angelic response.

"You rode in here on a Harley so loud it made the windows shake, then looked at the hot, leather-clad rider like he just made your whole life. Then *he* looked at *you* like you were the hottest little thing he'd ever seen.*You* did that. My stylish, high-maintenance sister was riding a *motorcycle*."

"High maintenance?" Her voice squeaks. "Who are you calling high maintenance?" She uses a manicured hand to flick her perfectly styled hair over her shoulder. Even after a motorcycle ride, her hair looks like she just walked off a photo shoot.

My sister is many things…and high maintenance is definitely one of them.

I don't mean it as a bad thing. It's actually one of the things I admire most about her. She's unapologetically girly. She takes care of herself—always has. She's always loved clothing and fashion and pampering. Look at this morning! Mom told me she was going to pick up the car, and she's standing in front of me in figure-hugging jeans, a simple white tank top, and enough silver bangles that she sounds like a wind chime when she sips her coffee. She's wearing smudged eyeliner, mascara, and a bit of blush across her cheeks. She looks edgy and cool and totally not like a hungover person doing the walk of shame to their car in the pub parking lot.

No wonder Mr. Motorcycle looked like he wanted to throw her over his shoulder and take her to his lair.

I grin at her outrage. "You know you're not *low* maintenance, Trina."

"And there's nothing wrong with that!" a voice calls out from the doorway. Dorothy and Margaret, the elderly twin ladies who own the town hotel, are standing at the entrance, hands on their hips.

Margaret cocks a brow. "I've been called high maintenance all my life, and always take it as a compliment." She pats her perfectly coiffed hair with an elegant hand, her silk blouse and pressed salmon-colored trousers adding to the overall effect.

Her sister, Dorothy, is the wild child of the two, with long silver hair braided over her shoulder and a leopard-print wrap dress. Different style, but no less stylish. She nods at Margaret's words and tuts at me.

I just grin and jerk my chin at Sven, who starts making coffee.

Dorothy glides toward Trina and hooks her arm through my sister's elbow. "Now, you're next, mm?"

Trina frowns. "What?"

"Your motorcycle man." She beams.

Trina, looking slightly freaked that Dorothy already knows about her escapades this morning, shoots me a panicked glance.

I just laugh. She'll get used to this town quick enough.

Dorothy leans her head against Trina's. "He's going to sweep you off your feet and ride off into the sunset with you. First Fiona, then Simone, then Candice, now you! We just need to get Jen and Fallon to stop messing around, and everyone will live happily ever after!"

Trina wrinkles her nose, and for a brief moment looks exactly like her daughter, Katie. "I don't believe in happily-ever-afters, Dorothy."

"Oh, that's just the divorce talking." Dorothy waves a hand. "Look at Candice. She was mopey for *years*!"

Um, excuse me? Mopey? "My husband died, Dorothy," I deadpan.

Dorothy ignores me. "Lottie!" She crosses the café to go kiss my mother on both cheeks, then takes her time hugging Blake, squeezing his shoulders, kissing both of *his* cheeks, patting his hair, stroking his arm...

I grin and shake my head while Margaret studies Trina.

"You okay?" Margaret asks quietly.

Trina nods. "Yeah. Fine. But I'll probably need a new car in the not-too-distant future."

"Get that good-for-nothing ex-husband of yours to pay for it." The older woman harrumphs, and I hide my grin while she orders a coffee.

Then, like a hurricane, Simone and Fiona—the two women who co-own the café along with me and Jen—blow through the door. Simone pumps a fist in the air. "Fiona's venue just confirmed! She's getting married to the man of her dreams at the old cannery on the coast! It's happening on the first of December, and we're going to have the *best* time!" She squeals and throws an arm around Fiona's waist, leading the laughing woman to the counter.

My mother jumps up to congratulate Fiona, who's already being smothered by Dorothy and Margaret.

Trina glances at me, a sad smile playing over her lips.

Then Jen appears in the doorway to the kitchen. "Have you decided on a cake flavor yet, or what?"

"Oh, give her a break, Jen!" Simone calls out, laughing as Dorothy hugs her tight. "You made my wedding cake in twenty-four hours! You have like a million weeks to do this one. You're a master baker. You can do it!"

Jen purses her lips, but I think it's mostly to stop from smiling. As congratulations are exchanged and coffees are made, I drift closer to my best friend and the most talented baker I've ever met. "You okay?" I ask Jen. "What's going on with your recipe book?"

"Amanda is coming back next week to go through the recipes I have so far." Her lips twist, and her eyes dart back to the kitchen. Fallon, our amazing chef, dances around the space like he was born to make food for people. When Jen looks at me, she lets out a long sigh.

Amanda works in publishing, and she happens to be Fallon's ex-girlfriend. With Jen agreeing to work with her, she's basically torpedoing whatever budding romance was occurring between her and Fallon. Now Amanda visits Heart's Cove on the regular, and everyone can see the way she looks at Fallon. I don't blame Jen for stepping back.

"You don't know that they'll end up back together, Jen."

She gives me a quick, jerky nod. "Yeah. Whatever. Better get back to work."

"Let's have a celebratory dinner! Our place," Simone calls out. "Everyone's invited. Wes will fire up the grill." She beams at me, then shifts her eyes to Trina. "And don't think you're getting off without telling us all about your motorcycle ride this morning, Trina. You're one of us now. That means you got beans, you spill 'em."

Trina gapes. "How in the *world* do you know about my motorcycle ride? It happened a few minutes ago!"

Simone taps the side of her nose. "Welcome to Heart's Cove, honey."

I just laugh, and Dorothy lets out a loud squeal of her own. "I almost forgot! The pottery master class is going ahead on Monday." She looks me, Fiona, Simone, and finally Trina in the eyes. "You're all coming. Monday, eleven o'clock in the morning." She points a finger at Trina. "And I know the kids will be at their day camp every day next week, so you have no excuse."

Trina's shoulders drop. She bites her lip. "Look...pottery? I'm not artistic. That was Kevin's thing."

"Oh, *puh!*" Dorothy bats the comment away. "You will be there and you will enjoy it, if only for the fact that Mr. Blair is easy on the eyes. His pieces sell like crazy, you know. He's a big name in the pottery world. Did you hear about the big pop-up gallery opening happening in January?" She doesn't wait for anyone to answer. "Mr. Blair agreed to show a few pieces." Dorothy beams. "It's going to be great. And"—she leans closer to the two of us—"he has the hands of a *god*."

For some reason Trina's eyes glaze over for a brief moment, and color sweeps high over her cheeks. Then she blinks it away and lets out a breath. "Fine."

Dorothy just grins and winks at me. "I'd get him to do classes here year-round, but he works at—"

"Dor! Come taste Jen's new recipe," Margaret calls from the kitchen.

"Can't resist a demand like that!" The older woman laughs and sways her hips toward the kitchen. "See you all on Monday."

I exchange a glance with my sister, who just blows out a breath.

"Guess I'm doing pottery then, huh." Trina shakes her head, resigned, then moves to give Fiona her congratulations.

4

MAC

I RIDE FOR OVER AN HOUR, but it still doesn't cool the embers burning on my skin. I feel her everywhere. Pressed up against my back, wrapped around my waist, her thighs plastered against mine. I feel the memory of her silky, soft skin against my fingertips.

Trina.

I've been wanting to learn her name for weeks. All summer, I've spent more time than usual at my father's bar in the vain hope that she'd show up again. It's pathetic, really.

But she came back. She has my number. I felt the sharp intake of her breath when I started the bike. I know she'll want more.

Or at least, I hope so.

The engine cuts as I pull in next to my father's bike in the parking lot of the Cedar Grove. Then I groan as a minivan door opens, and a tall woman with chocolate-colored hair and a sultry smile slides out.

"Well, if it isn't Mac Blair. Funny seeing you here." Belinda sways her wide hips toward me.

"Were you waiting for me to show up?" I jerk my head to her minivan.

She rolls her eyes and lets out a coquettish laugh. "Of course not. I was just stopping in. I haven't seen you in so long, and you know, the kids are in junior high now, so..." She lets the words hang, and I don't take the bait.

Belinda was a mistake. A big, *big* mistake that I do not intend to repeat. Ever.

See, I'm a teacher at the local elementary school. I teach second grade, and I'm damn good at it. But—not to sound like an arrogant jackass—there are certain mothers who tend to be interested in me beyond my role as their kid's teacher. They see the motorcycle, they see my age, my body, and they think I can give them a good ride.

It's inappropriate.

Belinda and I...

I hate admitting this, but it's true. I slept with her. Her kid was in my class, and on the last day of the school year, she showed up at the school with a bottle of whiskey in her hand and fuck-me shoes on her feet. I took her home and obliged. I won't pretend I didn't enjoy it.

If it had happened even a day earlier and people caught wind of it, I could have been in big trouble. There's no explicit rule against parents and teachers seeing each other, but it's highly, highly unprofessional. It was a mistake. Inappropriate, obviously, and the only thing that saved me was that I was no longer teaching her child.

The problem is, I ran into her all the time for the next four years. School drop-offs, pick-ups, theater nights, sporting events, science fairs...she was always there.

And now she's here.

Four years, this woman has been batting her lashes at me.

And she's not unattractive—not at all—but it's just not something I want to do again. I can't handle the whispers, the looks from other mothers, the stain on my reputation.

"How's Michael doing? Looking forward to the new school?" I take a sidestep away from Belinda to keep some distance between us.

"I'm not here to talk about my kid, Mac." She tilts her head. "Aren't you going to ask me if I want to take you up on that motorcycle ride you promised me four whole years ago?" Her eyes flick from me to my bike, and there's no mistaking the heat in her gaze.

"Listen, Belinda." I take a deep breath and comb my fingers through my hair, looking for the right words.

It was never going to be more than sex with her. It's never more than sex with anyone. I can't do that lovey-dovey bullshit. It doesn't make sense to me that people actually *want* that. To open up. To be vulnerable. Why give someone else the chance to hurt you? Why show someone else all your softest, weakest places?

Even if Belinda tried to convince me she just wanted sex, I can tell by the desperate edge to her voice that she wants more, and I simply can't give it to her. I don't have that in me to give.

Not to mention she was the first and only time I'll ever hook up with a parent. It's not worth the torture afterward, when they inevitably want more than I can give. It's not worth throwing my job away. My reputation.

Then, just as I'm wracking my brain for the right way to tell this woman to leave me the hell alone, a car comes screeching into the parking lot and slides into a spot across the pavement from me. Four white-haired ladies shuffle out of it.

One of them is about four feet tall with eyes that shoot

flames as she glances at another woman over the hood of the car. "Dorothy, you wouldn't know good wine if I smashed a bottle of it over your head."

I know Dorothy. She owns the Heart's Cove Hotel with her twin sister, Margaret. She's wearing an animal-print dress, cinched at the waist with a belt studded with turquoise. She gets out of the opposite side of the car and plants her hands on her hips. "And how would *you* know good wine, Agnes? I didn't know they had sommelier classes in hell."

Agnes sticks out her tongue.

A short-haired woman puts her hands up. "Ladies—" She stops talking when she sees me, points in my direction, and screams, "He's here! It's him! It's the motorcycle man!"

Belinda lets out a huff. "Do you know these women?"

"Uh..." I frown, my eyes darting between the three women shuffling toward me, then to the driver who's following behind. It's Margaret, Dorothy's twin sister and co-owner of the Heart's Cove Hotel. "Yeah," I finally say. "I do."

"Mac Blair is the motorcycle man?" Dorothy screeches. She turns to Margaret, then swivels her head back to me. Then she squeals and jumps. "Yes! Mac Blair is the motor-cycle man!"

"Excuse me, Belinda." I walk away from her, angling toward the women in front of me. "Ladies. Can I help you?"

"Don't know who you're calling a lady, but I'm hoping it's not this old hag," the short woman, Agnes, says, jerking her chin at Dorothy.

I frown. "Um..."

"Oh, don't mind her." The pixie-cut lady with purple reading glasses around her neck grabs my elbow and yanks me closer. She peers into my eyes, then takes a step back and studies me from head to toe. Then she nods. "You'll do."

"I'll...do?"

"What are we waiting for?" Dorothy cries. "Mac, we're here for a drink. Lead the way." She thrusts her arm toward the bar, then proceeds to lead the way herself.

The five of us enter the Cedar Grove in a whirlwind of silver hair and animal print. My father is behind the bar counting the till while Lee, my younger brother and part-time fill-in bartender, wipes bottles down with a white cloth. They both look up and freeze. My father's brows inch down over his eyes.

"Ooh, moody," Pixie Cut says. "I haven't been in a dive bar in decades."

"What are you calling a dive bar?" my father growls, but there's no bite to his words. His lips tip up as he meets my gaze, tilting his head in question. *Who are they and why are you with them?* his eyes ask.

"She meant it as a compliment," Margaret cuts in smoothly, looking utterly out of place in her peach pantsuit and pearls. "Didn't you, Lottie?"

Pixie Cut—Lottie—still has her arm hooked through my elbow. She leads me toward the bar and hums her agreement. "Of course it's a good thing." Propping her reading glasses on the end of her nose, she glances at the bottles on the wall before removing the glasses and looking at Dorothy. "I thought you said this place had good wine."

"This is what I was trying to tell you," Agnes huffs. "She wouldn't know it from vinegar."

"No, I said I *hope* they have good wine," Dorothy says with a roll of her eyes. "But I'm thinking maybe I'll just have bourbon."

Margaret groans. "Dor...are you sure that's a good idea?"

"Of course it's not a good idea." Dorothy plonks herself on a barstool right next to a grouchy old regular.

"New friends of yours?" my father asks me with a grin

while the other ladies take their seats. His eyes linger on Margaret, watching the way her fingers run over her pearl necklace while she peruses the beer-stained menu. Having her in here is like having the First Lady visit my father's bar. She makes everything seem grubbier. Suddenly, I see every speck of dust, every bit of dirt, every beer stain and layer of old grease.

"Something like that," I answer, then glance over my shoulder and let out a long breath when I see Belinda hasn't followed me in. I'll have to buy the first round to thank these ladies for that.

"We have full attendance for your class on Monday, Mr. Blair," Margaret tells me. "The students can't wait to learn from a talent such as yourself."

"Call me Mac. He's Mr. Blair," I tell her, gesturing to my father.

My father really plays up his fading Scottish accent when he leans a broad palm across the bar to shake with her. "Pleasure to make your acquaintance, Mrs..."

"Margaret," she replies, slipping her hand into his while she pats her hair with the other. "Call me Margaret."

"We should do shots," Lottie states with a decisive nod.

"Good idea!" Dorothy cries, while Margaret and Agnes bark out a "No!" in unison.

"First round is on me," I tell my father, who nods.

"Oh, I like him," Lottie says, lowering her reading glasses to look me up and down again. "I *definitely* like him."

"Have a little shame, woman," Agnes huffs, but she gives me a long, assessing look just the same.

Grinning, I meet my father's gaze across the bar and nod toward the door. He gives me a slight dip of the chin while my brother surveys his new patrons with an arch of the eyebrow, and I slink out before the four ladies can crowd around me and tell me more about how "I'll do." Whatever that means.

When I get outside, I poke my head out to check for a certain minivan, then slip out when I see the coast is clear.

Then, grinning, I get back on my bike and ride.

5

TRINA

THE WEEKEND IS SPENT HOSTING multiple kitten viewings for half the residents of Heart's Cove. Toby and Katie are over the moon. Katie does, in fact, empty the litter box. There's a deep wrinkle in her nose while she does it, but to her credit, my daughter doesn't complain once.

My car magically appears in front of the Four Cups Café sometime between Saturday night and Sunday morning, to the delight of everyone in town. Candice calls me to let me know she has the keys, and I bite my lip when I see it, knowing—just *knowing*—it was Mac who left it here. Candice, of course, only gives me a mischievous grin when I ask her who dropped it off, which all but confirms it was Mac. And seriously—how thoughtful can one man be? Now I don't need to figure out how I'll pick my car up from the mechanic.

I don't quite have the courage to call or text him, though. Not right now. Maybe on Monday, once the kids are busy at camp and I have time to take a breath. After the pottery class. Maybe Tuesday, when I have free time. Just...later. I'll do it later.

But before I know it, I'm dropping the kids off at a nearby

summer day camp and getting ready for a pottery class I never signed up for.

What does one wear to a pottery class? Dorothy said old clothes that I don't mind ruining, but I'm the type of person that has a strict policy on house clothes staying at home. I stand in front of my closet and finally choose a pair of loose khaki-green, drawstring-waisted pants that are somewhere between sweats and cargos, and a tight, white, cap-sleeved tee. My hair, which I curled yesterday and still has good volume, gets swept up in a high pony. I brush on a little makeup, then grab my purse, casual Converse shoes, and my favorite pair of oversized shades to complete the look.

Okay, fine. Maybe I am high maintenance. But is that really a bad thing? I like clothes. I like makeup. I like looking nice. So what?

I used to have to defend myself to Kevin all the time. He didn't understand why I got manicures, why I spent my time blow-drying my hair, why I wanted to look stylish when I was going to the grocery store. He thought it was frivolous.

Any time I tried to explain to him that it made me feel good to look good, he'd tell me he preferred me in sweats with no makeup on. As if *his* preferences on my appearance were more important than how *I* felt. These days, when I think back on my marriage, I wonder how much I settled for someone who didn't really care about me, my thoughts, or my feelings. Is it any surprise he was unfaithful? I sometimes wonder if he ever saw me as my own person at all, or if I was just an accessory to his perfect life.

Not to mention the person who would finally launch his career was a woman I'd met and befriended at the nail salon —did he acknowledge that maybe my manicures were a good thing?

I'll let you guess the answer to that one.

Shaking my head, I find my mother humming to herself in the kitchen. "You coming?"

She arches her brows. Her eyes glimmer with hidden delight, but I don't have the time or the energy to figure out why. With my mother, sometimes it's better not to ask. "Oh, no, honey, you go ahead. I'll stay here and do some laundry." She smiles, the mirth in her gaze softening into something warm. "You look gorgeous, Katrina."

At least my mother appreciates it. Smiling, I call out a goodbye and head to the Heart's Cove Hotel.

The art studio is at the back of the building, accessible through a lush, jungle-like courtyard. I find Candice, Simone, Jen, and Fiona in the lobby, and the five of us do the usual greetings and hugs, then head back toward the studio.

I've been in town most of the summer, but it still feels weird to be accepted so seamlessly into a group of friends. I haven't had girlfriends since college.

"You okay?" Fiona glances at me as we walk. "You're looking very serious for someone who's about to have her hands covered in clay."

I force a smile and shake my head. "It's nothing. I'm fine." When she arches her brows, I let out a laughing huff. "Fine. I'm nervous. I haven't done anything artistic in years. It's silly, I know, but it's true."

She's quiet for a few steps, then her lips curl into a smile. "You know, my first couple of hours in Heart's Cove were spent in this studio. That's how I met Grant." Her eyes glimmer. "I was so completely overwhelmed, because I'm as far from an artist as you can get, but now I love it. There's no pressure in there. You can be as bad or as good as you want. There's no rules to creativity."

"Kevin used to mock my lack of artistic skills," I blurt, then snap my mouth shut. I hadn't meant to say that. But he did, didn't he? Little snide comments whenever I'd try to join him in the studio in the early days. I stopped going after a year or so, and he never asked me back. Art was his thing, and I wasn't invited.

Fiona tuts. "Girl, one look at your face and I know you've got more creativity in your pinky finger than I've got in my whole body." When I frown in confusion, she smiles. "Your makeup, Trina. It's art."

"It's not fair!" Simone says, turning around to grin at us. "I can barely manage to put mascara on without poking myself in the eye, and here you are looking like a million bucks."

My chest warms at their comments, even though I wave them away.

Then we enter the studio, and I scream. Literally.

Because Mac is there, wearing an old blue button-down with the sleeves rolled up to show off his mouthwatering hands and corded forearms. He's got a brown apron wrapped around his muscular body, and it looks positively sinful.

The man wears leather, and I want to jump him. I never thought he'd look like pure sex in an apron.

I was wrong.

Mac's face registers surprise, but it's not the bad kind (I hope). He straightens up from the pottery wheel where he'd been positioning a stool and rakes his fingers through his hair, his eyes running down the length of my body.

I—

Wow. I want him to look at me like that every hour of every day for the rest of my life. It warms me from the inside out, makes me feel like the most beautiful, sexiest woman in the world.

That's when I realize that everyone *else's* eyes are on me, too. Simone and Fiona look like they're having the time of their lives, fighting grins behind raised hands. Jen lifts her gaze to the ceiling. Candice is just unabashedly laughing like the evil older sister she is.

"Ladies," Mac greets us in his deep baritone, eyes still on me. "Here for the pottery class?"

"You're Mr. Blair," I say stupidly.

Mac's eyes gleam. "You know my name, Trina, but if you want to call me Mr. Blair instead, I won't complain."

Now Simone is laughing too. Oh no. I turn my red face away from Mac and stare at the fiery-haired woman who's quickly becoming a good friend, then shift my gaze to Candice. My sister just grins.

There are a few students in the class I don't know, and they're all looking at me. Wonderful.

Mac saves me by introducing himself to everyone and starting the class at a long table at the back of the studio, where a few bags containing rectangular chunks of clay are positioned at regular intervals around the table. After we all get situated with paint-stained aprons on, he instructs us to open the bag and use a wire to cut off a big hunk of clay. We massage it to get the air out, which feels like a workout and a half, then cut it again and roll it into four balls. Mac demonstrates as he talks.

I was wrong about the tire changing. That wasn't a show. *This* is a show. Those hands—I need help. I can't stop watching them. My mouth waters as he handles the clay with confidence, shaping it into four equal-sized balls with a few expert movements. The slapping of his palm against the clay almost sounds like skin slapping against—

Nope. Not going there. Not in public. Not right now.

Then I realize everyone has already started, and all I've been doing is staring at Mac's hands.

With trembling movements, I make four wonky-shaped balls, then wrap them back up in the bag to stop them from drying out. We're led over to the wheels set at equal intervals in a circle in the center of the studio, and somehow, with all the other ladies moving at light speed before I can grab a seat on the opposite side of the room, I end up sitting beside Mac.

They seem totally impervious to my withering glares, avoiding my eyes as they take their seats. Jerks.

So I sit, and I wait for Mac to start teaching...but I'm not prepared for what happens next. Turns out shaping the balls of clay was only the start of the show.

"Place your ball in the center of the wheel. Smack it down hard." Simone snorts, and Mac's eyes flick to her, then to everyone's clay. "Good. Pat it down a couple of times, then wet your hands and start your wheel. We're going to center the clay, which will allow us to shape it into what we're trying to create. If it's off-center, you won't be able to shape it properly. You'll end up with one side thicker than the other."

I can't look away as Mac takes those huge, broad hands and dips his long fingers into a small pail of water. His forearms flex as he shakes off a few drops, then Mac starts shaping the clay. He's saying something, explaining the process of centering the clay, but all I can do is stare.

Wet clay moves between his hands, smooth and sensuous. His fingers press, release, move like magic over the clay, making it dance up and down and through the gap in his hands. He cups the clay and shapes it in a smooth, tall— listen, there's no other word for it—*phallic* shape. It looks like a massive grey dong on the center of his pottery wheel, and the sight of it makes me want to combust. I have to look away.

My face is red-hot.

Candice is biting her lip, and Simone's face is as red as mine, except she's not blushing. She's trying not to burst out laughing. Traitor.

With nothing else to do, I start centering my clay. It's

smooth, wet, and it feels calming to put my hands around it. Keeping my eyes firmly on my own wheel, I listen to Mac's deep voice rumble through me as he gives instructions, encouragements, and tips.

My clay wobbles. I chance a glance over at Mac and reposition my hands, wetting them, moving them over the smooth material. After a few moments, I think I've got it.

Once the clay is centered, we start opening it. Mac demonstrates as he explains, but all I can do is watch the way those hands fondle the clay as a bowl appears on his wheel.

My panties are wet.

That's so damn embarrassing. I'm turned on by the man doing *pottery*, for crying out loud. What is wrong with me?

It's just... I can't even explain it. He's just so *capable*. He shifts his fingers ever so slightly, and the opening in the center of his clay widens. Then he shifts again, with water and clay running over his hands as the wheel goes around and around and around, and he pulls the sides up as if he's commanding the clay to move. Soft, gentle strokes. Firm touches. Stiff, muscular upper arms, with his elbows braced against his wide-spread legs.

It's erotic. Every movement. Every touch. Every focused, beautiful line of his face.

Tearing my eyes away from the sex-on-a-pottery-wheel show, I try my hands at opening my lump of clay. It's harder than it looks.

Within a few seconds, there's a warm presence at my back. Mac pulls his stool over next to mine. "May I help?" he asks.

"Of course," I reply, my voice a croak.

Those gorgeous hands move closer, fingers pressed against my own, palms warm and broad against the backs of my mine. His touch is confident, warm, and it sends my mind reeling.

"Firm, even pressure works best," he says, his head bent next to mine, so close his breath ruffles a rogue strand of hair.

"Ain't that the truth," Simone quips, and Fiona lets out a cough that sounds suspiciously like a laugh.

I don't even have the brain capacity to look up and glare at them.

Repeat after me: *Murder is wrong. Do not murder your sister's best friends. Murder will get you put in jail for the rest of your life, even if they deserved it.*

"Here, like this." Mac moves his hands over mine again, showing me exactly how to move them to shape my lump of clay into a bowl. The clay responds to him, and so do I. I can barely breathe at the feel of his hands on mine, his sleeve brushing my arm, his thigh pressed against my leg.

And our hands, wet. Touching. Stroking. Clay, cold and soft and malleable, moving exactly where he wants it to.

I can't breathe.

He smells so damn good. I'm close enough to inhale it, bask in it.

My heart thunders against my ribs, and it's all I can do to watch...and enjoy. My insides clench around the painful emptiness between my legs, and I try to hide the way he makes me want to squirm. I want to squeeze my thighs together, but Mac tells me to brace my elbows against them, so I have no choice but to keep them spread wide on either side of the wheel. When he picks my hand up and shows me how to place it to pull up the sides of the bowl, my breath hitches.

Mac notices. He glances at me, turning his head so his lips are only a couple of inches away from mine. Sinful, stormy eyes meet mine, then drop to my mouth. His gaze lingers, tracing the shape of my lips, and I almost expect him to kiss me.

Then I remember we're in a room with women who won't think twice about teasing me for the rest of eternity, not to mention a bunch people I don't know. I've been divorced for all of four days. I can't kiss Mac. I can't kiss *anyone*!

I jerk away from him, gouging the side of my bowl in the process.

Mac just grins. "Luckily, wet clay can be reshaped." He nods to the gouged clay. "Show me." His command shivers through me, and I make the mistake of meeting Simone's eyes.

She wiggles her eyebrows, mouth forming the words *show me* in a much more suggestive way. And damn it, I'm blushing again.

I turn my attention to my wheel as Mac rinses his hands in my bucket of water and watches me. I wet my own hands again, then shape the bowl just like he taught me.

"Good, Trina," he says, and oh, my name on his tongue sounds sinful. "You're a natural." Mac's eyes darken, and for a few long seconds, I'm caught in the crossfire of his gaze.

Then someone—Candice, maybe?—clears their throat, and Mac jerks his gaze away. He mumbles something about helping the other students, and I busy myself shaping and reshaping my bowl.

I END UP WITH A BOWL, a cup, and a little flat jewelry tray by the end of the class. Mac will have to fire our creations in his kiln once before we can glaze and fire it again, which means we'll be coming back next week. I pretend that doesn't make my heart leap. Most of the students except for my crew have filed out of the class by the time Mac removes his apron.

He smiles at the five of us. "Good work today, ladies."

"We had a good teacher." Simone winks at him, then winks at me.

Subtle. Real subtle.

"You should see an optometrist for that eye twitch," I tell her.

Simone just laughs.

Mac clears his throat, then his lips tip up in that cheeky grin that makes my cheeks burn hot. "How do you feel about that pool lesson this weekend, Trina? My father's been asking about you. Said you need to come by the Grove before he gets too lonely out there."

"Oh, I—" I'm about to come up with an excuse—any excuse—when Simone and Fiona exchange a glance, and Simone lets out a little *whoop*.

"Girls' night!" She grins, then arches her eyebrows at the rest of us. "Yeah? Yeah."

"I'll book the salon for some blowouts," Fiona says. "Jen, make sure you have the evening off. Wait, what evening are we doing this?"

"We?" I ask. "Girls' night?" When did my pool lesson with Hamish—which I fully intended on avoiding—turn into a full-on girls' night out that somehow includes blowouts at the salon?

"Saturday," Candice answers Fiona. "The Cedar Grove, right?" This, she directs at Mac.

Mac's grin spreads into a full smile. "The Cedar Grove." He nods.

"We can get our hair done, then head to Katrina's to get ready. You can do our makeup, right?"

"I don't... Toby and Katie..."

"Clancy and Allie can watch them," Candice cuts in, waving a hand. "They're pretty much in love with Mr. Fuzzles

48

anyway, so any excuse to spend time at your place will be enough for them."

"Mr. Fuzzles?" Mac asks, eyebrows arched.

I shake my head. "New kitten. Don't ask. It's been an eventful week."

"He's *the cutest*. Little white paws." Simone lets out a squeaky noise. "You should come meet him, Mac. I can just imagine a big, strong man like you holding a little, tiny, furry kitten. That's the stuff dreams are made of."

"He should come meet him?" I repeat dumbly. I feel like I have whiplash from staring down everyone who talks. Mac should absolutely not, ever, not in a million years come meet my new cat. No way.

"This is going to be so fun!" Candice says, and I'm ashamed to say I'm tempted to be violent with my own beloved sister.

Murder is wrong. Do not murder your sister. Murder will get you put in jail for the rest of your life, even if she deserves it.

"You can say that again. Saturday night! Yay!" Simone hooks her arm through Fiona's. "I'll make mini quiches. You bring wine. We should get our hair done just after lunch so we can meet up at Trina's early enough to get ready. Then we can have some kitty time too."

"Definitely." Fiona nods decisively. "We could do an early dinner. Charcuterie boards!"

Biting my lip, I turn to Mac. "I guess everyone will be at the Grove on Saturday." I give him an apologetic smile. "Hope that's okay."

"I'll tell Dad to batten down the hatches in preparation."

"I heard that!" Simone calls out from the doorway. She pauses, turns, and grins. "Not a bad idea, actually. I'm feeling like letting loose."

Jen, Candice, Simone, and Fiona leave, and all of a

sudden I'm alone with Mac. Tension stretches taut between us. I should walk away. I really, really should. But somehow, my feet stay anchored to the ground. My body burns in every place he's ever touched, from my hands to my hips to the thighs that were pressed against his only a few days ago.

He stands there, just a couple of feet away from me, and it feels like every cell in my body is drawn to him.

I clear my throat and jerk my thumb over my shoulder. "I should..."

"Yeah." Mac rubs the back of his neck, and neither of us make a move to leave. His grey-blue eyes meet mine, and a little smile tips up his lips.

I don't want to leave. Not even a little bit. "I didn't know you were into pottery," I say. "Dorothy said you were kind of famous."

Color rises high on Mac's cheeks, and he shrugs the comment away. "I don't have much time to do it during the school year, but summers tend to be productive."

"Oh! Do you have kids?"

"No, I—"

"Hey Trina, you coming?" Candice pokes her head through the door. "Sorry to interrupt, but apparently Fallon is putting lunch on at the café to celebrate our newfound love of pottery."

"Yeah. Sure. Of course." I glance at Mac. "See you Saturday."

He nods, his eyes lingering on mine, then dropping to my lips. Before I can do anything stupid, I turn on my heels and walk away, but I stop when I get a few steps away. Glancing over my shoulder at him, I tilt my head. "My car—was that you?"

"Was what me?" Mac picks up a stool and stacks it on top of another, not meeting my eyes.

"Did you drop it off in town this weekend after Remy fixed the tire?"

Mac looks at me then, his eyes crinkling at the corners. He lifts a shoulder, then bends over to pick up a stack of stools. "You seemed like you might need a break. It was the least I could do."

My heart grows so fast I can barely catch a breath. Through a thick throat, I squeeze out enough air to speak. "Thanks, Mac."

He just nods. "See you on Saturday."

"Yeah," I answer, lingering, before finally getting my butt in gear and leaving before I *really* do anything stupid.

6

TRINA

CANDICE WAS RIGHT. Allie and Clancy, Fiona's stepdaughter, are more than happy to spend time with my kids—and the kitten, of course.

Mr. Fuzzles, despite my grumbling about taking care of a pet, hasn't been a bad addition to the household. Last night, after the kids had gone to bed and I was zoned out watching *The Bachelor* on TV, he jumped up on the couch beside me and stretched his little body next to my thigh, curling his tiny white paws under his chin. It was the first time he'd approached me, and it made my heart thump harder than it should. When I used a gentle, timid finger to scratch behind his ears, he made the cutest purring sounds I'd ever heard while his tail flicked over and back across my thigh.

Then, out of the blue, he jumped off the couch, gave me a look over his shoulder that I can only describe as pure, unadulterated sass, and sauntered away. As if he *knew* he was winning me over. Little shit.

Now it's Saturday afternoon, and Toby and Katie are playing outside with Allie and Clancy. I just got back from the salon with the girls, and I can only hope that Hamish did, indeed, batten down the hatches. These ladies are not messing around. It's barely past six o'clock in the evening and we've already made our way through three and a half bottles of wine and an industrial amount of mini quiches. The charcuterie boards have long since been demolished.

While I sit at my vanity, Simone lounges on my bed and Candice peruses my closet. Fiona is in the bathroom doing her makeup while Jen reads a book on my armchair, legs hanging sideways off the arm as she waits for everyone to get ready.

Candice lets out a long sigh and finally turns to me. "Trina, can you do that thing you do where you wave a magic wand and make me look amazing?"

I frown, laughing. "What?"

"You know, you tuck my shirt in and cuff my jeans and then do stuff with accessories and hair and I go from frumpy and old to a super-hot MILF in like ten seconds?"

"You want me to style you?" I tilt my head.

"Yes!" She stands in the middle of my room and spreads her arms. "Fix this."

I smile and do as she says. She's wearing a silky, draped top with an asymmetrical neckline, but her skirt sits too low on the hips. It doesn't show off her tiny waist at all. I tap my chin, then dig through my closet for a high-waisted, faux-leather skirt that will hit Candice just below the knees. I tell her to put it on. That skirt is hot. On me, it hits scandalous mini-skirt territory and used to make Kevin cluck about my age.

Once she has it on, it only takes a bit of tucking, a few bobby pins in her gorgeous ombre hair, and a touch more blush.

"There." I stand back and smile.

"Holy shit." Simone sits up on the bed, glass of wine dangling between her fingers. "Do me next!"

Candice moves to a mirror, looks at herself, then shakes her head and beams at me. "You are so freaking talented, Katrina. You should do this professionally."

"What, dress people?" I snort and shake my head, but Fiona walks out of the bathroom and whistles.

"I'd pay for someone to tell me how to dress if I ended up looking like *that*," Fiona says.

"Same." Simone stands up and spreads out her arms. "Do me! Do me!"

Jen looks up and nods. "You could make it a business." When I frown at her, Jen shrugs. "If I can bake, and Candice can do yoga, Simone can do social media and websites, and the four of us can run a café, then *you* can do *that*. People would pay." Then she returns to her book.

I blink. For some reason, her words hit me hard. Jen isn't the type of person to mince her words. She's incredibly logical, methodical, and hearing her say that I'm good at styling... I don't know. It means a lot. It shouldn't, but it does.

So, I take a sip of wine and get to work. I put Simone in a gorgeous orange wrap dress that sets off her hair and eyes, then add lots of gold jewelry. Then Fiona puts on a tight, short-sleeved green top and the same slim-fitting black pants she had on before. Jen refuses my services, but she does let me touch up her makeup and when she glances in the mirror, I see a hint of a smile on her lips. The three others twirl and laugh and flick their hair, then tell me I'm a genius.

All I did was dress them, but sure. I'll take the compliment.

I feel twenty years younger than I am right now. Girls' night? I haven't had a girls' night in far, far too long. And I haven't had someone actually appreciate the fact that I'm good at hair and makeup and styling clothes in even longer. I'd started to feel like my interest in "girly" things was something to be ashamed of. Lord knows Kevin mocked it often enough for me to doubt myself.

Never mind the fact that I managed all our household affairs and even did his bookkeeping and management before he got big enough to hire a team. But I learned that when you want to be typically feminine, you have to deal with people assuming that you left your brain at the door.

I smile, then turn to my closet and suddenly remember what I'm doing. I'm going to see Mac. I'm going to play pool. In his presence. At a bar. With all these crazy women egging me on.

Oh, no.

"What the hell am I going to wear?" I turn to my friends, panic suddenly rising inside me. What am I even doing? I should be spending time with my kids and making sure they're okay with the divorce, not going out and meeting strange, sexy, pottery-throwing, motorcycle-riding hunks.

"Okay." Fiona puts her glass of wine down and lifts her palms up, entering what I can only describe as Fiona Gets Down to Business Mode. "We're going for sexy but not trying too hard, but so smoking-hot Mac won't know what hit him. I want his jaw to hit the floor as soon as you walk in. I want him to forget how to speak. Your outfit needs to totally lobotomize him."

"Yes. Big hair, big makeup, tight clothes," Simone announces. "Hooker-chic."

"Whoa, um, no," I cut in.

"Oh! Wear that white bodysuit with the low back!" Candice says, eyes brightening. "You know the one. It's super flattering and has those long sleeves and the low scoop. No cleavage, but damn sexy."

I tilt my head. "With jeans and heeled boots. That could work."

"Candice, be honest," Simone says seriously. "Is it truly sexy? Is it lobotomy-inducing sexy?"

"The man's brain will leak out of his ears. I promise. You haven't seen my sister when she tries hard."

Fiona chokes on her wine. "Wait...all this time, all these outfits I've seen you in—that's you *not* trying hard?" She gapes at me, then at the rest of them. "Am I just a frumpy person, or is that not shocking to you all?"

I blush and try to hide how much I appreciate what they're saying.

I am a girly girl, hear me roar!

Getting dressed distracts me from the worry of seeing Mac again. I give my hair a little zhoosh, curling it out a bit bigger than the stylist did as per Simone's instruction, and brush on some smokey makeup as my wine glass gets filled and refilled as if by magic.

When the five of us are ready, we head downstairs. The kids are in the living room with Clancy and Allie, and my mother, Dorothy, and Margaret are in the kitchen eating dinner. I'm not quite sure when they arrived, but I have a sneaky suspicion they wanted to see the five of us off.

Dorothy whistles as my mother grabs her phone. "Photos! I want photos."

"Mom, this isn't prom." I grab my purse from the kitchen counter and check for my things while my mother ignores me and starts creative-directing a photo shoot right there in the hallway.

Katie skips to me and wraps her arms around my waist. "You look like a princess, Mommy. So pretty."

Annddd my heart melts. I place a soft kiss on my daughter's head. "You going to be okay tonight without me?"

My sweet daughter who just called me a pretty princess rolls her eyes and snorts. I guess that answers that.

Then, with one last look at my friends and one last goodbye kiss for my kids—and fine, a little scratch behind Mr. Fuzzles's ears—I bid goodbye to the ladies in my kitchen and head for the waiting taxi. As I slip inside, crammed in the back seat with three others, I can't help but smile.

It's been ages since I've had a night out like this. *Years.* In fact, I don't remember the last time I went out with girlfriends without worrying if Kevin would be okay with the kids—or as he called it, "babysitting," even though they're his own children—or without him turning his nose up at such "pedestrian" activities as going for a drink. If it wasn't a gallery opening or a poetry reading, Kevin would act like it was beneath him.

But this...this is fun. And I'm going to enjoy every minute of it.

And maybe I've had too much wine, but when we arrive at the Grove and tumble out of the cab, I can't help but laugh when Simone struts up to one of the many motorcycles parked outside and poses beside it. Fiona starts snapping photos—much like my mother was doing a few minutes ago—and I finally let go of that little niggle telling me I shouldn't be doing this.

I'm a grown woman. I'm allowed to have fun. I may be recently divorced, but I'm not dead. I can go meet a sexy man at a bar if that's what I feel like doing. I can learn to play pool in my forties. I can have nights to myself.

And—after fantasizing about that pottery class for nearly a week—I can say with complete honesty that this is *exactly* what I feel like doing.

7

MAC

As I TIP a bottle of beer into my mouth to take a sip, my eyes drift to the door for the millionth time tonight.

She'll show up. I know she will. Her friends wanted to come here, so she has no choice. She'll be here.

Another sip of beer; another glance at the door.

"You got it bad," my brother says from behind the bar. He's taller than me by an inch and has the same thick, dark hair, usually messy from the way he runs his hands through it. Lee sees one of the regulars jerk his chin and is a good enough bartender to know that means the man wants another drink. As he pours the pint, he arches a brow at me. "Dad told me about your woman."

"She's not my woman."

Yet.

Wait. No.

She's not my woman, ever.

My father claps me on the shoulder. "Help me change a keg, will you?" He jerks his head to the storeroom where we keep the spare barrels.

I nod, slipping off my stool to follow him across the bar. My father has a bounce in his step that I haven't seen in a long time, and I wonder if it has anything to do with the long phone calls he's been taking in his office with a certain refined, sophisticated older woman he recently met.

The thought makes a void tear open in my chest. My father is a man of contradictions, but he's always been predictable. Steady. He owns a bar, but doesn't drink. He rides a motorcycle, wild as anything, then goes home to spend long hours reading by the window that overlooks his backyard. He flirts with women, charms them within moments, but he doesn't get attached. Never has.

Not since my mother left him with us boys and never came back.

It was me, Lee, and Dad against the world. I learned early on how easy it is for women to walk away. I felt the pain of those wounds like bloody, ripped blisters on my feet. Constant, throbbing aches that got worse with time, not better, and I learned it by seeing my father drink himself to near-death, then crawl his way back to sobriety.

When he bought the Grove, I thought it was some awful form of torture, some penance for the years he spent drowning in his own pain, but it was just another of his contradictions. Being near alcohol didn't make him relapse. It's like he needed the constant reminder of what would happen if he did.

It always made sense to me that Dad was on his own, the same way it made sense that *I* was on my own. Like the sun rising in the east. It was the only way we could be.

But my father glances over his shoulder, a broad grin on his lips. "Don't look so worried, son. She'll show."

I pretend not to know what he's talking about. We keep

the new kegs near the back of the building, in a room where the delivery truck can easily access the door. My father, wisely choosing to drop the subject of who may or may not show up at the Grove tonight, tells me which beer needs to be changed, so I grab one of the big silver kegs and start rolling it across the floor to get to the keg room behind the bar. From there, I swap an empty for a full one and haul the empty keg over my shoulder to take it back to the storage room.

It's a trip I've made hundreds of times, especially as my father has gotten older and struggled with the weight of the full kegs. I know every step of the journey from the keg room to the storage room by heart. I could walk this path in my sleep.

And it's when I'm halfway across the bar that I see her.

Trina walks in wearing tight jeans, the hottest fucking knee-high boots I've ever seen, and a white top that's somehow not revealing while leaving nothing to the imagination. Holy *fuck*. My brain stops sending signals to the rest of my body and everything inside me malfunctions. I trip over a chair, my body pitches forward, and the keg clangs against a table. Beer goes flying everywhere.

Screams, flailing arms, empty kegs rolling away, and then I'm on the floor. There's a chair on top of me and a table descending toward me, until a hand reaches out and catches it—but not before every bottle and glass on the table comes clattering down around and on top of me. One of them smashes nearby.

Great. Wonderful. I blink, afraid to move in case I cut myself on broken glass. Also, I might be in shock.

My father's face appears in my field of vision, his eyes glimmering with humor. "That was quite the dismount."

"Be quiet and help me up, yeah?" I extend an arm, which my father grabs to help me to my feet. Thankfully, the glass that smashed was a couple feet away from me, but I still brush out my hair in case of shards.

"Are you okay?" a sweet-as-honey voice says from behind my back, and I brace myself before turning around.

It doesn't help. Trina is still as drop-dead gorgeous as she was a minute ago, when I wasn't covered in dust and spilled beer and a sheen of hot embarrassment. Her long-sleeved white top hugs every inch of her tight, curvy body. I run my eyes down to those mile-long legs, internally groaning again at the sight of her heeled black boots. I can't help but imagine asking her to wear them for me—and *only* them—somewhere more private.

When my eyes slide back up to meet her eyes, I have to fight the instinct to shift my pants against the growing tightness near the placket of my zipper. She did something with her hair, her makeup. It makes me hard as hell, as if my body knows this is the woman I've been waiting for. This is the woman I want.

Then I realize I've been staring at her for a really, really long time. My father clears his throat as someone sweeps up glass nearby.

"Hey," I manage.

Her lush, pink lips—glittering with some kind of shiny gloss that makes me want to lick her mouth clean—curl into a smile. "Hi." Her gaze slides to my father, standing to my left. "Reporting for duty, Hamish. I brought a few willing students with me." She points her thumb over her shoulder, and that's when I see her friends.

Battening down the hatches might have been a good idea.

Simone, the redhead, has her arm around Harold, a grouchy regular that's as much of a fixture as the stool he sits on. But the weird thing? Harold is *laughing*. I've known the man eleven years, and I've never seen him laugh.

The dark-haired woman—Fiona, from memory—is passing her card over the bar to pay for a round of drinks while Trina's sister, Candice, has drifted over to the electronic jukebox by the wall. Then, "Fantasy" by Mariah Carey starts blaring over the speakers, causing every regular patron—all male, all older than me—to snap their heads up in confusion.

But the women—including the quiet one, Jen, that barely said anything at the pottery class but made the best bowl I've seen from a beginner—throw their hands in the air with a collective scream and immediately start singing and dancing. They know every word. Every little trill. And they're singing at top volume—and not necessarily in key.

"Oh, God..." Trina looks horrified.

It makes me laugh. I pick up the chair I'd crashed into while my father replaces the customer's spilled beer, and when I grab the empty keg, I clear my throat. "I need to put this away," I tell Trina. "Don't... Don't disappear, okay?"

Her smile spreads wide across her face as she tilts that pretty head of hers. "Where would I go? I have very serious business to attend to." Her eyes slide to my father, who nods.

"Damn right you do. First thing's first, grab a pool cue. I'm going to show you how to chalk it up."

With a grin, Trina follows him to the back of the bar where the pool table resides. I watch her walk away and nearly stumble over that damn chair again when I see the back of her outfit. There's her ass, which is glorious, cupped by those jeans like they're painted on...

And then there's her top. Somehow, by some female fashion voodoo, there's no back. Her hair cascades down in golden-brown curls to mid-back, and when she takes a hand to lift it off her neck, I groan at the sight of her spine, the creamy expanse of flesh on display.

The woman's *back* is making my cock throb, for fuck's

sake. I readjust my belt, but I can't tear my eyes away from Trina as she grabs a pool cue, chalking it up under my father's watchful eye. Then he demonstrates how to prop the cue against his left hand, and I'm the luckiest man in the world, because I get to watch Trina lean over the green felt, her heart-shaped ass and exposed back glowing gold under the lights above the pool table.

That pose...

I stifle a groan. I'm not going to make it through the night if this continues.

A face appears at my side. Fiona. She squints at me, then lets a slow smile spread across her face. Then she just starts laughing. "It's a lobotomy, ladies!"

The rest of them cheer, then go back to singing and dancing.

I glance over my shoulder and nearly fall over again when I see Harold bopping along to the music, his feet shuffling beside his stool as Simone swings his arms from side to side while she sings Mariah's lyrics off-pitch in his face. And Harold loves every minute of it, judging by the broad, gap-toothed smile on his face.

Shaking my head, I grab the keg and make my way to the keg room for a moment of peace. I put the empty barrel with the rest of them and pause before exiting the small room again. It's a long, rectangular room with an exterior door at one end and an interior door to the bar at the other. Empty kegs line the wall on one side, with full ones on the other. I stand between the silver barrels, hand on the interior door, and I drop my chin to my chest.

Trina... She looked... I'm not...

I can't even form coherent thoughts. My cock is so hard I feel like I'm fifteen years old instead of forty-five. I squeeze my eyes shut and press my palm to my shaft against the zipper of my jeans, willing it to go down—but it only swells in response, throbbing against the pressure of my touch.

Fuck.

I can't go out there like this. I already tripped over my feet and nearly knocked a table over. How am I supposed to watch her bending over the pool table every few minutes while my body feels heated to the core?

And—look, I'm not proud of this. But I either have to wait for this to pass, knowing my shaft will grow painfully hard as soon as I walk out there again, or...

Ah, fuck it. I hunt through my pockets and, not finding what I need, I kick off a shoe and pull my sock off. Then, like some sex-crazed hormonal mess, I lean my back against the door and unbuckle my belt with quick, jerky movements. My cock is a heavy iron bar when I pull it free from my pants.

Fisting myself with a tight grip, I close my eyes and think of those shiny, pink lips. Of that body leaning over the pool table, hair spilling over her shoulder with her back on display. Of Trina's bright eyes, and how good they'd look if they were lazy with pleasure. I think of notching my shoulders between those thighs while discovering what kind of noises she'd make with her legs wrapped around my head. How she'd taste, earthy and sweet and fucking perfect. I think of spreading her wet heat with my hardness, feeling her milk my cock with every hard stroke—

My orgasm rips through me, pulling heat to my groin and spurting it out in thick, long ropes. I grunt low and rough, catching my seed with my fucking sock, of all things, wishing it was her skin. Her mouth. Her soft, pink folds.

I lean against the door, panting, letting my head fall back with a soft thud. I should be fucking ashamed of myself for this, but all I feel is relief. A few gulping breaths, and my heartbeat starts to slow. When I close my eyes, I still see her, but I no longer feel like I'm about to burst out of my skin.

Then I tuck myself in, zip myself up, slip my shoe back on, walk out of the keg room, and throw my soiled sock away in the first available trash can. Finally, with a deep breath, I walk back out into the bar.

8

TRINA

"It's all about angles," Hamish says for the millionth time when my shot hits the felt just beside the pocket, ricocheting halfway across the pool table. "Focus on the angles."

"I get that," I answer, trying hard to keep the frustration out of my voice, "but I'm not understanding what angles I'm supposed to be focusing on."

A hand lands on my shoulder, and Simone appears at my side. "Can I try?"

"Please." I give her a smile in thanks, needing a sip of my drink—badly. Between seeing Mac fall flat on his face when he saw me, to the heat in his eyes when I approached, to this surprisingly serious lesson on how to play pool, I'm not exactly feeling like myself.

Not to mention this backless bodysuit requires undergarments that are a combination of Spanx, a girdle, and a full jumpsuit with built-in cups—no way in hell am I ever going braless in public, not after breastfeeding two kids—and all these layers are starting to feel a little too warm. A bit too tight...especially down there.

Simone sights a ball as Hamish directs her, but I have a

feeling she doesn't need his help. She hits it with practiced ease. Not only does she pot the ball she was trying to hit, but the white ball rolls to nudge a second ball into a corner pocket.

"Show-off," I mumble, but there's no animosity in it.

Simone grins. "Try thinking less. When you do an eyeliner flick, do you calculate the angles in your head, or do you just go for it and trust your instinct?"

"Instinct," I answer. "Also, I've done it a zillion times, so I know what looks good on my face."

"So do the same thing here. Look at the ball and line up, then hit through it with a smooth stroke."

Why did the words "smooth stroke" just make me blush? Is it perhaps because Mac just walked out of the hallway where he disappeared a few minutes ago, and he looks good enough to lick?

Simone titters, then winks at me. She thrusts the pool cue into my hands and gives me an encouraging nod. "Go for the orange." She points to the solid orange ball lined up perfectly with a pocket.

It should be an easy hit. Even for me.

But I can almost *sense* Mac approaching. The distance between us shrinking. His eyes on my body, my skin, my hair.

Squeezing my eyes for a moment, I think of eyeliner flicks. Easy. Intuitive. The more confidence, the better the wing.

And I hit the cue ball, smiling at the satisfying thunk of the orange hitting the bottom of the pocket and rolling into the internal mechanism of the table.

"Nice shot," a deep voice says behind me. I turn to see Mac grinning at me. "You're a quick study."

"Thank goodness for eyeliner," I respond, and laugh at

the tiny frown that appears on Mac's forehead. I shake my head. "Never mind."

"Boys versus girls?" Simone asks, sipping her drink as her eyes gleam at me. "I'll rack 'em up." She gets to work, accepting the keys that Hamish hands her to unlock the table and allow us to play for free. I watch as she gets the triangle and starts expertly swapping balls around with—in my eyes —no rhyme or reason, trying my best to ignore the heat of Mac's shoulder as it nudges mine.

"How was your week?" I ask, my voice going up uncontrollably at the end. I clear my throat.

Mac takes a sip of beer. "Long." His eyes flick to mine, then to my lips, then away.

Lordy.

Is it hot in here, or is it just my shapewear?

"Ladies first," Hamish says to Simone. "You break."

Simone shrugs and throws me a wink over her shoulder before turning back to the old Scot. "Your funeral, old man."

Then, with a flourish and more confidence than I've had in all my life, Simone lines up and hits the pack of balls hard enough to make me jump. The satisfying crack of the balls snaps across my skin, and the balls explode outward. Two of them drop into pockets, and Simone blows on her nails.

Mac chuckles, moving his hand to brush the small of my back. His broad, warm palm makes heat pool low in my body, and I do my best not to let my heart run away from me. "Are you always this nervous?" he asks, his thumb making a slow sweep across my spine, his eyes dancing as he glances down at me.

I study the strand of tousled hair that falls down over his temple, a bit of silver gleaming in the low light of the bar, and I shrug. "Only when I'm about to make a fool of myself."

"It's a week to try new things," he replies, and I know he's talking about pottery and pool, but it really, *really* sounds like he's talking about something...else.

His hand stays where it is, thumb making slow, steady movements over and back across my skin. His thumb is near my spine, but his other fingers feel dangerously close to my jeans. To places so private, they haven't been touched in a long, long time. It's making my head spin.

I watch Simone miss a shot and whisper a curse under her breath, then Hamish lines up and hits three balls in a row. Then, he leaves me with the white on the opposite end of the table as all our balls, with all my targets hidden behind the boys' balls.

I bite my lip, not moving from my spot even though both Simone and Hamish look at me expectantly.

"Your turn," Simone says with an encouraging smile.

Just then, Fiona, Candice, and Jen wander over. Simone gives them a quick recap, and Fiona lifts her glass. "Go Trina! Are you stripes or solids?"

"Solids," I answer, still not moving from the wall.

Mac hasn't moved his hand either, and his thumb keeps stroking, slow and steady. It's erotic, that touch, sending every thought fleeing from my head as heat builds low in my stomach. Back and forth, soft but firm, feeling his big, warm hand pressed against my skin. I think, given enough time, I could probably come from it. From him touching the small of my back. My skin feels tight, prickly. All I can do is throw back a gulp of my drink and tear myself away from him. The space where his hand was a moment ago burns. I want more of it. More of him.

I line up for a shot that Hamish helpfully points out for me, and then promptly miss.

Mac grins. He holds out his hand for the cue, his fingers brushing mine while he takes it from my hands. Then I watch his corded, muscular body lean over the table to expose a little strip of skin on his lower back, the arms in his muscles stark against the green felt beneath them.

And he pots a ball.

"Well, we know who the dud in this round is," I say, rolling my eyes. "Aren't you guys supposed to be teaching me?"

Simone just laughs and takes her position when it's her turn. I find myself at the bar, ordering a round for everyone, then watch Hamish do his thing.

My turn again already. When I stand next to the table, pool cue grasped in my hands, I bite my lip and look at the battlefield. I don't have high hopes.

"Here," Mac says as he sets his fresh beer down and approaches. "I'll help. You're keeping too much tension in your right arm. Line up for that shot." He points to one of the balls and waits for me to position myself.

I feel him move behind me, his fingers leaving trails of fire over my hips as he shifts me over slightly, repositioning the pool cue. His hand on my elbows is like a brand, squeezing gently to get my attention.

"Good," he says quietly. "Relax."

"Kinda hard in this position," I say, glancing over my shoulder in frustration.

Oh. Big mistake.

Mac is standing just inches from me, his hips near my ass, one hand on the waistband of my jeans while the other still grips the pool cue. Words fail me. I don't want to admit to myself how good it feels to have him behind me like this, or how much it turns me on to be bent over this table with him behind me.

Especially when he's looking at me like he's thinking the

same thing. Hooded eyes, dark gaze. After a beat, he nods to the table. "Take the shot, Trina."

I turn back around, still so intensely aware of every inch of him so close to me. But I take the shot and to my surprise, I pot a ball.

Simone whoops, and all the girls cheer. I start laughing, standing and leaning back slightly into the warmth and strength of Mac's chest.

He puts his hands on my shoulders and leans his lips close to my ear. "Nice shot." A soft squeeze of my upper arms with those sinful hands, and he steps away from me.

I miss my next shot, but that's less because I suck at pool and more because my brain is scrambled. But still, when I slide onto a barstool next to Fiona, my eyes across the pool table on Mac, I can't help but smile.

I'm having fun. I can't remember the last time I had fun. My kids are safe, my new home will be ready soon, and the sexiest man I've ever seen looks at me like he might think I'm sexy too.

I met Kevin thirteen years ago, when I was twenty-nine years old, and I wonder if it's been that long since I had a night out like this. A night that's just for me.

THE BOYS WIN, and Jen and Candice take our spots to play them. Unsurprisingly, Jen is even better at pool than Simone. She tries to tell me something about angles, but I've had two drinks—not to mention the wine I had at home—and all I can do is nod along and pretend I understand what she's explaining.

Feeling overheated, happy, and a little buzzed, I end up going to the bathroom before slipping outside for a bit of fresh air. It's August and the air is warm, so I stand just outside the Grove and let out a happy sigh.

The door opens behind me, and I turn to see Mac exiting the bar. His eyes crinkle when he sees me. "You okay? I saw you slip out on your own and was worried you were running away from me again."

"Needed some fresh air," I explain, grateful that the dark is hiding my blushing face. "I'm wearing too many layers."

Mac's eyes flash as an eyebrow pops up. "I can think of a few ways to rectify that."

I laugh, swatting at him. "You're naughty."

"Only when I want to be. Now, tell me the truth. You were out here because you just wanted to ogle my bike."

Laughing again, I tilt my head up to meet his gaze as he approaches. "Maybe," I admit.

He closes the distance between us and takes a deep breath. "I'm glad you came. Earlier, I was thinking maybe you wouldn't show."

"Is that why you had that spectacular fall when I walked in? Pure shock?"

Mac's lips tilt, but his eyes grow lazy. "No, Trina." He reaches over and hooks a finger into my belt loop, tugging me closer. "I fell over because you're the most beautiful woman I've ever seen."

Heat rises up my neck and over my cheeks. He gives me another tug and I catch myself on his chest, fingers curling into his black tee. "No need for flattery, Mac."

With one hand still hooked around my belt loop, Mac lifts another to tuck a strand of hair behind my ear. He lets his fingers slide down the strand, then shifts his gaze to meet mine. "It's not flattery if it's true."

Suddenly, I realize where I am. Half-drunk with a man I barely know, standing outside a bar his father owns. My two kids are at home in bed, and I'm here. Doing...whatever it is I'm doing.

"Look, Mac, I..." I take a deep breath.

Mac slides his palm over my neck, curling his fingers into the hair at my nape. He leans his forehead against mine, effectively silencing me. "If you're about to give me some sweet rejection, do me a favor and just...don't."

I close my eyes for a moment and try to find the words to say what I need to say. I've been divorced for approximately three seconds. I spent thirteen years with Kevin and I don't know myself anymore. I have kids and school and money and housing to worry about.

And a cat. I can't forget the cat.

I can't handle a man! Even if he looks like sex on legs. *Especially* if he looks like sex on legs. I'm a divorcée with two kids and boobs that are a lot less perky than they were twenty years ago. Why the hell would a sexy, badass, pottery-throwing motorcycle man like him want someone as normal and boring as *me*?

"Trina," Mac says softly, lifting his head from mine. I open my eyes to meet his gaze. "Whatever's going on in your head right now, I'm going to need it to stop."

Annoyance sparks at his words. "You can't just tell me to stop thinking what I'm thinking, Mac."

His lips tilt. "I can, and I did."

"Listen. I don't know the type of women that you usually hang around with, but I'm not—"

He shuts me up with a kiss. His mouth takes mine as the pressure on my neck increases, and I tilt my head where he wants it. Then he deepens the kiss, sliding his tongue across mine as a low, guttural grunt escapes his throat. The hand on my belt loop slides around my body to rest on my lower back. The heat of his skin, the pressure of his kiss, the way his tongue strokes and teases—it's too much.

I melt.

Or maybe I implode.

Whatever happens, any thoughts of rejection fly away, and I forget all the reasons I can't do this, because every part of me can only focus on how much I want it. My hands hook around his neck, fingers tangling into that tousled, dark hair as another groan slips through his lips.

I love those noises. I love that he's making them with *me*. I love the way his hand presses against my lower back when I slide my tongue against his, how he tightens his fingers into my hair to bring me nearer.

Then his hand slides lower and he palms my ass to tug me closer. I gasp when I feel the steel in his pants. Mac breaks the kiss, moving his lips to my jaw, my neck, his teeth tugging at my earlobe.

"Mac."

He pulls back just far enough to meet my eyes. "I fucking love the way you say my name."

My insides turn molten at the intensity of his gaze, his voice. "How do I say it?" I ask, my voice barely more than a rasp.

He closes his eyes for a moment, his nose sliding along the side of mine. When he kisses me again, Mac's lips are soft, tender. Then he speaks against my mouth, shaping the words as his lips brush mine. "You say my name like it means something."

My heart thunders. My legs wobble. Mac's hand stays splayed over my ass, the tips of his fingers just brushing the crease between my inner thighs and the swell of my curves. I'm going to spontaneously combust. His other hand moves from my neck down to my breast, and his thumb starts making slow, deliberate circles over my furling nipple.

Gasping into his kiss, I realize I'm clinging to him, sinking my fingers into his shoulders and grinding my hips against his hardness. His tongue slides over mine, exploring my mouth as that thumb—that *thumb*—continues its slow torture of my breast.

I want him to use his mouth. I want him to bend his head down and suck my breast through my top, tug my nipple between his teeth and make another one of those guttural noises. I want him to drag me to the side of the building, tear my jeans down and shove inside me. Every filthy, dirty fantasy I've ever had is a living thing inside me now, hot and needy and alive.

Then someone opens the bar door, and we scramble apart. The old man with the missing front tooth who had been dancing up a storm with Simone stumbles out, catching himself on the side of the building. He looks up at me, then at Mac, nods, and makes his way toward the road.

I put a hand to my forehead and chance a look at Mac.

His lush, kiss-bruised lips curl up at the corners.

"We should go back inside," I blurt.

A pause extends between us, and I wonder if Mac might not want to go inside. If he might want to go somewhere else...with me.

But he lets out a breath and slides his hand across my shoulders to pull me close to his side. It's the perfect place for me, and all I can do is hook my arm around his waist to hold on. Then he places a soft kiss to my temple, and my heart gives a mighty thump. "Yeah," he says softly. "Let's go back in."

9

TRINA

I WAKE up to the mother of all hangovers and a godawful smell. What the—

Vomit. There's vomit on my carpet.

Did I...?

I blink. No. I didn't get *that* drunk. I had five drinks. I counted! I remember everything, including a certain kiss that feels like a universe away from where I am now, and I know for a fact I did not vomit on my carpet. I left not long after the kiss, swept away by Candice in Mom Mode, who insisted we'd regret it if we stayed out for one more drink.

I didn't puke.

Which means...

"Mom..." Katie is at the foot of my bed looking pale, sweaty, and ashamed. "I'm sorry. I wanted to come to bed with you, and then I didn't make it to the bathroom in time, and—" She interrupts herself, clapping a hand over her mouth.

You know when you hear those stories about mothers lifting cars off their babies with superhuman strength? Well, my hungover ass moves with superhuman speed. I throw my blankets off and don't even blink when I realize I'm wearing a pajama shirt and nothing else. I scoop Katie up under her armpits and sprint to the en-suite bathroom just in time for her to spew all over the toilet.

"Get it all out, honey," I say, pulling her hair back. "It's okay. You're okay."

Her little body shakes as another retch convulses through her. Oh, jeez. Leaving my hand on her back running small circles over her, I reach for a washcloth and run some cool water. Then I run it over her head, her neck, trying to soothe my little girl.

After washing her up and tucking her in my bed, I get to work cleaning the vomit-soaked carpet, glancing once every few minutes at my daughter, fast asleep in a pile of blankets on my bed.

It's hard not to feel guilty about going out last night when I have a pounding headache and a sick little girl. Watery light starts brightening through the curtains as dawn approaches while I spray some carpet cleaner on the stain to soak.

Giving Katie a kiss on her clammy forehead, I go out in search of my son.

He's usually up by now. Toby is a morning lark through and through, just like me. But when I push open his bedroom door, I find him burrowed in a nest of blankets and pillows of his own. Sitting down on the edge of his bed, I push hair off his clammy forehead as he groans, looking so young it makes my heart squeeze.

"I don't feel good, Mommy."

Uh-oh. He hasn't called me mommy since he was a toddler. He must be feeling really ill. My son curls himself around my hip, putting a hand across my thigh.

I stroke his hair for a few moments, then grab a bucket to set it near the bed. Then, my morning is swallowed up by sick kids and lots of vomit. My mother wakes to the sound of Toby retching into his bucket. She gives me a horrified look and gets to work helping me.

All those times I complained—either out loud or in my head—about being a grown woman living with her mother? Yeah, just...forget about those. Lottie is a superhero right now.

It's not until the sun is well and truly up, the kids have had a bit of juice for hydration, and I feel worse than I did when I awoke that I'm finally able to sit down at the kitchen table. Mom puts a cup of coffee in front of me and feeds the cat while I sit, listening to birds titter as a beautiful day unfolds just out the window.

"You think they caught a bug at day camp?" I ask as my mother joins me with a coffee cup of her own.

"Who knows?" She leans back and lets out a long sigh. Then she blinks and glances at me. "How was your girls' night?"

I let out a huff. Girls' night feels like eons ago. Did I really half-drunkenly kiss Mac? Calling it a kiss doesn't exactly feel accurate. It felt like sex. I shake my head. "It was fine. I'm not twenty anymore. I can't drink like that. I had five drinks and I feel like garbage."

My mother chuckles. She tilts her head. "Was Mr. Pottery there?"

Don't blush. Don't blush. Don't blush.

"Yeah." My cheeks heat. Damn it.

She holds my gaze. "And...?"

"And what?" I play dumb, knowing it won't get me anywhere with her.

I'm saved by a knock on the door, and that's when I realize I'm still not wearing any panties. My T-shirt hits high on my thighs, so I sprint—well, hobble—upstairs to grab a pair of old pajama shorts.

Candice is in the entryway when I come back downstairs, frowning at me. "You're not dressed."

"The kids are sick."

Her reply is automatic. "Oh, no! Can I do anything?"

Have I mentioned I love my sister? Why the heck didn't I move here ages ago? I haven't had this much help with the kids, *ever*.

I shake my head.

"I was coming to get you to go glaze our pottery, but I'm guessing you want to stay here."

"Yeah." Does it make me a terrible mother that I'm partly glad my kids are sick? Not glad they're sick, but glad I have a decent excuse. The thought of seeing Mac when I look and feel the way I do...

"I'll tell Mac you say hi."

"That's not necessary—"

"You do that, honey," my mother interjects. "Tell him to stop by here sometime during the week too. I'd like to see him again."

"Mom, no," I practically shout, then frown. "Wait. '*Again*?' What do you mean by 'again?'"

Lottie, in classic Lottie style, totally ignores me. Why is it that I feel like a kid any time she's around? I'm a grown woman! I'm forty-two!

"This Mac boy might be just what she needs. Don't you think, Candice?" She shuffles back to the kitchen for more coffee while I swing my gaze to meet Candice's laughing one.

My sister shakes her head. "Now you know what I went through for the past three months. She was insufferable when Blake and I first started seeing each other."

"Careful!" Mom calls from the kitchen.

Grinning at Candice, I say goodbye, then go check on my kids again.

I DON'T SEE anyone until the next day. I'm too busy taking care of two sick kids, and when Candice and Fiona stop by with big platters of food, soup, and a box with my mediocre pottery, I give them a grateful smile. "I haven't eaten in forever. Thank you. The kids are sleeping, but the soup will be great."

"Fallon made it from scratch," Candice says, opening the fridge and propping it with her hip while she puts the food away.

Fiona lifts my slightly misshapen bowl, glazed in bright pink. "It was supposed to be green but somehow turned pink when it was fired in the kiln. Don't ask me how."

I snort. "That's fine. I'm not exactly going to frame it or anything."

"You should see what Mac made. It was gorgeous. He brought a few samples of different glazed pots and mugs to show us what was possible, and I think I'm going to order all new crockery for the café," Fiona says, running her fingers over the uneven edge of my new jewelry tray.

"Apparently he's famous in the pottery world," I say, putting my new bowl in the cupboard.

"It shows. I think his stuff would fit the Four Cups' aesthetic."

"Definitely," Candice says. "And with the extra money we made with the catering contract at the beginning of the summer, I'm fully supportive of upgrading." Without me having to ask, my sister starts cleaning. She glances at me over her shoulder and nods to the messy mop of hair on my head and grubby athletic clothes I'm wearing. "Go shower. We'll clean up and check on the kids."

What would I do without them? Sometimes, I worry that moving the kids away from Kevin was a bad decision, but I'd discussed it with him prior to the move, and he seemed almost relieved that he wouldn't have to take care of them fifty percent of the time. When we were married, he could barely manage a few hours without calling me to rescue him. He was happy enough to get a weekend a month with them.

Still, I worried that it was a bad decision.

Now, though, when I have more of a support system than I've had in years—decades? Ever?—I know coming to Heart's Cove was the right thing to do. I take a long, hot shower, and come out feeling like a new woman.

Then I dress and head downstairs to find my mother, Candice, and Fiona lounging in the living room with tea and cookies laid out.

Fiona points to the plate of treats. "Jen made these. New recipe. Double chocolate with salted caramel. Amazing."

I haven't eaten a vegetable in forty-eight hours, but whatever. I pour myself a mug of chamomile tea and grab a cookie, curling up on the couch next to my sister.

"How are you holding up?" Candice asks.

I glance at her and shake my head. "I was just thinking how grateful I am for you guys."

Candice pats my leg. "We're family, Trina. It's what we do."

I lean my head back on the sofa. "Yeah, but I'm still grateful for you all. I haven't had help in a long time." Staring at my tea, I shake my head. "I remember when Katie was born. Toby got some sort of stomach bug at the same time. He was nineteen months old and sick as a dog. Katie was three weeks old. It was totally overwhelming."

Candice's face scrunches up. "I remember that. I should have gone up to help you, but Paul was in the hospital, and..."

"It's fine." I wave a hand. After taking a sip of my tea, I let out a snort. "I remember this one specific day: I was breast-feeding Katie on the sofa. Toby was lying next to me, so sick I was considering taking him to the emergency room. Kevin walks into the house with his mother, and—"

I have to stop myself from talking, because the anger and shame well up inside me without warning. Tears build behind my eyelids, and I swallow them down with a gulp of tea. I meet Fiona's eyes across the room.

"What happened?" she asks.

"His mother walked in," I repeat, "and saw me on the sofa with Katie at my boob, and made this big song and dance about turning away in shock. Then Kevin—my fucking *husband*—told me I needed to cover up. In my own house! I was feeding our daughter and taking care of our sick son, and he had the nerve to tell me I needed to cover my own boob up. I wasn't sunbathing topless for the whole neighborhood to see. I was on the couch in the freaking living room! *My own* living room! But his mother wouldn't shut up about it. She even told Kevin's sister, and the whole family made me feel like I'd done something wrong. I was postpartum and sleep-deprived and totally overwhelmed, and they made me feel ashamed for feeding my own daughter."

"That *dick*," Candice says with more vitriol than I've ever heard from her. "And his mother! How fucking *dare* she? She's a mother herself!"

Seven-year-old anger boils inside me. I snort and shake my head. "I should have known then that he wasn't the man for me. I probably did know, but what was I supposed to do with two young kids?" My finger toys with the edge of my mug. "The worst thing is, I felt so, so ashamed. It was like a burning lump of coal in my chest. He kept badgering me, and his mother made so many snide comments about me covering up, and I was actually convinced that I was in the wrong."

"I'm going to kill him," my mother says before taking a vicious bite of her cookie. She masticates violently while shaking her head. "He's coming next weekend to be with the kids, right?" When I nod, she points her half-eaten cookie at me. "Well, he's going to get a piece of my mind."

"Mom," I protest, even though I can't keep the smile off my face. "It was a long time ago."

"He deserves to get chewed out." Fiona shakes her head, gritting her teeth on my behalf. "What an ass." Getting up, she moves to sit next to me, putting her arm around my shoulders. Then Fiona—a woman I just met a few months ago—squeezes my shoulders until I soften against her. Emotion clogs my throat. Fiona holds me close as she says, "Divorce sucks, and it's painful and messy and awful, but you'll get through it. You'll be happier in a few months' time than you thought possible. I promise. Simone can attest to that too."

I don't know why I burst into tears. Maybe it's the fact that I've been so alone for so many years, and I didn't even realize it. I lived in Seattle with Kevin and drifted away from most of my friends as the years wore on. I knew *his* friends. The only person I could lean on was my mother, but Kevin didn't get along with her, so I ended up avoiding her too. I was so damn alone, and the man who was supposed to be my partner wasn't there for me. Ever.

I guess I'm crying because I never realized it. I didn't see what was right in front of my face until just now. With two sick kids, no job, the divorce finally done, and more external stress than I've had in years, I still feel better than I did when

I was married to Kevin and withstanding his belittling comments day in, day out.

I'm sad for myself. I'm sad that I actually put up with that. That I thought *I* was wrong. I'm sad that I felt ashamed for feeding Katie on my own damn sofa. I'm sad that when Kevin cheated, I blamed myself. I'm sad that I wasted so much fucking time on him.

But with Fiona on one side of me and Candice on the other, with my mother calling out threats against Kevin like it's her job, I let out a little teary laugh. My kids are sick, vomiting, and my life is a mess...but I have support. I have a family.

"There," Candice says when I let out a sigh. "See? We got you."

I look at my sister and give her a smile. "Remember a few months ago when you asked if Iliana was the one who had it all figured out?"

Our younger sister is a free spirit. She's been traveling for years, and always seems to land on her feet. I think she's had about a thousand boyfriends and none of them have stuck, but she's been happy. Free.

Candice smiles. "Iliana is different from you and me, Trina."

"I know," I reply, resting my head on her shoulder. "But I was just thinking that actually, she might be the one who's missing out by not being here with us."

Candice clicks her tongue, squeezing me tight, and my mother comes over to wrap all three of us in a big, motherly hug. When she backs away, she's got tears in her eyes.

Mr. Fuzzles, who has been out of sight most of the day, appears from under the sofa. With a surprisingly powerful jump, he leaps into my lap and curls up on top of me, promptly falling asleep. My heart nearly gives out at the feel of his little warm body snuggled up against me.

Maybe I am a cat person.

After a few minutes, conversation drifts to more neutral topics. Candice's house will be ready for me, my mother, and the kids to move into in two weeks, just in time for the start of the school year. Fiona is helping Clancy choose colleges to apply to, and she's brimming with pride for her stepdaughter. Her wedding preparations are well underway. My mother bought a new outfit from a local shop and can't wait to wear it when she's out with Margaret and Dorothy next week.

When I ask where they're planning to go, she grins. "Well, a certain Scottish bar owner seems to have taken a liking to a certain hotel owner, and she seems to be enjoying the attention."

"Hamish?" I ask, not sure how to feel about that. "And...Margaret?"

My mother smiles wide. "Dorothy wants Eli to meet him." Eli is Dorothy's partner. They met a couple of years ago, when Simone and Wes started dating. They're perfect for each other.

Then Candice glances at me. "Mac was asking about you today." Her eyes twinkle. "He offered to deliver your pottery in person."

I stare at her, horrified.

My sister cackles. "I figured that would be your reaction, which is why I said it probably wasn't the right time to come visit you."

"Thank God."

"Do you think he'd let me ride his motorcycle?" my mother asks, reaching for another of the admittedly addictive chocolate-caramel cookies.

I freeze. "Mom..."

"Trina, I'm in my seventies, and there's a sexy younger man with a hot bike. What kind of person would I be if I *didn't* ask him to take me for a ride?"

"Um, the normal kind?"

Candice snorts, then throws me a sideways glance. "Pick your battles, Trina. If Mom wants to ride on Mac's bike, I'd put money on the fact that she'll end up on it."

The worst part is, I know it's true.

"I just need to get through Kevin's visit this weekend. Can we leave the motorcycle riding until after that?"

"I'm not making any promises," my mother announces.

Then, the four of us hear movement upstairs, and my mother—nutty, thrill-seeking, but incredibly loving and supportive—puts out a hand. "My turn. I'll go check on them. You relax, Trina."

Having moved to stand up, I pause, glance down at the kitten in my lap, and lean back again. After a brief hesitation, I help myself to another cookie. Mr. Fuzzles purrs against me, lifting his head to demand more scratches. I oblige, and finally let a smile curl over my lips.

"What?" Fiona sips her tea, arching a brow.

"I was just imagining the look on Kevin's face if he saw my mother riding a motorcycle." I laugh, shaking my head. "He'd be horrified." When the two of them don't answer, I give them a grin. "That's a good thing."

"I'm sure it can be arranged," Candice says, kicking her feet up on the coffee table. "Or better yet, he could see *you* riding on the back of Mac's motorcycle. I'd pay good money to see *that* expression on his face."

"Asshole," Fiona mumbles.

And maybe this makes me a bad person, but hearing Fiona calling my ex-husband nasty names puts a great big smile on my face.

10

JEN

THERE'S something wrong with the leavening agent in my chocolate layer cake recipe. Crossing my arms, I stare down the offending baked goods with narrowed eyes. Dense on the bottom and crumbly on top, this recipe just doesn't want to play ball.

And, of course, it's the recipe Fiona and Grant chose for their wedding—and one Amanda thinks we should include in the book.

But the recipe isn't working. It's too finicky, it's not consistent, and definitely not friendly for home bakers. And it's driving me crazy.

It's nearly eleven o'clock at night, and I've been baking chocolate cake for six days. It's now Thursday night, and I'm running out of time. Developing recipes is a rabbit hole I never expected to be so all-consuming. My mind is brimming with baking chemistry, procedures, ingredient quality. Last night, I had a stress dream about a talking meringue. It called me a fraud then burst into flame, and I woke up sweaty and breathless.

It's bad.

But by the end of it, there will be a book with my name on the front and my recipes inside. That's worth a few sleepless nights, no?

At least I'm not thinking of him. Fallon Richter. The man who kissed me like I was the only woman he ever wanted.

Too bad his ex-girlfriend, Amanda, wants him too—and that she's the one person who can make my recipe book a reality. So with Fallon on one side, and Amanda (and my recipe book) on the other, I was forced to choose. Unsurprisingly, I chose not to get in the middle of an old relationship.

I may not be the smartest person in the world, but I know that poking that hornets' nest will only hurt one person: me.

The back door to the café opens, and I let out a little yelp. "Fallon. What are you doing here?"

"Looking for you," is his answer, which makes my heart seize and thump at the same time, which then makes me wonder if his presence is dangerous for my health.

"Why?" I'm holding a spatula for some reason. When did I pick that up? It's brandished between us like it can protect me from the power of his gaze.

"Two months ago, you kissed me like there was nothing else in the world you'd rather do, Jen." Fallon takes a step inside and lets the door close behind him.

Despite myself, I take a step back. "Look, Fallon—"

"Why are you avoiding me? We work together, yet you've said not two sentences to me in the past month."

"I've been busy. The book..." I shrug. "Developing recipes is a lot of work."

It's a weak excuse, and we both know it. I'm avoiding him because his ex-girlfriend looks at him like he hung the moon, and she's also supposed to be the one to deliver my dream on a silver platter. Even if he *does* want to be with me, how can I pursue that? I've seen jealous women lash out before. I'd be putting my own career at risk.

Plus, there's a part of me that just refuses to believe that a man as sexy and charming and handsome as Fallon would want to be with a nerdy, nearly celibate forty-five-year-old baker like myself. It just doesn't fit logically in my mind. I can't make it make sense.

But seeing him here...it makes my heart skip. I won't say how many times I've thought of our kiss, or how many times I've dreamed of doing it again.

Those dreams are much, much better than judgmental, sentient meringue.

Fallon seems to be thinking the same. His eyes drop to my lips. "You know, I contacted Amanda because I knew she'd jump on the opportunity to do a book with you. I didn't think it would make you run away from me."

"Fallon"—I roll my eyes and turn back to the sub-par cake —"you emailed her and invited her to town, and didn't even mention me until she was here. You don't need to coddle me. It's fine."

"What's fine?" He sounds exasperated, so I glance up at him. Uh-oh.

Those dark, nearly black eyes are trained on me. His big, broad body looks impossibly bigger, and he moved closer to me without me even noticing. His palm lands on the stainless steel counter beside me, and he leans his muscular chest into my space. "What's fine, Jen?"

"For us to leave things where they are," I finally say, still holding the rubber spatula between us. Fallon doesn't even look at it. "We kissed. So what? I'm not going to ask about your past with Amanda, and all I ask is that you leave me alone and let me finish this book."

His eyes flash as he lets out a dry snort. "You know, some

days I regret calling Amanda at all, then I come in here and see how hard you're working on these new recipes, and I feel like an asshole for ever letting those thoughts cross my mind. You *deserve* this, Jen. But Amanda being the one to publish your book doesn't mean you can't explore what exists between you and me."

Another spasm grips my chest. My mouth grows dry as I blink up at Fallon, still holding that stupid spatula between us like it can save me from whatever he's about to say next.

"I don't know how else to say this, Jen, so I'm just going to say it as slowly as I can." He leans forward. "I'm not interested in Amanda. I'm interested in you. Can you get that to sink in? Am I being clear enough?"

I resist the urge to roll my eyes. The man sure does have an overbearing, condescending way of professing his affection for me.

"And what about her, *hmm*?" I ask, tilting my head. "What does she think about that? She's still staying at your house, no? She's still flicking her hair over her shoulder and giggling at every stupid comment you make, yeah?"

His eyes slide away from me.

I'm on a roll. I cross my arms—spatula still gripped in hand—and cock a hip. "And what about the book, Fallon? Have you thought about that? How do you think Amanda would react if she came to Heart's Cove to check on my progress with the recipes, only to find out I'd shacked up with the man she was pining after?"

"She's a grown woman, Jen. She'd deal with it."

"Yeah? Or maybe she'd pull out. Maybe I'd end up with no book deal, then you'd wake up next to me one day and realize you're bored because I'm *literally* the least exciting person in this town, so I'd end up with no book and no relationship."

Fallon's body goes rock hard. His eyes flash, anger written on every line of his face. "Is that what you think? You think you need to choose between me and your career? You think I'd just move on from you without looking back?"

"I don't *think*, Fallon. I know." I turn back to the cake and with a sigh, pick up the cake board and tip the whole thing into the garbage.

"You're a coward." He says the words quietly, but they still hurt like hell. "You're afraid of what we could have together."

Swiveling my head to meet his gaze, I can't help the hurt and anger zinging across my chest, carving that nasty word into my bones.

Coward. Coward. Coward.

His teeth grind as he watches me, and I will myself not to cry. I won't cry. I can't.

Lifting my chin, I grit my teeth to stop my bottom lip from trembling. It takes all my energy to keep my eyes from filling with tears.

How dare he march in here and say those things to me? After one kiss, I'm supposed to just drop everything and be with him? I'm supposed to put my dream at risk so he can have his fill of me and then probably toss me aside in a few months' time?

Yeah, right.

I've worked for this. *Me.* Sure, he introduced me to Amanda, but she was impressed with *my* recipes. *My* baked goods. *My* skills.

What happens when he gets bored of me? What happens when he changes his mind?

Not worth it.

"You should leave." My voice is icy when I say the words, and Fallon clenches his jaw at the sound of it. But you know what he doesn't do? He doesn't *move.* I tilt my head. "Leave,

Fallon. I have work to do, and I don't feel like having insults hurled at me while I do it."

His arms drop to his sides and he releases a long sigh. "Jen, I didn't... I'm not... I'm sorry. I shouldn't have said that."

"No, you shouldn't have. Now if you'll excuse me, I need to troubleshoot this recipe and bake another batch before your ex-girlfriend shows up here tomorrow morning asking for a progress update. Maybe when you go home tonight, you can give her that progress update yourself."

Then I, very maturely, bang a mixing bowl down on the counter and start pulling ingredients closer. My jaw is tight, eyes are burning, but I *will not cry*.

"Jen, listen."

"No, *you* listen," I grind out, letting anger sweep over me. "You can't just pick me up and put me down at will, Fallon. I'm not your toy. And I'm not going to sacrifice the one thing I really want—this recipe book—for some unknown relationship with you that might last no more than a day." Eyes blazing, I take a step forward and poke his very broad, very solid chest. "I get that you like wanting things you can't have. I get that you're probably used to women fawning over you because you know how to cook and you're hot and you have a body like...like *this*. But listen to me good, Fallon, because this is important. *I am not those women.* I choose my book. I choose my career. I've worked my ass off and restarted my life over when I was thirty-five to pursue baking, and I'm not going to let some infatuation ruin that. I'm *good* at this. For the first time in my life, I feel like I've found what I'm meant to do. So, yeah, maybe I'm a coward, but I'm not going to make Amanda hate me just for the chance to kiss you again. Not today, not tomorrow, not *ever*."

I'm panting hard now, and I think that may be the longest speech I've ever made in my life.

Fallon, somehow, looks angrier than when I started. "An infatuation?" he asks slowly, enunciating the word with careful precision.

"Well, what would you call it?"

He holds my gaze for a few long moments, then lets out a bitter snort. "Fine," he says, and turns on a heel to walk away. When his hand is on the door handle, he pauses and glances over his shoulder. "For the record, Amanda's staying at the hotel this time, just like every other time she comes to town from now on. I made sure of that."

He waits for me to reply, and when I say nothing, he strides out into the night.

I jump when the door bangs, then stick my tongue out at it. Yes, I'm a grown woman. But I'm not thinking straight.

How else am I supposed to react when I have to choose between a man and my career?

I take my aggression out on baking more cakes than I'll ever need.

11

FIONA

THE FIRST THING I notice when I walk into the Four Cups Café on Friday morning is that Jen has been busy. Like, really, *really* busy. The display cabinet is so full of baked goods there's barely any space left. There are baskets of muffins, jars of cookies, and new, handwritten little cards proclaiming half a dozen new recipes scattered over the counter.

There's a three-tiered chocolate cake displayed on top of the glass cabinet under a cake bell. It looks incredible.

Jen shuffles out of the kitchen with a tray of croissants, her mouth set in a grim line. Angry, purple bags have bloomed under her eyes, and she doesn't even lift her head to greet me.

That isn't unusual in itself—Jen isn't much of a talker—but there's something about the hunch of her shoulders that doesn't sit right with me.

"You okay, hun?" I round the counter and grab an apron off a hook on the wall, tying it around my waist as Jen places the croissants in the overflowing display cabinet. "Did you stay up all night baking all this?"

"Yeah," she replies. "Figured out my chocolate cake recipe

and needed to take some anger out on baking for a little bit longer."

My eyes run over the hundreds of new baked goods littered all over the place. I bite my lip. "Looks like you succeeded."

Jen snorts.

I tilt my head. "Want to share what made you so angry?"

The door opens, and Fallon strides through with a face full of thunder.

I glance at Jen, whose eyes have narrowed to slits. The air in the café is so thick, it feels like soup. Welp. There's my answer.

"I gotta go," Jen mumbles, then drops her empty tray in the kitchen and leaves out the back door.

Fallon watches her go, jaw set in a grim line, then starts wordlessly helping me take chairs down from tables and open the café up for business.

"Everything okay?" I ask.

"Peachy." A chair bangs onto the floor, then Fallon stomps to the kitchen with long, angry strides.

Okay, then.

Thankfully, Sven, our barista, arrives wearing his usual pink T-shirt with a glittery *Heart's Cove Hottie* written across the chest, sleeves ripped off to reveal his tattoos and a carefree grin tugging at his lips. At least someone is in a good mood.

I open the café and get swept up in the usual hubbub of early risers needing their daily dose of the black stuff. It's not until ten o'clock in the morning or so that Grant, my soon-to-be husband, walks in looking good enough to eat.

Pushing a strand of hair off my forehead, I let my lips slide into a smile. I love that man. I love the way his broad body moves so gracefully. I love how he has eyes only for me, and even though I'm sweaty and frazzled from the morning rush, he still looks at me like I'm the most beautiful woman he's ever seen.

His thick, corded arms wrap around me as his lips dip down to kiss the soft skin below my ear. "I enjoyed this morning," he growls softly.

My cheeks warm, and a curl of heat knots in my stomach. I woke up before Grant this morning and decided to use an—ahem—*creative* tactic to wake him up which involved my mouth...and not for talking, if you know what I mean.

"Me too," I tell him.

"Do you have time for me to return the favor?" Grant asks, pulling away slightly before dropping a kiss on my lips. "I can't focus on work when I'm like this."

"Get a room, you guys!" Simone, my fiery-hearted and fiery-haired best friend, calls out as she enters. "We get it. You're in love." She rolls her eyes but gives me a sly wink. "Morning!"

"Morning," I say, giving Grant a quick squeeze before pulling away. A squeeze that says, *Later.*

Simone grins, then takes in the explosion of baked goods behind me with a raised eyebrow. "Jen's been busy."

A man enters the café, and I don't have time to answer Simone because I'm slipping behind the counter to take his order. With a receding hairline and long, lanky limbs, he looks like any other middle-aged man in need of caffeine. But there's something in the way he glances around the café, like he's looking for someone but he's not supposed to be here.

"Can I help you?"

"Uh..." He glances at the chalkboard menu behind me, then at the multitude of grinders and coffee carafes on the counter at my back. "Black coffee?"

"Comin' right up." I smile brightly, glancing briefly at

Grant, who still looks ready to throw me over his shoulder and take me away. Blushing, I pour a black drip coffee for this customer and try to wrap my head around the fact that I'm getting married again.

It scares me, obviously. My first marriage was such a disaster, such a slow stripping of my confidence and sense of self that committing to a man again makes the primal part of my brain blare in fear. But Grant leans a big boulder shoulder against the wall, his full lips teasing into a smile as he scrubs his scruffy jaw with a wide palm, and the fear subsides.

He loves me. I love him. His daughter loves us. Our little family is more than I could have ever hoped for.

The man takes his coffee and drops it at a table before putting his jacket on the back of a chair, then wanders past Grant—giving him a quick glance and a wide berth, probably because Grant has about fifty pounds more muscle than he does—and ducks to the bathrooms.

That's when the café doors open again, and Lottie, Trina, her kids, Candice, and Blake come barreling through. The kids are seven and nine, and they recovered from their illness this week and are now begging for a muffin from the over-flowing basket by the till.

Lottie corrals them to a table while Candice tilts her head up to Blake for a kiss, and Trina lets out a long sigh and leans against the counter. "We ran out of coffee. Do you do intra-venous drips here, or no? I need it in my bloodstream like, now."

Grinning, I take her order as Sven gets to work.

Then, I watch in slow-motion as the man in the bathroom returns to the main space. He spots Lottie first, and freezes. Lottie takes a step as if to shield Toby and Katie from him, a look so fierce on her face that I already know something is wrong.

It's him. It's Kevin. It's the asshole who shamed her for breastfeeding her own damn kid in her own damn house.

Then Trina sees him, and she goes rock solid too.

Then it's Candice's turn to freeze.

Blake frowns, following her gaze to the balding man at the mouth of the bathroom hallway.

"You're not due until tomorrow," Lottie growls.

The man puts his hands up as if to placate her. "I had a day off. I thought I'd come down early."

His voice makes the two kids turn around, and Katie launches herself at him. "Daddy!" She wraps her little arms around his stomach and looks up at him with stars in her eyes. "You're here! Are you staying? Toby and I got a cat! His name is Mr. Fuzzles and he likes catnip. Don't worry, I change his litter box and everything."

The man frowns. "Why doesn't an adult do that?" He finally lifts his gaze to Trina, who somehow goes even more immobile. "You let her handle a cat's excrement? No wonder they got sick."

"They didn't get sick from doing chores, Kevin." Trina's voice is flatter than I've ever heard it.

"It's okay, Daddy, I ate lots of soup and now I'm all better. Toby too."

My eyes flick to the little nine-year-old boy, who's still sitting at the table, staring suspiciously at his father. He stands up, glances at Trina, then at Katie, as if he wants to go to his mother but doesn't want to leave his sister behind. My heart spasms. What a beautiful, protective boy.

I clear my throat, but Simone throws me a glance from the opposite side of the café, shaking her head.

Trina takes a step forward. "You can't have them until tomorrow."

"Not even for ice cream?" Kevin says, looking at his daughter.

"Ice cream! Ice cream!" Katie screams, jumping up and down and turning to Trina. "Please, Mom?"

"You haven't even had breakfast, Katie."

"Are you not feeding them?" Kevin's question is sharp enough to cut.

Trina flinches.

"Okay, that's enough." Lottie puts a finger up in Kevin's face. "Not one more word. Toby, Katie—with me." She snaps her fingers, and the two kids jump beside her. Lottie takes one of their hands in each of hers. "We're going to walk back home and wait for Mommy and Daddy to have a conversation. Okay?"

"Fine." Katie drops her chin. "But can we have ice cream later?"

"Maybe," Lottie concedes. "Come on. Let's go."

"Good," Toby grits out, mean-mugging his own father. My heart squeezes at the sight of the anger in that little boy's face. My divorce was painful, but seeing these two kids in the middle of Trina's separation makes me grateful I never had little ones to go through it with me.

Lottie starts walking with the kids, and when they're outside, Kevin turns to his ex-wife. "Are you trying to keep me from seeing my own goddamn children, Katrina?"

Katrina stiffens and opens her mouth, but before she can answer, a loud, rumbling noise starts growing outside. And growing. And growing...until half a dozen motorcycles appear outside the café windows, parking in a neat line against the curb. The first rider to dismount and remove his helmet is a very familiar, very sexy man who I last saw when I was slightly inebriated about a week ago.

Mac Blair is sex on a bike. The man handles clay like he was born to do it—and apparently motorcycles too.

He walks into the coffee shop like he owns the place, all leather and attitude, closing the distance between him and Trina in a few long strides. He wraps his arms around her shoulders and tugs her close, brushing his lips against her cheek in greeting.

Trina looks shocked. Horrified. A little flustered—and I'd bet anything she's more than a little turned on.

"Hey, gorgeous," Mac says loud enough for everyone to hear—probably because no one is moving a muscle as this little spectacle unfolds. "You want to go for a ride this morning?" His voice drops, but I don't miss a word. "Been thinking about having those legs hooked over the seat of my bike all week."

Holy *moly*. I'm about to get married, and even I feel a little turned on. Eyes wide, I glance at Simone, who looks about ready to faint. Then I look at Kevin, who looks ready to explode. Then I glance at Grant, who has a little grin teasing over his lips when he watches the flush creep over my cheeks, as if he knows he'll reap the rewards of anything that turns me on when we're alone.

Trina just opens and closes her mouth like a goldfish until her ex-husband, Kevin, now red-faced and flustered, takes a step toward them.

"Who the *fuck* are you?"

12

MAC

TRINA SNAPS OUT of her trance. "Kevin, watch your mouth."

"How about you don't whore yourself out to a fucking biker gang, huh? How about that?"

Trina flinches against me, and I feel about ready to rip this motherfucker's head off. Tucking her behind my back, I turn to face the sniveling, sorry excuse for a man in front of me. "That's not an appropriate way to speak to a lady."

The man scoffs. "Lady? That's rich."

A hand on my shoulder makes me pause the slurry of insults about to spew out of my mouth. Trina appears by my side, taking a step sideways to put a bit of distance between us. I try not to let it sting.

She crosses her arms. "I wasn't expecting you until tomorrow, Kevin."

I frown. She was expecting this shitstain?

Trina glances at me. "Thank you for the offer, Mac, but I won't be able to ride your motorcycle today. Unfortunately, something came up. Maybe another time." Her spine is steel-straight, her chin held high. Admiration warms my chest at the sight of her, strong and proud in the presence of the man across the room who no doubt wants to cause her pain.

"I'm going to tell my lawyer about this, Trina," the shit-stain says, his lips curling in disgust.

"Last time I checked, motorcycles weren't illegal, Kevin," Trina snaps. "And last time I checked, you signed the divorce papers. Oh, and *last time I checked*, you *definitely* have no right to speak about my relationships. Or have you forgotten that you cheated on me for *years*?"

Is it wrong that I'm kind of turned on by this? I glance at the door, where my father, brother, and Harold are standing near the entrance.

Then the door opens with a loud bang, and the White-Haired Lady Crew comes rushing in.

Dorothy greets my father with a loud kiss on the cheek. "Welcome! Oh my, what an entrance! We heard you all the way from the hotel and had to come say hello." She waves another man in, a tall, grey-haired gentleman with a kind face and a shiny bald spot on his crown. He shakes my father's hand.

Then Margaret enters. My father clears his throat, tugging the ends of his motorcycle jacket before smoothing his hair down. When Margaret extends a hand, he takes it and presses his lips to her knuckles.

A screw in my chest tightens, which makes guilt worm through my veins. I should be happy for my father. Any normal person would be delighted to see two people falling for each other.

Margaret turns the same shade of blush pink as her tweed suit jacket. Meanwhile, Dorothy is calling out for coffees all around, Trina looks like she's about to faint, and Shitstain Kevin has turned red with anger. His fists open and close, eyes darting to me every few seconds.

Finally, the short, sharp-tongued woman with the helmet-like grey hair waddles in—Agnes, I think—sneering at Dorothy, who ignores her, and letting out a huff. "What's this racket about? It should be illegal for you bikers to come roaring through a quiet town like this. I was having a quiet coffee in the bookstore, and you lot—"

"Oh hush, you boring old hag," Dorothy says with a smile on her face. "You wouldn't know fun if it slapped you on the ass and called you Bonnie."

Agnes rolls her eyes. She's the first one to spot Kevin across the room, and she walks toward him, stopping a few feet away before crossing her arms. "Who the hell are you?"

He starts. "What?"

Agnes drops her arms to the side, looks over her shoulder to meet Dorothy's gaze, and rolls her eyes. I don't understand the relationship between these women. They insult each other, but they also go drinking and are able to communicate with nothing more than a look. Agnes turns those admittedly slightly scary eyes back to Kevin and speaks slowly. "Who... the hell...are you?"

"Agnes, this is my ex-husband, Kevin," Trina cuts in. "It's his weekend and he's here a day early, and we were just figuring out our schedules for the next couple of days."

His weekend? Does Trina have kids? She hasn't mentioned them. She mentioned her cat, but not her kids... But now that I think of it, I vaguely remember her mentioning some names when they were planning their night at my father's bar. I frown, glancing at Trina.

I only met the woman a couple of weeks ago. She has every right to keep her kids away from anyone she chooses. Still...I'd like her to trust me.

I clear my throat, drawing everyone's gaze.

Dorothy squeezes the older man's elbow and points at me.

"Eli, that's Mac. Isn't he handsome? I told you he was hand-some, didn't I?"

"He's a looker," Eli responds, and Dorothy's lips curl into a smile.

She claps. "Well, what are we waiting for? Hamish, you're supposed to be offering to take us out on those mean machines out there."

"Is that so?" my father answers with a grin and a wink at Margaret.

"Yes, that's so. You can't come roaring into town and not offer us a lap around the block on those things. Look! Marge is wearing pants. We're all set." Dorothy points at me. "You take Eli. I'll go with Harold. Marge, you're with Hamish. Agnes, you take that young stud over there—"

"My son, Lee," my father cuts in with a small smile tipping his lips.

"Well, Hamish, you sure do know how to make 'em pret-ty," Dorothy says. "Lee, unfortunately you're stuck with Agnes. I'd say she doesn't bite, but I don't like to lie." Then she looks at Trina. "And you take care of yourself. Yeah?" Then Dorothy looks past my shoulder to the counter. "Get our coffees ready. We'll be back in ten minutes. Coffee's on me, boys!" She ushers everyone out, holding the door open as she glances back at me. "Yoohoo, Mr. Handsome! Come on, Eli isn't going to ride himself around the block!"

I can't help the grin from tugging at my lips. Glancing at Trina, I lift my brows. "You okay?"

The harsh lines of Trina's face soften, and I wonder how often she's had to stand on her own without anyone checking on her. She nods. "I'm good. You okay? You don't need to drive them around if you don't want to."

"He's fucking fine," Shitstain Kevin cuts in. "What I want to know is why he thinks he has the right to fucking talk to you like that?" Aggression is written in every line of his face, carved into every muscle of his soft frame. "You're fucking him, aren't you?"

Before I can do anything, the old ladies *move*. Dorothy comes flying in the door, followed by Agnes and Margaret, already wearing their motorcycle helmets. They form a line between him and Trina, and Dorothy lifts a finger. "You watch your mouth, buddy. One more word, and you'll be barred from every business in town."

Kevin splutters. "You can't—"

"Oh, would you look at that," Margaret cuts in. "Unfortunately, we double-booked your room. You'll have to find somewhere else to stay for the weekend." She looks up from her phone, which I can see is just a blank screen. Out of the three of them, she's the last one I'd expect to threaten someone.

Fighting to hide my grin, I glance at my father.

He's standing in the doorway, looking as smitten as I've ever seen him, hand clutched to his heart.

"Ladies, it's fine," Trina says, putting a hand on Margaret's shoulder. "Go. Enjoy your motorcycle ride. I'll be okay."

The ladies give Kevin one more nasty look, then shuffle out toward the waiting bikes. My father whispers something in Margaret's ear, and I can't help but notice the extra swish in her hips as she makes her way toward his bike.

Trina glances at me and gives me a nod.

Every part of me wants to stay, tuck her into my side, and protect her from whatever garbage will spew from Kevin's mouth. I don't want her to stand alone against him.

But she didn't even tell me she had kids. This isn't my fight. We barely know each other, and she doesn't want me here.

Isn't that for the best? Doesn't that suit me just fine?

I don't do complications. I'm not the type of guy who can stand by a woman's side through thick and thin. Not when I know I should be on my own.

Still...instinct blares at me to stay. To protect.

But Trina just gives me a nod, and with a sigh, I make my way outside to the line of bikes and passengers waiting for their scoot around the block.

When we get back, Trina and her asshole ex are gone.

LATER, I end up driving to the Cedar Grove with the boys, but as soon as I walk in, all I can think about is my evening with Trina in here. The place seems duller, darker without her, and I can't bear to be here. I turn right around, then freeze.

"Hey, handsome," Belinda says from the doorway. She's wearing a tight top that shows off far too much cleavage, and I can't help comparing it to the classy, effortlessly sexy clothing Trina usually wears. The two of them are like night and day.

"Belinda." I clear my throat, wondering if I can get outside without speaking to her.

"You never called me after last time I came to see you." She pouts, and it's not cute.

I glance over my shoulder at my father and brother, who are most definitely listening to every word. Turning back to Belinda, I sigh. "Can I speak to you outside?"

She gives me a seductive smile, and I fight the urge to roll my eyes. "Of course, big boy," she purrs.

We walk out into the late afternoon, and I know there's no excuse now. I need to find the words to get Belinda to leave me alone, once and for all.

If I took even a second to examine that thought, I'd realize that it's because of Katrina. I'd realize that it's important to me to cut ties to all other women, as stale and tenuous as they might be.

If I took a moment to admit to myself that what I feel for Trina might not be your run-of-the-mill need for a hard fuck, I might hesitate and lose my nerve. I might retreat and push Trina away.

But I don't think of any of that.

I look at the woman in front of me. "Belinda, I've told you time and time again that it's not appropriate for us to see each other."

"My son isn't even at this school anymore, Mac." She scoffs, rolling her eyes.

"I'm not interested." My voice is hard, and Belinda's face changes in an instant. She goes from sultry and flirty to furiously angry.

Her lips curl down and her eyes grow dark. "Excuse me?"

"I'm just being honest. This has gone on long enough."

Belinda arches an eyebrow. "Oh yeah? I'll go to the principal and tell her all about our affair together. You'll lose your job."

"Our 'affair' was one night after the end of the school year, and it was a mistake."

She flinches. With a hand on her hip, Belinda purses her lips and shakes her head. "I waited around for you for four years, Mac, and this is how you repay me?"

"I didn't ask you to do that. I told you I didn't want to see you anymore."

"No, Mac. You told me it wasn't *appropriate* for us to see each other. You kept me on the hook for *years*, only to turn around and tell me you don't want me now that my son is out of your school. You couldn't have done that four years ago? You couldn't have been honest with me?" She scoffs, shaking her head as she stares at the sky. "You're an asshole and a tease, Mac." Then she turns on her heels and stomps toward her minivan.

I stand rooted to the spot until she's out of the parking lot and out of sight.

Closing my eyes for a brief moment, I push away the uncomfortable truth in her words. I *did* dodge her advances for years, if only to avoid awkward confrontation at my work. Maybe it would have been better to be honest—but would I have risked repercussions at work? Would it have blown up in my face?

I did the best I could do at the time. I tried to let her down as gently as I could.

When I get on my bike, though, all thoughts of Belinda get left behind as the wind whips over me. The only thing on my mind is when I'll get to see Trina again.

13

TRINA

I COLLAPSE into a sofa in the library above the Four Cups Café. Everyone's here. Simone is regaling us with a hilarious story about her college boyfriend breaking up with her because he thought she ate too much cheese. Jen is making tea for everyone. Fiona is bustling around throwing a blanket over my legs, tidying a few books that have been left out, overall just acting like a mother hen. Candice is sitting next to me, a quiet, supportive presence.

It's nice being taken care of. It's not something I experience very often.

When Jen puts a chamomile tea in my hands, I inhale the scent of the steam and let out a sigh.

"You good?" Simone asks.

I shrug. "As good as can be."

"I still think you should have refused to let him have the kids tonight," Candice says as her lips curl downward. "The absolute *gall* of that man! To barge in here a day early to his planned visitation and turn the kids against you by promising ice cream and fun. He's going to play 'Fun Dad,' and I wouldn't put it past him to shit-talk you behind your back."

"I gave in because I want us to have a good co-parenting relationship. If I put up a big fight about one night, then what? We get adversarial and nothing works."

"The minute he called you a whore, you should have punched him in the throat. Screw good co-parenting when someone verbally abuses you like that." That harsh comment comes from Fiona, and everyone hums in agreement.

My brows arch. "That's a particularly violent statement. Have you been hanging out with Agnes lately?"

Fiona laughs. "No, but cheating spouses who then get mad about you moving on to something better hits close to home. He has no right to make you feel bad about what's going on with Mac."

"Nothing's going on with Mac," I respond, even though after almost a week, I can still feel the taste of his lips on mine.

"What happened after you left the café?" Simone asks.

Stalling for time, I lift my mug to my lips. It's too hot to drink, and I grimace when I burn the roof of my mouth. Since everyone is still waiting for me to respond, I release a sigh and shrug. "We went back to my place. Kevin booked an AirBnB since his room at the hotel was 'double-booked.'" Everyone snickers at the comment, and I just shake my head. "When Katie heard his new place had a pool, I'd pretty much already lost the battle."

"Yep." Candice nods, lips pinched. "He's playing 'Fun Dad.'"

Fiona lets out a disgusted snort. "What an ass."

"He's not a bad father. I can't keep him from seeing the kids. I want them to have a good relationship with him." I don't know why I'm defending him. Kevin cheated on me. I found out when I saw tickets to an art gallery opening and thought they were for the two of us, only to discover he was taking his mistress instead. I spent years supporting him while he pursued his passion for painting, and then was left behind when he finally made it.

He never appreciated the work I put in at the start of our marriage to support us, and he definitely didn't appreciate the work it took to raise two children. He'd stay in his studio until late at night, then reappear and be the World's Best Dad for a few days.

I don't know why I put up with it before, and I'm not sure why I'm not as outraged as my friends. Maybe I'm just tired.

"Anyway, it's fine," I tell them. "I'll be able to get some job applications done this weekend."

"Have you put any thought into starting a stylist business?" Fiona asks, tucking one leg under her butt as she sits down.

I frown. "Well...no. You guys weren't serious about that, were you?"

Fiona shrugs. "I'd pay you for advice on how to dress. You're really good at it, Trina."

I shake my head, dismissing the thought immediately. "No. No, I'll look for a real job."

Simone and Candice exchange a glance. Simone gives me a soft smile. "Girl, none of us here have real jobs. They're overrated, anyway."

My heart thumps, but striking out on my own and doing something related to fashion is just too much for me. It's too far out of my comfort zone. What happened this morning with Kevin has me reeling, and the thought of starting a business when my life is in such upheaval? I shake my head. "I'm not... I don't... I wouldn't even know where to start."

"Start small," Simone says. "With me or Fiona—"

"Or me," Candice cuts in.

"—and figure out how you'd structure your services.

Then just start a social media page and *boom*. You're in business."

I shake my head. "It's not that simple."

Fiona tilts her head. "Why not?"

"Because..." I drift off, then frown. I *know* it's not that simple, but I can't quite think of all the reasons. Because...the kids! The divorce! Because I couldn't possibly do something like that all on my own...could I? Close to panic, I look at all their expectant faces. "Can we talk about something else, please?"

"What's going on with you and Mac?" Jen arches her brows, kicking her legs up onto the coffee table.

I groan.

Candice laughs. "Atta girl, Jen. On to more important things." My sister turns to me with an expectant look on her face. "So? Has Mac called you since this morning? That *entrance*, my God. I wish we could have recorded it."

I bite my lip. "No, he hasn't called."

"We should go to the Grove," Simone says, brightening. She puts her mug down on the coffee table and looks at each of us in turn. "Allie is with Clancy and Grant at your place," she says to Fiona and Candice. "And Jen, you're done baking for the day."

Jen frowns. "I still need to—"

"You're *done* baking for the day, Jen," Simone cuts in. "Have you seen how many baked goods are overflowing from their containers down there? Amanda can't possibly expect you to do more."

"The lemon meringue pie recipe isn't quite right, though, and—"

"Jen." Simone lowers her brows.

I clear my throat. "Look, it's fine. I'm not sure going to the Grove is a good idea. I shouldn't be seeing Mac anyway—"

"Why not?" Fiona screeches, sitting up on her armchair. "Why the hell not, Trina?"

"He's..." I trail off, not really knowing what to say. I flap my hands around a bit as if that'll explain things. "I'm... It's too soon."

"Bullshit." Simone stands up and gathers everyone's mugs. "Let's go."

My protests fall on deaf ears. We stumble down the stairs together and spill onto the sidewalk, only to pause when we hear the sound of a couple of loud engines.

Two motorcycles come rumbling down Cove Boulevard, the main street through the center of Heart's Cove. My heart leaps, then I let out a surprised laugh when I see the passengers on the back of the two roaring bikes.

Dorothy's silver hair streams behind her from under her helmet, her oversized leather jacket making her look massive on the back of Mac's bike. She's holding onto him tight, her face split open with a smile. But it's Margaret that surprises me. She's on the back of Hamish's bike, holding onto him just as close, a high, bright flush on her cheeks.

The men stop their bikes in front of us as the ladies dismount. Dorothy lets out a squeal. "Again! Again!"

Mac just laughs, then lets his gaze slide to me. His lips tip up at the corners. "Hey."

Why did my clothes just suddenly get rougher? I can feel every fiber of fabric scratching me, every scrap of material abrading my too-sensitive skin. "Hi."

My gaze darts to Margaret, who's still blushing as Hamish helps her with the clasp of her helmet. "That was lovely, Hamish."

"The pleasure was all mine." His eyes are soft as he responds.

I exchange a glance with Candice, who hides a smile

behind her hand. Margaret's husband passed away years ago, and I've never seen her flirt with anyone. It's nice to see.

Mac takes a step toward me, and my whole body reacts. How does he manage to move like that? Grace and strength in every inch of his body. With his helmet under his arm, he combs his fingers through his hair and nods toward his motorcycle. "Want a ride?"

More than anything.

The thought pops into my head before I can stop myself, and my lips drop open. I suck in a breath and release it slowly, trying to figure out how to put my feelings into words.

Yes, I want to press my thighs against Mac's and wrap my arms around his torso. I want to feel the warmth of his body at my chest and let him guide me around every bend in the road as the sun sets over the ocean. I want him to take me somewhere private and kiss me silly, if only to forget about my horrible, awful, terrible day and the fact that I don't have my kids tonight.

But I shouldn't.

Kevin was a jerk, but he was also right. What if I'm getting involved with Mac too soon? I should be focused on my kids, preparing for the school year, finding a job.

But Mac's eyes slide down my body, taking in the tight jeans and the draped, loose-fitting tee that exposes one of my shoulders. There's heat in his honey-colored eyes that I can't ignore, and I find myself speaking.

"Yeah," I hear myself say. "I'd like that."

I'm rewarded with the sexiest grin I've ever seen. Mac's full lips curl up at the corners as his eyes glimmer, the crinkles at their corners deepening. It should be illegal to be that sexy. With dark jeans, his leather jacket, his motorcycle boots, and hair that looks like it would feel good to run my fingers through, is there any wonder I agreed?

And before I can change my mind, Candice's hands appear on my shoulders. She not-so-gently nudges me closer to the sexy motorcycle man in front of me as Mac extends a helmet.

I glance over my shoulder to see Simone giving me a big thumbs-up. So, with a sigh and one last look at Margaret and Hamish, whose heads are still angled close together, I turn to Mac and nod. "Let's do it."

His grin widens to a smile, and a thunderbolt hits me right in the middle of the chest. Way, *way* too sexy for his own good. It should be illegal.

Helmet fitted over my head, and Dorothy's oversized leather jacket—which I discover is actually Mac's—over my shoulders, I swing my leg over Mac's bike and shimmy forward, sliding my hands around his waist. This time, I don't hesitate. It feels all too natural to have my arms around his waist and my cheek pressed up against his shoulder.

"Hold on tight," he reminds me, and I can't quite hide my smile as I turn to rest my chin on his shoulder and let him take me away.

WHEN MAC finally stops the bike, I feel like I just ran a marathon. My blood is heated, my arms sore from squeezing him so hard, and my thighs permanently branded with the feel of his legs against them. There's something intensely erotic about being on a bike with him, feeling the roar of the engine between my legs, knowing I'm completely at Mac's mercy.

He took us around bends, on the highway, and wove through the forest until we got to a familiar lookout point above the Pacific Ocean. I stumble off the motorcycle and giggle, giddy with adrenaline as I remove my helmet and take a deep breath.

"Better?" Mac asks, studying my smile as if he wants to remember it. As if he'd never get sick of looking at me.

I nod. "Much better."

"Your ex is an asshole."

A surprised laugh falls from my lips. I clap my hand over my mouth and shake my head. "You shouldn't say that."

"Why not?" He takes a step toward me, grabbing the helmet from my hands to rest it on the motorcycle seat. "It's true, isn't it?"

I shrug, turning to the ocean crashing at the foot of cliffs below, if only to avoid his piercing gaze. "I... I don't know. I don't like bad-mouthing people."

"Even if they deserve it? Even if they insult you in a room full of people? Even if they say things that no man should ever say to a woman?"

I bite my lip and ignore how much his words affect me. When was the last time a man actually defended me like that? Actually *cared*?

Mac meets my gaze for a moment, then angles his head toward the edge of the parking lot, where a small shed-like building stands.

My eyes light up. "Ice cream!" Then I laugh, because I had the exact same response to the treat as my seven-year-old daughter.

Mac, smooth as anything, intertwines his fingers with mine (swoon!) and leads me across the lot. There's an old couple in front of us who order with expert precision, and I wonder how many times they've gotten ice cream together. Then Mac steps up and leans a muscled forearm against the chest-height counter.

The young girl behind the counter arches her brows,

color rising high on her cheeks at the sight of the man in front of her. "Wh-what can I get for you, Mr. Blair?"

Somehow, it doesn't surprise me that she knows him. Mac flashes a smile. "Hi Kaylee. How has your summer been?"

"Really good, but my arm is pretty sore from scooping." The girl lets out a little giggle, her cheeks turning a brighter shade of red. I bite my lip. It's cute seeing her reaction, but I'm glad I'm no longer a young teenager. She points to the buckets of ice cream in front of her. "What would you like?"

"Double-scoop waffle cone. One scoop cookies 'n' cream, one scoop double-chocolate brownie blast. Trina?" He looks at me.

I step up and hesitate, even though I know exactly what I want. I grin at Mac, feeling like a little girl again. "Butter pecan, please."

"One scoop or two?" The girl is already putting Mac's cone together with a few expert movements, dunking her scoop into a jug of milky-looking water between each new mound of ice cream.

"Oh, what the hell. Two. In a waffle cone as well, please."

At my words, Mac's lips tug. He slides his hand around my waist and gives me a squeeze.

My smile widens, and I duck my head to hide it. I haven't been out for ice cream in a long, long time, and for the past few years it's always been with kids in tow. Kevin would always click his tongue if I got more than one scoop, and he'd grumble at the extra dollar for a waffle cone.

This feels so indulgent, I can't wipe the smile off my face.

Mac pays before I can reach for my purse, ignoring my protests and handing me my cone. Then we walk to the edge of the parking lot, where a few benches are set out to admire the view. I take a seat next to Mac, keenly aware of the way his thigh is pressed against mine, the movement of his tongue over his ice cream cone, the way his hand is slung casually along the back of the bench behind me.

This feels like a date. When was the last time I went on a date?

Wait—no. I don't want to think about that. It'll make me feel too old.

"So," Mac says after a while, "when are you going to let me see that pussy of yours?"

That's when my ice cream decides to go down the wrong hole. Choking and spluttering, I cough out a shocked, "Excuse me?"

Mac keeps his eyes on the horizon, the setting sun turning his skin golden-brown while the corner of his lip twitches. "Mr. Fuzzles, was it?" When he meets my gaze, his eyes are dancing. "Why? What did you think I was talking about?"

Laughing, I nudge him with my shoulder and shake my head. "You're unbelievable."

Mac's smile widens, turning my stomach into delicious knots. He drops his arm from the back of the bench to my shoulders, tugging me closer. "At least I put a smile on your face this evening. Mission accomplished."

Oh. Everything from neck to navel warms inside me at his words—at the sincerity of them. He's just...so damn *sweet*!

And as Mac lifts his treat to take a bite out of the waffle cone, then glances at me and gives me a cheeky wink, I know I don't stand a chance to resist him.

Would it be so bad if I just...didn't?

14

TRINA

WE STAY at the lookout until the sun sets and a chill creeps into the air. Our ice cream is long gone and there's a lingering taste of sweetness in my mouth. When Mac takes me by the hand and leads me to his bike, my heart gives a mighty squeeze.

I like this.

I like being treated like a princess. I like having my hand held. I like simple pleasures like ice cream and sunsets.

And, apparently, I also like motorcycles.

We stand beside the bike and Mac puts my helmet on, his lips tugging once the latch is clicked beneath my chin.

"What?" I ask, seeing the glimmer in his eyes.

"You look cute in a motorcycle helmet."

"I am not *cute*."

His lips curl a bit more. "Okay, you look hot as fuck in a motorcycle helmet." A chuckle falls from his lips when he sees the startled expression on my face. "Better?"

"You have strange preferences, Mr. Blair."

That makes him laugh outright, and my heart clenches

again. And when Mac leans down and presses his lips to mine in a soft, sweet kiss that quickly devolves to something deeper and wetter? Well, my heart nearly gives out completely.

When he pulls away, Mac brushes his thumb over my swollen lips and shakes his head. "I don't think my preferences are strange at all."

With practiced, easy movements, he mounts his bike and nods for me to follow. Then, we're off onto winding, forested streets all the way back to Heart's Cove, to the temporary rental my mother and I are occupying for the next week until we can move into Candice's old place.

Mac pulls out in front of the house and we dismount. A deep well of disappointment opens up inside me as I remove my helmet, once again doing my best to smooth down the rat's nest on top of my head.

The house keys are cold in my hand as I fiddle with them, watching the way they spin around the key ring just to avoid glancing up at Mac's bottomless eyes. "Thanks for this evening," I finally say. "I didn't realize how much I needed it."

Mac lets out a breath, and I look up to see him combing his fingers through his hair. His eyes are on me, and just as I predicted, the sight of them makes my blood heat.

If I didn't live with my mother, I'd invite him in. If I had any sense of adventure, I'd ask to see his place.

But I have kids, responsibilities, and my life is such a jumbled mess that I need to think things through. What if I'm just latching onto the first decent man I meet? Shouldn't I be focused on being single for a while? Getting to know myself again? Finding a job, moving forward, being independent?

There's nothing but conflict inside me. On the one hand, Mac is a brawny, sweet, sexy man the likes of which I've never even *seen*, let alone dated. He makes pottery and rides a motorcycle. He doesn't complain when kooky old ladies like Dorothy and Margaret demand rides around the block. His kisses are like dynamite.

I'd be a damn fool to turn my back on that.

But on the other hand…I'm a mess. I'm barely out of a bad marriage. The ink isn't even dry on my divorce papers and I'm ready to throw myself into another man's bed. That's wrong, isn't it? Shameful, in some way?

Mac cuts through my turbulent thoughts by placing a hand on my neck, his strong, warm fingers curling around my nape. "I want to see you again," he says, and I can't help but bite my lip.

At the sight of it, Mac lets out a low groan. "Remember what I said about the lip biting, Trina? It'll get you in trouble if you aren't careful."

Lungs catching, I gaze up at him. I'm sure he can feel the pulse thundering in my neck. I'm sure he can see the heat in my eyes. He knows the effect he has on me.

So, telling him the truth is just voicing something he already knows, even if it comes out a bit breathy. "What if I want to get in trouble?"

Another groan, and his fingers tighten. Then I'm wrapped up in his arms and I'm kissing him again, just like we did outside the Cedar Grove. Melting into his chest, I let out a moan at the warmth and strength of him, the feel of his strong, broad body curved around mine.

And his lips—oh, his lips are magic. He parts mine with his tongue and deepens the kiss, the hand on my neck shifting to tangle into my hair.

I curl my fingers into his shirt, then claw them up to wrap around his shoulders, wanting more closeness. Needing it.

I'm making out like a horny teen on my mother's doorstep, and I don't even care. He tastes too good. He feels too good. *I* feel too good.

When his hand slides down my back to grip my ass, I swear it nearly sends me over the edge. The sheer possessiveness of the movement, the way he grips my body like he needs to feel it under his palm—it's too much for me to handle.

I break the kiss, panting, resting my forehead against the side of his jaw as he releases a low groan. "Kissing you is dangerous, Trina."

"Why?" My eyes are closed as I inhale the scent of his skin, loving the way he holds me close. My nose nudges against his throat, rasping against the stubble there.

"Because it makes me forget myself. Makes me never want to stop." He shifts, brushing his lips against mine. Then he pulls away and gives me a soft smile. "I'd better go."

"Oh." I don't mean to sound as disappointed as I do, so I force a brave smile onto my lips. "Okay. I'll, um, see you around."

"Count on it," he tells me, and it sounds like a vow.

Then—perfect timing as always—the front door opens and my mother yelps, "Oh, Trina! You're home!" She puts a hand to her heart. "Mac! Lovely to see you."

I don't believe for a second that my mother wasn't watching through the curtains, but I still pull away from Mac and give her a nod. "Hi, Mom."

"Well, did you have fun? That's some machine you got there, Mac." She smiles, toddling over to us in fuzzy slippers complete with bunny ears on them. The rest of her outfit consists of bright red jeans and a polka-dot top.

Movement catches my eye behind her. Little, black, furry movement.

Like a bullet, Mr. Fuzzles darts out the open door, through my mother's legs, and makes a break for freedom. Mom screams, trying to catch the cat while promptly tripping over the floppy bunny ears on her slippers. Momentarily distracted, the cat pounces on the floppy slippers, then changes his mind again and darts toward the road.

"Mom!" I cry, rushing toward her as she stumbles and falls into a flowerbed.

She lands with a low *oof*, then points to the road. "I'm okay. Get the cat!"

That's when Mac *moves*.

I thought watching him change a tire was hot? I thought pottery was sexy? How about lightning-quick speed and Olympic-level agility? Mac lunges for Mr. Fuzzles and scoops him up in one hand before the cat can make a break for the road.

"Oh, thank God," my mother says from the flowerbed.

I help her to her feet and wipe the dirt and flower petals from her clothing before finally turning to see Mac walking up the path toward us.

And my ovaries just lay down and surrender.

One of his big, broad hands cups the quickly-growing kitten to his chest, a little ball of black fur purring loudly against him. I watch tiny little paws kneading his thumb as Mr. Fuzzles nuzzles his face against Mac's other fingers, the rest of his body lying on Mac's wrist and forearm. Mac stops in front of my mother and me, a soft expression on his face as he uses a finger to scratch behind the kitten's ears. It sounds like he's holding a little engine.

"Oh, he likes *you*," my mother says. "He's never let me pick him up and hold him like that."

Mac's lips tilt up, his eyes still on the little ball of fur. Then he glances at me and nods. "Here." He extends his hands and deposits the cat into my arms, to Mr. Fuzzles's great displeasure. The cat yowls and reaches for Mac, flailing and scratching so hard I nearly drop him.

Mac to the rescue once again. He grabs Mr. Fuzzles with a deep chuckle and nods to the door. "Maybe I should bring him inside."

"Great idea!" My mother claps, retrieves one of her slippers from the plants, and leads the way to the house. "Have you two eaten? I can whip something up for you."

Oh...no. I don't want a family dinner with Mac and my mother. No way.

Panicked, I whip my head toward Mac, who just gives me a wink and a smile. "I have plans, unfortunately, but thank you for the offer, Lottie. I'll have to take a rain check."

"Another time." Mom waves a hand for us to follow her to the living room. "Keep your shoes on. Mr. Fuzzles's scratching post is in the guest room. We can drop him in there"—she turns to the cat and lifts a finger as if she's scolding him like a child—"so he can think about what he's done."

I notice the way Mac's eyes linger on the kids' shoes by the door, the jackets, the colorful backpack with Disney princesses all over it, and I bite my lip.

I haven't actually told him about the kids. It's not that I've withheld the information, it just...never came up. The time that I've spent with Mac has felt like an escape from my life. Not that I'm ashamed of my kids, but just that... I don't know. It's just so much easier to be a divorced woman meeting up with a hot badass without thinking about all the implications of actually being with him.

But Mac says nothing about the kids' clothes. He just deposits Mr. Fuzzles next to his food and water bowls, grinning when the cat does a figure-eight through his legs, then softly closes the door.

"I'll walk you out," I tell him.

When we get to the motorcycle again, the curtains twitch, and I know for sure my mother is watching. I clear my throat. "Look, Mac. I, um... I haven't actually mentioned this before, but I've got two kids."

Surprisingly, Mac just smiles. "I know."

"You know?"

"Your ex mentioned something about it being his weekend. I figured it out."

I let out a little snort. "Ah," I say, and give him an awkward smile.

"It's fine, Trina. I like kids. Obviously." He smiles back, as if what he just said makes sense. Why would it be obvious that he likes kids?

Frowning, I just nod. "Right. Well, look, Mac—" I take a deep breath. Time to be a big girl. "I haven't actually dated anyone since Kevin, and I'm not really ready to introduce the kids to anyone. It's not anything about you. It's just, I don't want men in and out of their lives while the divorce is so fresh, and..."

"I get it." Mac reaches over to take my hand, then places a soft kiss against my knuckles. "You're doing the right thing. I wasn't going to ask to meet them."

"Oh. Well...good." I bite my lip and nudge the pavement with my toe. That was a much easier conversation than I imagined.

That makes him chuckle. "I'll call you, Trina."

My lips curl, and I nod. "Okay."

With one more soft kiss on the lips, Mac dons his helmet and slings a strong leg over his bike, gives me a wink and a smile, then rides off down the street and out of sight.

I turn to see my mother at the door, a cheeky grin teasing her lips. "Trina, honey, that man is something else. If you don't want him, I'll have him any day of the week. Hell, I'll have him *every* day of the week!"

"Mom, gross." I frown, and Lottie just laughs.

But the scariest part is, I feel the same way.

15

TRINA

THE WEEKEND that follows is busy. I spend two days packing with my mother while the kids are away so we're ready to move into Candice's old place on Monday.

Kevin drops them off at the rental on Sunday evening, peering over my shoulder to the house beyond. His lips curl in disgust. "Is your new boyfriend there? I hope you're not letting some creep around my kids."

I stare at the man on the doorstep, wondering who the hell I was married to for so long. Is this really the same man I thought I'd grow old with? Someone so vindictive and bitter? Someone who cheated on me *while we were married*, and now gets mad that I might be moving on *after* the divorce?

Maybe it's the fact that I have a girl gang behind me, a bit of space, and the attention of a sexy, sweet, motorcycle-riding badass, but I'm finding it hard to be small and civil and meek with Kevin now. I square my shoulders and stare him down. "He hasn't met the kids, and he won't meet them until I'm ready for that to happen."

Kevin snorts. "Yeah, right. He's probably in there now. Tell me, Trina. Do you think of me when you suck his cock?"

Startled, I blink. Did he just say that to me? *Did he just say that to me?*

Oh, *hell* no.

Cocking my hip to the side, I arch a brow. "Honey, I don't think of you ever, and definitely not when Mac's big, beautiful cock is involved."

Then I slam the door in his face.

Then I start shaking, and tears leak down my cheeks, so I hide in the powder room in the hallway until my mother knocks on the door.

"Trina? Everything okay?"

I open the door so fast my mother stumbles back, wide-eyed. "Kevin just asked if I think of him while I suck Mac's cock."

Mom's jaw drops. "He said *what*?"

"So I told him I don't think of him ever, and definitely not when Mac's big, beautiful cock is involved." The words are coming out of my mouth for the second time, and it's just as horrifying as the first.

But Mom doesn't look horrified. Her eyes widen for a beat, then she throws her head back and laughs. When she wraps me in a hug and pats my back, I pull away and shake my head.

"Mom, I haven't done anything with Mac. I don't know anything about his penis. It could be tiny. He could have a micropenis!"

My mother arches a brow as her lips twitch to keep a smile down. "Sweetheart, I don't think Mac has a micropenis."

"I don't know if I even want to find out!"

"Of course you want to find out. Don't be silly."

I'm living in an alternate universe. That's the only explanation I can come up with for the fact that I'm talking to my mother about Mac's...*equipment*. My mother and I don't talk about sex, ever. I definitely don't discuss specifics, like, *ever* ever. But for some reason she seems to think this is all a big joke.

That is, until she pats my cheek with a soft look in her eyes. "I'm proud of you, Katrina."

"You're *proud* of me? For saying *that*?" Definitely an alternate universe. I've fallen through a wrinkle in the space-time continuum.

Mom huffs. "You let that man dim your shine for years. He walked all over you and it broke my heart to see it. Let him imagine you in bed with a handsome man like Mac. Just let him! He deserves to squirm."

"I don't want to be vindictive. Why can't we just co-parent like adults? He was more than happy to sign off on me moving here. Said it would be better for his work, but maybe I should have stayed closer to him. Maybe the distance is hard on him, and he's regretting it."

"Good." My mom gives me a decisive nod. "He should regret it. He ruined a good thing and he treated you like crap."

"Nana said crap!" Katie screams from down the hall. "Toby, Nana said crap! She said a bad word!"

I close my eyes for a beat, and when I open them my mother is chuckling. She turns toward Katie's voice. "I did say crap. Crappity, crap, crap!"

"Mom," I cut in, exasperated.

Katie just squeals. "*Crap!*" my daughter yells, then bursts out laughing.

My lips twitch despite themselves. "Now look what you've done." I try to keep my voice stern, but my mother sees right through me.

She just winks and heads down the hallway. I give my

eyes one last wipe and exit the powder room, suddenly not caring about my daughter saying a bad word. She's laughing, even though her life has seen more upheaval than I ever wanted her to. She said goodbye to her father today, and it broke my heart to see her teary. But she's laughing now, so maybe one little inappropriate word is a compromise I can live with.

WHEN WE MOVE into Candice's old house, the kids are over the moon. They choose their rooms, and my mother insists that I take the master bedroom even though I think she should have it. We spend the week cleaning, unpacking, and preparing for school to start on the following Monday.

I also end up looking for—and finding—a child therapist for the kids. Seeing Toby's hostility toward his father and Katie's tears when she said goodbye to Kevin put my butt in gear. Enough thinking about myself. Enough worrying about a hottie like Mac. Time to do right by my kids.

Candice, at first, tries to refuse to charge us rent. When I insist on having a lease and paying her rent, she relents, but charges us such a small amount for a four-bedroom house that I almost break down and cry.

Once the kids are in school, I'll get a job and I'll pay her back somehow—but she's all loved-up with Blake, building her dream home while Allie prepares for college next year, and I have a feeling she truly doesn't care. She's happy, and she's paying it forward.

Mac and I don't get to see each other, but we do text frequently over the course of the week. I send him updates on the cat, telling him how Mr. Fuzzles is adjusting to the new home.

Not surprisingly, I don't mention the last conversation I

had with Kevin, and I don't ask him about the status and size of his junk.

Mac sends me pictures of his pottery projects, of sunsets he sees on his motorcycle rides, and everything in between. Every day I wake up to a good morning text, and every evening he sends me a sweet goodnight. It makes my heart flip every time I see it.

It doesn't feel wrong to be talking to him. Even though I'm recently divorced and Kevin keeps making snide comments every time he calls the kids or sends me a message, they wash over me without burrowing under my skin. It's like a switch flipped, and I can see the kind of man he truly is...and rise above it.

By the time Friday rolls around, I haven't seen Mac in a week, and I feel like I'm about to burst out of my skin. Thank goodness for moving and busy kids. At least I haven't had time to pine after him too much.

But on Saturday night, when the kids are bathed, have their teeth brushed, and are having story time with Nana, I pick up my phone and stare at the screen. The moving and cleaning is done, the kids have everything they need for school on Monday, and my weekend is free.

I need to woman up and do this.

So, I find Mac's number and with a trembling hand, hit the call button.

His deep voice makes butterflies explode in my stomach. "Hello, gorgeous."

"Hi, Mac."

"I've been wondering when you'd call."

"Doesn't seem like *your* phone is broken." I smile as I talk, my eyes on the gorgeous backyard of Candice's—no, *my*—home. I could live here. I could be happy here.

"Wanted you to be sure you wanted to see me."

"Well, I'm sure." When did I get so bold? I glance over my shoulder, listening for any little footsteps; hearing nothing, I turn back to the window. Movement near my feet makes me look down to see Mr. Fuzzles circling through my legs before jumping up onto my foot. "I think Mr. Fuzzles can hear your voice. He just came by to say hello, and he usually gives me a wide berth."

Mac chuckles, and the sound of it makes everything inside me clench. Why did I wait a week to call him, again? I want to feel like this all the time.

Gathering my courage, I take a deep breath. "Look, I was wondering if you wanted to meet up tomorrow?"

Mac groans. "I'm working tomorrow. Have a lot of prep to do before Monday"—what happens Monday, I wonder?—"and the Four Cups pottery order is way bigger than I expected. I told them I'd have samples for them tomorrow, and—"

"Oh, that's fine." Heat rushes to my cheeks. I clear my throat. "It's cool. Whenever you're free. Or not. Whatever."

I should have known he'd blow me off. Yes, we've been texting, but would a man like him really want to get involved with a single mom? He probably saw the kids' stuff, saw my mom, and decided it was just too much work to hang out with me. I shouldn't have called. How embarrassing. How utterly, completely embarrassing.

I'm never dating again.

"Trina." Mac says my name in a low, rumbly voice, and I have to grip the wall to stop myself collapsing.

"Mm-hmm?"

"I'll see you tomorrow."

"You will?"

"Yes."

I close my eyes at the word, heart still thundering.

Mac hums, then keeps talking. "I'll get my work done and I'll pick you up after dinner. That work for you?"

"Um..."

"It doesn't work for you?"

"It's just that the kids start school on Monday, so the evening will probably be busy." I bite my lip and squeeze my eyes shut. Why didn't I just call him yesterday? Or earlier today?

"How about right now?"

My eyes snap open. "What?"

"Are you busy right now?"

"Uh...no?"

I can hear the smile in his voice when he speaks. "I'll be at your place in half an hour. Okay?"

"Okay," I whisper, and when we hang up, I look down at my yoga pants and the shirt I reserve for cleaning, then hop into panic-fueled action. Turns out when you only have a few minutes to get ready for a date, it only takes a few minutes to get ready for a date.

When my mother sees me emerge from my room in jeans, a black sheer blouse over a black lacy cami, and the quickest makeup I could muster, she arches a brow. "I'm guessing you're not having a glass of wine with me tonight?"

"No. You don't mind watching the kids for a few hours?"

"Honey, they're in bed, and I live here. Of course I don't mind. I'm guessing this"—she motions to my outfit—"is related to a certain motorcycle man?"

The sound of a Harley approaching answers the question for me.

Mom grins. "Have fun, Trina."

"I will," I tell her as I plant a kiss on her cheek, and I already know it's the truth.

16

MAC

THERE'S nothing better than feeling a beautiful woman's arms around my waist while I ride through hilly, wooded landscapes on a warm summer evening. Trina's thighs press against mine as we bank around a corner, her chest plastered to my back.

We ride for forty minutes, taking the long way back to my place, a wooded property I bought over a decade ago. I park outside my pottery studio and Trina dismounts, giving me a broad smile as she removes her helmet.

"I don't think I'll ever get over how much fun that is." She combs her fingers through her hair and shakes it out as I get off and put our helmets away.

"You've got the bug." I grin as I intertwine my fingers with hers to lead her to the studio. I don't know what it is about this woman, but I have to be touching her whenever I'm nearby. It's like there's a magnetic pull between us, and I can't resist holding her hand, touching her back, curling my arm around her shoulders. I just want to be close.

This growing need to be near her should scare me. Under

normal circumstances, it would. But with Trina, it feels too easy to be around her to question it.

Rolling open the big, corrugated iron door, I smile at Trina's sharp intake of breath.

"Mac," she breathes as she steps into the space.

I flick on the warm yellow lights and steal a glance at her. It's the first time I've had anyone in here, apart from my brother and my father. Definitely the first time a woman has stepped inside the space. My studio is usually my sanctuary. It's where I come to be alone, to create. But when Trina called me earlier and asked to see me, I knew I wanted to show it to her.

She walks up to the wall of shelving, where pottery projects are displayed from floor to ceiling. She touches a glazed plate that has a seam of gold paint running through the center before standing in front of a tall, fluted vase, shaking her head. "You're really talented, Mac."

Heat rises over my cheeks. I rub the back of my neck and turn away, reaching for one of the bags of clay I bought earlier today. "You want to make something with me?"

My voice comes out gruff, and in the few silent moments that follow, I realize I really, *really* want Trina to say yes. I want her to sit with me and throw a bowl or a pot or whatever we decide to make. I want her to sit here and soak in the magic of this space, the meditative qualities of the pottery wheel. I want her close to me.

When I lift my gaze to her, a bag of clay hanging from my hand, I see her face split into a wide smile.

She nods. "Yeah. But only if you're ready for my mediocrity."

My brows twitch into a frown at her words. Mediocre? Trina is the furthest thing from mediocre. Sure, she kind of sucks at pool, and she's a beginner at throwing pottery, but one look at the woman and you'd know *mediocre* is not a word that describes her in any way.

Jerking my chin to the wheel, I cut a piece of clay, prep it, and tell her to pull up a stool. Then I realize she's dressed for a nice dinner out, with her designer-looking jeans and lacy black top. "Hold on." I put the ball of clay down and grab a pair of coveralls.

Trina grins. "And he cares about my clothes too. I'm liking you more every minute I spend with you, Mac." She says it in a joking way, but I can't help the warmth snaking through my chest at her words.

"The feeling is mutual."

And it's the truth. All my worries about getting involved, about committing to someone...they just disappear whenever Trina's around.

She blushes, then gets to work putting the coveralls on over her clothes. When her arms are in, I can't resist stepping closer to her and zipping her up. Her eyes meet mine as my hands linger at the top of the zipper, that lush lower lip caught between her teeth.

Clearing my throat, I nod to the stool. "Sit down."

"You sure like ordering me around, don't you?" An arch of her eyebrow makes me want to kiss the sass right out of her. But she still does what I say.

"Woman, you have no idea." My voice is full of gravel, and Trina's cheeks blush pink.

"I should smack you for calling me woman." She sticks her tongue out at me and laughs, sitting in front of the pottery wheel with her hands on her lap. "Okay. Now what do we do?"

I grab another seat and place it behind hers, pressing my thighs against her hips and reaching my arms to rest on her legs. It's a reversal of how we ride the bike, and I love the way

Trina leans back into me and fits her head into the crook of my neck. She, too, can't stop leaning into me. Wanting more contact.

It's almost enough to make me forget about the clay and rip those coveralls right off her body. But Trina looks at me expectantly and dips her hand into the bucket of water beside us.

With a grin, I follow her lead, sliding my hands over hers as I turn on the wheel and start centering the clay. This is something I've always done by myself. I don't teach many classes, and I've never invited anyone to work in my studio. Pottery-making is something I do alone in the woods with nothing but my thoughts and maybe a stereo blaring my favorite songs. I can sit here for hours, and on a warm night like tonight I love keeping the studio doors open while yellow light spills out into the night.

This is new for me. Having a beautiful, magnetic woman wrapped up in my arms, feeling every little moment of delight as she feels clay moving under her touch. Knowing she's experiencing this for only the second time, and I get to experience it with her.

It's turning me on.

The way she leans into me, then gets caught up in what we're doing and moves forward, eyes on the spinning wheel, on our hands, on the water and clay running over our fingers. For a few long minutes, we don't speak. We center the clay together, the stubble on my jaw rasping against her cheek as I lean over her shoulder, my body wrapped up around hers.

I wonder if she can feel how hard I am. I wonder if she knows every time I catch my breath. I wonder if this moment feels as intimate and spellbinding to her as it does to me.

When I curve my fingers over hers and start opening the clay, Trina's body relaxes into mine. Her hands turn pliable in mine and we work together, our bodies so close we move as one. We don't speak. There's only the noise of cicadas outside and the pottery wheel whirring inside, our quiet breaths, the rustle of the bucket of water any time one of us dips our fingers into it.

"What are we making?" Trina finally asks as I guide her to pull up the sides. "It's smaller than what we made in class."

"A cup," is my reply. My breath ruffles a strand of hair near her temple, and I feel her smile against me.

"Do I get to keep it?"

"Only if you come back to glaze and fire it."

She laughs. "Are you blackmailing me?"

"Is it working?"

Trina's smile widens as she turns to look at me, her lips just a few inches from mine. Eyes twinkling, she gives me the barest of nods. "Yeah," she says. "It is."

And in that moment, with her body relaxed against me, our hands messy with water and clay and her lips so close to mine, I can't resist any longer. My hand finds the crook of her waist, the thick material of the coveralls crinkling under my touch. I pull her close and crush my lips to hers.

Trina lets out the sexiest, sweetest little whimper as her lips part and her tongue searches for mine. Gripping her waist, I pull her close and cup my other hand to her jaw, my thumb sweeping over her cheek to keep her close.

I'll never get sick of this. Every time we kiss, it sets my body alight. I'm hard as steel right now, with her ass pressed against my crotch and her upper body twisted in mine. Her clay-covered hands find my shoulders. They curl around my neck, cool and slick from the pottery that now sits forgotten on the wheel.

She tastes sweet, perfect. When her fingers curl into the hair at the nape of my neck, I let out a low groan.

"You're going to be the death of me, Trina," I say against her lips before nipping at them and moving to her jaw, her neck. There's a grey smudge of clay over her cheek where my thumb swept across it, and her normally perfect hair is already streaked with it.

It makes my blood heat to see her like this. Messy. Undone. Eyes glazed and hungry, lips swollen with my kiss.

I pull back an inch to meet her gaze, studying her expression. "You want me to stop?" I ask as my control frays. I brush my lips over her jaw, nuzzling her ear as I inhale her scent.

Her brows tug together, confusion flitting over her face. "What?"

My fingers dig into her waist as she clings to my neck, turning in my arms in a way that her perfect, pert ass rubs up against my hardness. I groan, closing my eyes. "You're driving me crazy, Trina. I want you so bad I can barely think. If you want me to stop, you have to tell me."

That sinful lip gets sucked in between her teeth. Her fingers burrow into my hair, and then she says the words that undo me completely. "The last thing I want you to do is stop, Mac. Especially not now."

17

TRINA

THIS ISN'T LIKE ME. I don't go on motorcycle rides with men I've known only a couple of weeks. I don't let them take me to their house in the woods, then make out with them with clay-covered hands. I'm a mother. I'm responsible.

But right now, I feel the furthest thing from responsible. Recklessness heats my blood, drives me to the brink of madness.

When I say those words to Mac, the tension finally snaps like a dry twig. He shifts his hold on me to pick me up, spinning me around as he stands and lifting me so I wrap my legs around his hips. One of his hands slides down to cup my ass while the other grips my hair, pulling me in for a hard kiss.

He walks me to a workbench and sets me down, never once breaking our kiss.

I love the way his body curls over mine. How he tugs me closer to the edge of the workbench and notches himself between my spread legs. I love the way his hands tangle into my hair, how his stubble abrades my skin, how his muscular arms wrap around me so tight it feels like every part of him is touching every part of me.

I've never been manhandled like this. I've never had someone take control of a kiss like this, showing me just how much he wants me.

When we finally break the kiss, both of us panting hard, I laugh at the streaks of clay across his shoulders, his face, his hair. "Messy," I say between breaths.

"Perfect," is his response as his lips brush over mine once again.

I need more of this. I need to feel the muscles of his back clenching under my palms. I need to breathe in the scent of his skin and commit it to memory.

Clawing at his shirt, I tug it up and over his head before leaning back and letting my hands drift down his body.

He. Is. Magnificent.

Hard slabs of muscle cover every inch of his body. My fingers run through the rough hair sprinkled over his chest as Mac watches me, his hands gripped on my thighs. When I run my fingers over the flat discs of his nipples, I catch the small inhale of breath he makes. I smile when he does it again when I run my nail over the same spot, glancing up at him through my lashes.

Letting my hands drift lower, I run my fingers through the grooves of every abdominal muscle, sucking in a hard breath when I reach that deep V that disappears down into his low-hanging jeans. His body is thick, solid. So utterly manly. There's an unmistakable bulge in his pants and I bite my lip, hesitating for a brief moment before running my hand lower, over the zipper of his jeans to feel the steel-hard shaft beneath it.

Side note: my mother was right. It's definitely not a micropenis.

"Trina," Mac rasps, his fingers tightening on my thighs.

"You have a very nice body," I tell him, one hand still

cupped over his crotch. He throbs against me, sending a wave of heat crashing through my blood. I feel almost giddy. One touch and a few words have the power to make him throb like that. He's hard as rock—for me.

So, when Mac reaches for the zipper of my coveralls and tugs them down, it feels almost like an inevitability. Yes, I want to undress with him. I want him to touch and explore my body like I crave to explore his. I want to feel the silk-covered steel of his shaft wrapped in my fingers. I want to taste him on my tongue. I want him inside me. Every dirty fantasy I've ever had comes roaring to life inside me as the zipper of my coveralls parts and I pull my arms out of the thick blue material.

Once the overalls are hanging on my hips, Mac stops. "Don't move," he says, his hands squeezing my hips as I sit on the counter. He moves to the sink, washes his hands, then comes back with a damp rag, which he uses to clean my hands in slow, methodical sweeps. "All that effort to keep your clothes clean," he explains. "Wouldn't want to ruin them now."

"You're perfect," I blurt, and I'm not even sure I'm joking anymore.

Mac chuckles, fitting himself between my legs again, and with a quick kiss, moves those clean hands to my top. His deft fingers make quick work of the buttons on my sheer black blouse. When it's fully open, he surprises me by tugging at my camisole with a rough, hard movement, exposing my chest. I gasp. My breasts are pushed up by the bunched fabric, peaked nipples sensitive in the cool air. When his rough thumb brushes over my breast, an echo of the movement I made over his chest, a shiver courses through me. I arch my back into his touch, leaning my palms on the workbench as my thighs tighten around his hips.

I'm sure Mac can feel the heat between my legs, even through the multitude of layers that separate us. And when he lowers his lips to my breast, I close my eyes and tangle my fingers in his hair, wild with need for him. I'm rocking my hips against him, arching my back to crush my breast into his mouth, clawing at him. I'd be embarrassed if I wasn't so damn turned on.

And when he growls low at the back of his throat, palming my neglected breast as his teeth run over my other nipple, I let out an answering moan.

That's when Mac moves.

He pulls me off the workbench with a hard tug, catching me against his body. His chest hair is deliciously abrasive against my sensitized skin, but I don't have time to enjoy it before he's spinning me around so my back is to his front.

"Hands on the counter." His voice is harsh, commanding, and it sends fire rushing through my core.

I do as he says, pushing my ass into him as my fingers dig into the raw wood of the workbench.

And that's when I learn what Mac's hands can really do.

He unhooks the button of my jeans with a flick of his fingers, sliding his hand inside a moment later. With his fingers over my panties, he finds my bud and starts circling it with steady, confident movements.

A moan slips through my lips as the pleasure ratchets higher inside me. The lacy material of my panties—yes, I changed into my good undies for this—feels beautifully rough against that little bundle of nerves.

"Don't move, Trina," Mac says in my ear, banding his other arm across my chest so he can tease my nipple between his thumb and forefinger. "Keep your hands where they are."

"I will," I pant, my eyes glued to the space where his hand disappears beneath my clothing. As if he can sense my frenzy, his movements become firmer, faster. He slides his fingers down the gusset of my panties and grunts when he feels the dampness that has already soaked through. The heel of his palm grinds against me, and I can't resist the movement of my hips as I ache for more.

So, he gives it to me.

Tugging my panties aside, Mac slides those sinful fingers through the wetness between my legs. "You're so sweet and wet for me," he growls in my ear, nipping at my earlobe as his fingers slide along the slickness of my seam.

I don't even have the capacity to answer beyond a breathy moan. My hips are grinding into him, his hardness an ache against my ass. It somehow feels dirtier to be half-clothed, leaning against his workbench like this. I'm so turned on I can hardly think, let alone move. All I can do is keep my hands where he wants them and my legs spread as he works magic between my legs.

"Mac," I pant. Or maybe I'm begging.

In response, he takes one finger and slides it inside. I watch the back of his hand moving and his forearm flexing as he works another finger inside me until I finally have to close my eyes.

Here's a thing about me: I've never come from vaginal penetration alone. I sometimes didn't even enjoy it, really, unless I was incredibly turned on. In the past, I always needed direct clitoral stimulation, or I just resigned myself to not orgasming.

But I'm enjoying this. Maybe it's Mac's palm against my clit, sometimes grinding it hard while his fingers plunge inside me, sometimes barely brushing it, or his whole body curved around mine as his fingers thrust inside me. Maybe it's the soft grunts he makes near my ear, or the feel of his teeth brushing against my shoulder.

Whatever it is, an orgasm starts budding inside me. I drop my chin to my chest, eyes squeezed shut, as pleasure knots deep in my core, slowly building with every movement of Mac's hand between my legs. I'm trembling, bucking, jerking against him as his name slips from my lips in keening, breathy pants.

"More." I close my eyes. "Please, Mac. I want more."

His arm tightens across my chest as his fingers slip out of me, then right back in with an added third. I gasp, widening my stance as my hips grind against his hand. I'm going to come. I'm going to come. I'm going to come I'm going to come I'm going to come—

Then he stops.

I whimper as Mac pulls his hand from my pants, opening my eyes and turning to see him slip his fingers into his mouth. He sucks them clean, letting out a low groan as they slide free.

"Fuck," he says, one hand still wrapped around my chest. "You taste good, Trina."

I don't know what to say. There's something so intensely erotic about the orgasm he just denied combined with the look of pure lust on his face as he tastes my arousal. I can't think of anything except the emptiness between my legs.

"I want you." The words slip through my lips without thought as I spin in his arms, and I watch Mac's gaze darken. A sinful smile tugs at his lips right before he crushes them to mine in a hard kiss.

"Good," he says when we break apart for a breath. His hands feel rough when they grip my waist, and he spins me around to face the workbench again. "Hands on the counter."

This time, when his fingers slip down my pants, he doesn't hesitate to slide them under my panties. He reaches down to where I'm wettest, then brings his fingers back up to my bud. My fingers dig into the bench as I moan, the pleasure of his touch almost too much to bear.

When his other hand finds my breast again, pinching and tugging and teasing my nipple, I pray he doesn't stop this time. Pleasure builds and builds inside me, a knot of hot pressure in the pit of my stomach. His hand works magic over my clit until I don't even know what he's doing, I just know it feels incredible. Then his other hand yanks my pants down lower, halfway off my hips before moving between my legs. With one hand on my clit, he uses the other to thrust inside me, his whole body curved over mine.

And I explode.

I come with a moan, body arching into his as he groans in contentment, his hands delivering pleasure to my body like I've never felt before. It's like he knows exactly where to touch me. He knows how hard I like it. He knows not to stop as I writhe in his arms, his rough voice telling me to keep my hands where they are even as they drift closer to the edge of the counter.

He whispers dirty words in my ear, calls me a good girl, tells me to keep grinding on his hands. He tells me to use his fingers as much as I need to, tells me how good and perfect and sweet I feel. His words send another wave of heat through my thighs and stomach, and I do just as he says. I grind against his palm, ride his fingers, use his hands to take what I need until I'm mad with the feel of it.

And when I feel my orgasm fading, Mac growls in satisfaction. It feels so good I can hardly breathe.

"That's my girl," he rasps, his chin over my shoulder as he, too, watches his hand moving inside my pants.

It's only when I soften and squeeze my thighs that he pulls his fingers out of me, and the resulting emptiness makes me ache for something bigger.

Yes, I want him. I don't know if I'll ever get enough of him.

And maybe it's that feeling of being drunk on pleasure that makes me spin in his arms, that makes me kiss him once, then reach for his belt. Maybe it's my newfound freedom, this recklessness pulsing through my veins.

Mac wraps me in his arms and kisses me deep, sweeping his tongue into my mouth as a shudder wracks his body. "You're so fucking beautiful, Trina. I could watch you come a hundred times and never get sick of it."

I've never had a man be so selfless with pleasure. Mac hasn't even touched himself. He hasn't asked me to touch him. He's been hard since we sat down at the pottery wheel, but all he's wanted to do is touch *me*.

It makes me want to return the favor. I want him to feel as good as I do. I want to see *his* face when he comes. I want *him* to be wild with pleasure, to feel reckless and out of control with lust.

And when I lower myself to my knees, Mac's breaths grow shorter. "Trina, you don't have to—"

"I want to." And it's the truth. I open his belt and unbutton his fly, tugging the zipper down with trembling hands.

He helps me push his pants and underwear down to mid-thigh, then grips his shaft in a hand as it bounces free.

Turns out yes, it's beautiful. And yes, it's big.

It's a funny twist of fate that my ex-husband does, in fact, pop into my head for a brief moment as I reach to finally wrap my fingers around Mac's hardness. I realize that I never once wanted to take Kevin in my mouth. I did it, but I didn't particularly enjoy it. He made me feel like I owed it to him. Like it was his right.

This is different. Mac brushes his hand over my cheek as he releases a breath. I glance up at him, and the look in his eyes makes me feel like the sexiest woman in the world. His eyes are at half-mast, dark with pleasure as he watches me bring my mouth to his cock.

"Hands on the counter," I tell him with a grin, my lips brushing against his tip.

"Trina." He lets out a little huff, but does as I say. Both hands rest on the workbench on either side of my head, then I wrap my lips around his cock and suck.

By the time I've run my hands over his shaft a few times and taken him as deep into my mouth as I can manage, I realize I'm wet again. I glance up at him and see him watching me, the look on his face telling me he's nearly undone. The muscles of his arms are hard and bulging as he grips the edge of the counter, his hips moving with slow, steady thrusts as I take him in my mouth.

I've never felt so in control. So sexy. I've never been so turned on by doing something like this, but I can't help the way my hips rock in time to his.

"Touch yourself," Mac growls, as if he can tell how wild this is making me. As if he doesn't want me to spend one minute without feeling good.

I only hesitate for a second. With one hand wrapped around his shaft as my tongue laps up the salty taste beading at his tip, I slide my other hand between my legs. And that's when the control Mac had been keeping on himself snaps. He thrusts his hips as he moves a hand to the back of my head, hard enough to make my eyes water but not hard enough to hurt. His hand tightens in my hair as I touch myself, drunk on the taste of him, the knowledge that he's watching me pleasure myself while I pleasure him.

When he tells me he's about to come, he tries to pull away but I just suck him deeper. He pants my name in a way that makes me moan around the shaft in my mouth. His hands tighten at the back of my head, then his hips still as he throbs against my tongue.

I come as he does, my hand moving almost frantically between my legs as he spurts onto my tongue, down my throat, the salty, musky taste of him driving me wild.

Never in my life have I enjoyed doing this. Never have I ever been turned on by swallowing a man's pleasure. Never in my life have I brought myself to orgasm while I was on my knees like this.

But it feels right with Mac. Right and so, so dirty. I cry out, the sound muffled by him, my body bucking until finally I pull away, releasing him from my mouth with a soft pop.

Mac picks me up with one swift movement, wrapping me up in his arms and burying his face in the crook of my neck. I cling onto his hard biceps, breathing hard, the remnants of my orgasm still sending spears of heat through my thighs and stomach.

He says my name again, his arms trembling as he wraps them around my limp body. Mac kisses me then, and it feels nothing like our other kisses. It's not feral and needy. It's tender, but still hard and hot and wet. It's like he's trying to tell me how much he loved what we just did. Like he can't get enough of the taste of me.

When we finally fall apart, I lean against that famous workbench and stuff my breasts back into my bra. The coveralls are still hanging off my hips and my pants are undone. My sheer blouse is half-off, revealing one shoulder. Mac has clay all over his shoulders and hair. I'm sure I do too.

I watch him lift his boxer-briefs back up, followed by his pants. He leaves them undone as he lets out a long breath and lifts his eyes to meet mine. "Well," Mac says with a twitch of his lips.

"Well," I reply.

"That was fun."

I laugh. "Yeah. That's one word for it." I button my jeans and straighten my blouse as my eyes drift to the pottery wheel. The sad, half-finished cup sits as a misshapen lump of clay in the center of the wheel. It's already started drying out. I bite my lip. "We might have ruined that cup."

Mac follows my gaze. His smile lights up his eyes as he shrugs his bare shoulder, reaching toward me to grab my hand and tug me close. His arms circle around my waist, hands cupping my ass as he nuzzles my nose with his. "I have to be honest with you, Trina, I don't give a shit about the cup right now."

"You should."

He pulls away, arching a brow as his lips twitch. "That so?"

"Mm-hm," I answer, my fingers running over his jaw. "How else are you going to bribe me to come back here?"

Mac laughs and tugs me even closer, his lips brushing mine so softly they barely touch. "I can think of a few ideas."

Heat knots deep in my stomach, and I smile against his lips before wrapping my arms around his neck and kissing him once more.

The truth is, it won't take much to convince me to come back here. Won't take much at all.

18

TRINA

AFTER MAC and I wandered over to his house—very neat, if sparsely decorated—and had a late-evening snack of crackers, cheese, and cold cuts, Mac drove me back home. Our goodbye kiss was lingering and sweet, and I'm still thinking about it now as I lean against my front door.

I can't believe I just did that.

After a week of moving, keeping the kids busy, getting therapy organized, and overall just running around cleaning and unpacking, I wasn't expecting to have a Saturday night like tonight. My lips curl almost unfamiliarly as I stand in my darkened house, and I realize I'm content. Happy, even.

That happy feeling continues into Sunday, when the kids, my mother, and I make our way to the Four Cups Café for a midmorning coffee and treat. As soon as we enter, the kids make a beeline for the counter, and my eyes dart to a huddle around a box at one of the tables.

"Ooh, what have we got here?" Mom sweeps past me to investigate.

Dorothy looks over her shoulder and waves her forward. "Look at this!" She brandishes a beautiful, handmade espresso cup, holding it by its teeny-tiny, delicate handle. My mother peers over her shoulder and grabs a saucer. It's a soft peach color, with seams of foiled gold running across it like the veins of a marble slab.

I know that saucer.

My heart thumps. Damn it! My heart goes wild over the sight of Mac's *pottery*. What the hell is wrong with me?

Simone and Candice are leaning over the box, chattering excitedly. "Gorgeous," I hear Simone say as she unwraps one of the new mugs.

I follow the kids and get them set up at a table in the corner with a muffin and small hot chocolates. Katie brought her coloring book, and Toby is reading a book. They'll keep themselves busy for a few minutes, at least. I walk back to the table to admire Mac's artful pottery.

"What's all this?" Agnes's voice says from behind my shoulder. She's got her hands on her hips in the doorway, looking down her nose at everyone from her four-foot-nine height.

Dorothy rolls her eyes. "Go back to your cesspit, Agnes."

"That cesspit keeps you well stocked with romance novels," Agnes returns. "I take order after order from you week after week, but do I judge the smut you read?"

It's supposed to be a rhetorical question, but Dorothy snorts. "Sure sounds like it."

Agnes runs the bookstore, and judging by the thousands of books housed in the library upstairs, I can imagine she's built her business on the women of this town. Agnes toddles past me and takes one of the larger cups in her hands. She inspects it with a raised brow, turning it over a few times before glancing my way. "Your man sure does make a nice cup."

I almost choke. "My man?"

Agnes rolls her eyes. "Will someone put Trina out of her misery? It's fine. You can sleep with Mac. No one will judge you. In fact, we'll all be happy that you're not both moping around town like lovesick teens."

"You know, Agnes, that's the first reasonable thing I've heard you say in thirty-five years." Dorothy plucks another cup out of the box to admire it, totally ignoring the death glare Agnes cuts her way.

Candice looks like she's trying not to laugh. Simone isn't even trying—she just cackles into the box. I'm mostly trying not to have my whole head burst into flames from blushing so hard.

"Have you been moping?" a deep voice says near my shoulder.

I scream.

Mac chuckles, his eyes sparkling when I turn to see him standing there. Stillness settles over the ladies at the table, the sound of crinkling paper and clinking pottery going suddenly quiet. My skin feels too tight. I have visions of Mac's hands doing delicious things to me, and now is not the right time to be having those kinds of visions.

I need to say something. Mac is *right here*, and he just asked me a question. Stop looking at his lips. Oh, God, he just licked them. Did I just have a mini orgasm? *Stop looking at his mouth.* "No! I haven't been moping. I've been busy." I've been real busy in the twelve hours since he had his hands down my pants. Since I had my mouth—

"Oh, please." Agnes snorts.

Dorothy, in an act that defies the blood feud the two women have maintained for many decades, lets out a loud belly laugh. "She's got you there, honey," she tells me.

My cheeks are burning. I close my eyes for a beat, try to regain control over my rioting body, and finally meet Mac's gaze again. "You...made...pottery?" I thrust my thumb toward the box.

Smooth.

Fiona walks over from behind the counter. "Remember, I mentioned it after our pottery masterclass? I ordered all new crockery for the café from Mac." She shakes Mac's hand, and even though I know she's about to be married a couple of months from now, a spear of jealousy still pierces my gut.

There's something wrong with me. This is out of control.

Mac isn't in his pottery-making garb. He's all motorcycle badass now, in black jeans and boots with a worn tee hugging every strong plane of his chest.

When did my mouth get so dry?

I clear my throat. "Oh, you ordered all new mugs for the café. Of course." I nod at Fiona. "I remember now. It's great that you guys promote local artisans so much." Is this how small talk works? Am I doing it right? Does my smile look weird? What do I do with my hands? When did it get so hot in here?

"I was actually hoping I could grab someone to help me with the rest of the first order. If you're happy with the samples, that is." Mac glances at Fiona, who nods.

"Couldn't be happier. It's got the stamp of approval from the ladies who matter most, doesn't it?" Fiona looks at the table behind her.

Dorothy beams. "Fantastic work, Mr. Blair. And oh, I wish I could help you with bringing the pottery over to the café, but look at the time!" She glances at her bare wrist. "I need to go see Margaret. We're meeting Hamish at the Grove. Agnes?"

"Well, what do you know? I'm parched. I need a drink. I'll come with you."

"I've got work to do," Simone says with an exaggerated sigh. "I'm late for a deadline."

"Allie's waiting for me at home," Candice throws in.

"I've got to watch the chicklets," my mother calls out, nodding to Katie and Toby.

Glancing at Fiona, I realize what's happening. They're setting me up.

"I have to stay here, I'm afraid," Fiona says with a mournful look. "Someone needs to work the till." She starts walking away and says over her shoulder, "Trina, would you mind helping Mac out?"

Yes, I would mind. I stare at the ladies, feeling utterly betrayed.

Do they not realize how much this man ties my stomach in knots by his mere presence?

Evidently not, because with barely a word of goodbye, Dorothy and Agnes are out the door and heading toward the hotel. Fiona is walking back to the counter, and Simone and Candice are avoiding my death stares by carrying the box of pottery back toward the kitchen. My mother winks at me, then walks over to the kids' table and gives Katie a kiss on the top of her head. She says something to the kids, who call out goodbyes without looking up.

Looks like they'll survive without me.

Heart thumping, I turn to Mac. "I guess that leaves you and me."

"Lucky me."

I blush, but secretly, I'm delighted. I gesture to the door. "Lead the way."

I COULD HAVE SAID NO. I *should* have said no.

Right?

That fact becomes apparent to me the minute Mac rolls the big, corrugated iron door leading to his studio. My eyes land on the workbench, that spot where I leaned my body and let Mac give me one of the best orgasms of my life.

Mac must see where I'm looking, because he clears his throat. "Are you okay being here?"

Okay? Am I okay? I'm basically having an orgasm by proxy just by being here, but yeah, I'm okay.

I try for a casual smile and hope it doesn't look like a grimace. "I'm good, Mac."

A bit of tension seeps out of his body at my words, and he rewards me with the sexiest grin I've ever laid eyes on. "All right, then." His eyes linger on my lips, then he clears his throat. "Better get to it."

We walk over to a shelf full of mugs, espresso cups, saucers, plates, and all types of pottery in the same peach-and-gold style. There's a handwritten list pinned to the wall, with half the items ticked off. Mac moves to stand beside me, the heat of his body an inferno at my side. "I've been rushing to get the first half of their order done before the start of the school year," he tells me, and I frown at his words. Why does he care about the start of the school year? It's the second or third time he's mentioned it. "It's one of the biggest orders I've ever gotten, and I know I won't have much time to work in the next few months. Glad the ladies liked the samples."

"They're beautiful," I answer. Before I can ask about the school year comment, Mac grabs a box from the corner of the room and brings it over, showing me how to wrap up the pottery in paper to keep it safe for the trip over.

"If we do the flat stuff first, we'll be able to pack the box a bit more tightly," he says, grabbing a stack of paper and placing it on one of the shelves. I watch him wrap a plate up with sharp, efficient movements, and start doing the same.

We work in silence for a few minutes, stacking plates in the box and packing everything tight. When the box is nearly full, Mac hauls it up and moves it closer to the door before grabbing another box from the corner. In the meantime, I pick up a large vase from another shelf, turning it over in my hands. It has a huge, round belly and a delicate opening. It's glazed in rich, royal blue with flecks of white across it, like a starry night sky.

It's gorgeous.

I'm not sure how it happens, but I'm so busy admiring Mac's work that I don't hear him come up behind me with a new box. I don't see him set the box down next to me. All I know is I'm holding a piece of art, and it's so completely incredible that Mac made this with his bare hands.

I can see a groove where Mac's fingers—or maybe some sort of tool—was held against the clay as it spun. I can *feel* the imprint of his hands on the piece, and there's some kind of magic in that.

Kevin was talented. I appreciated his paintings, and I know he deserved the praise he got. But there's something about holding this vase in my hands, touching the clay that Mac coaxed into this impossible, exaggerated shape, that makes my heart squeeze so tight. Maybe it's just how easy Mac's smiles are, and how much he seems to enjoy the fact that I've tried to do pottery with him. He wants me to enjoy it too. He's not gatekeeping his art from me.

The difference between the two of them is stark. Being in Kevin's studio always made me feel like I didn't belong. Like I wasn't welcome. Being here feels like there's nowhere else I'd rather be.

Then I feel a warm hand on the small of my back, and I'm jolted back to reality. I jump, and that beautiful, fat-bellied vase with the night sky painted on it slips from my grasp. I don't even have time to yell as it falls to the ground and smashes on the concrete floor. Shards and splinters and broken pieces of vase scatter halfway across the studio.

Gasping, I drop to my knees and scramble to pick it up, as if I'll be able to put it back together. As if I didn't just destroy something of Mac's that was beautiful and perfect. As if my clumsiness didn't just shatter something bigger than the vase, some intangible feeling I wasn't able to figure out.

Tears fill my eyes when I grab a large shard of pottery, my breath staying stuck in my throat at the mess I just made. "I'm sorry," I hear myself saying. "I'm so sorry, Mac. I'm so, so sorry. I didn't mean to. It slipped, I—"

A shaky breath slips through my lips as I try my best to hold back the tears. Maybe this is why Kevin didn't want me anywhere near his precious canvases.

"Hey." A soft, deep word. "Come on." Mac takes the shard from my hand and drops it to the floor with a careless flick of his wrist before taking my hand in his. He pulls me up and wraps me in his arms.

I melt into the strength and warmth and safety of him, trembling as I apologize to his shirt. "It was so beautiful, and I destroyed it," I whisper. "I'm so sorry."

Mac lets out a slow, deep chuckle. "It's fine, Trina. Really. If you had any idea how many things I've broken, you wouldn't be apologizing. It's one of the realities of being a potter. Lots of things break. Lots of things come off the wheel or out of the kiln less than perfect. It's just the way it is."

I lean my head back to look at his face, because I want to know if he's telling the truth. All I see in his eyes is warmth. No anger. No sadness. Nothing that would indicate he's upset with me in any way.

When I let out a breath, Mac's arms tighten around me. Then, he takes one of those beautiful, talented hands and wipes the tears from my face with his thumb. "Don't cry."

My fingers are curled into his shirt as if I'm clinging to him for dear life. His hand is warm, comforting, and I let out a shallow sigh. "I'm sorry, Mac. That was so clumsy of me."

"Stop apologizing. I don't care about the vase. It was lopsided and the neck was too thin for the vase to be useful for anything but collecting dust." His eyes shift back to me and he gives me a casual shrug. "It was a practice piece for an exhibit Dorothy and Margaret coerced me into doing in January, so no one was going to see that vase anyway." He smiles. "And even if it had been a paid piece, I still wouldn't give a shit."

He's not looking at me like I'm silly, or frivolous, or some air-headed woman. He's not judging my every move like my ex-husband used to do.

Mac is looking at me like no one else exists. His gaze darkens as it drops to my lips.

God, I love that look. I'm back here after less than twenty-four hours, leaving my kids with my mother so I can have some time alone with this insanely sexy man. That's...wrong, right? I should be more responsible.

But trying to keep hold of those thoughts is like grasping at tendrils of fog. I can't quite remember why I shouldn't fall head over heels for this man. I can't quite remember what it is about dating him that's a bad idea. Who cares if I just got divorced? Who cares if Kevin had a fit when he saw us together? Who cares if he's nothing like the soft, responsible, and supposedly loving man I married? Why can't I enjoy my life too?

I hold his gaze for a beat, two, and neither of us makes a move. That's when I realize I'm still wrapped up in his arms —and I never want to leave.

As if he realized it at the same moment, the arm that's banded across my back grows tighter. Mac's eyes lower, and the hand on my cheek moves to my jaw, sliding back to tangle into my hair.

I let out a little whimper, knowing I shouldn't want this as badly as I do but desperate for it anyway. I'm starved for his particular brand of affection. Hungry for it. For him.

Mac lowers his head and slants his mouth against mine. His lips brush my own in a tender movement. It's barely a kiss. More like a question.

And when my lips part and my hands move to his shoulders, he knows the answer.

The kiss that follows is like an unleashing. A dam breaking. It's feral, the way he grips me, holds me tight, parts my lips and explores my mouth with his tongue. It's like he's been dreaming of doing this, just as I have.

We've been apart just over twelve hours, and it feels like I haven't tasted his lips in an age.

Why should I hold back? Why should I take things slow? I can't remember why I haven't jumped into his arms daily from the moment I saw him change my tire. How can I ignore the way he sets my body alight? How can I resist when being in his arms feels like an ending and a beginning all wrapped up in one?

"Trina," he says, nipping at my bottom lip. "I want you."

"I know." My hands curl into his hair, tugging lightly. "I do too."

He groans. "I've thought about you every day since you came to the Grove all those weeks ago. I can't stop thinking about you."

"God, me too," I sigh, finding his lips again.

He tears himself away, eyes wild as he holds me. "Come to bed with me."

It's an invitation, a question, and a command. I know that if I said no, if I pulled away and told him to stop now, he'd listen. I could be the responsible mother. The chaste divorcée. I could focus on me—or whatever it is I'm supposed to be doing with the broken shards of my life.

But *I don't want that.*

Haven't I spent long enough denying myself? Haven't I spent thirteen years with a man who never cared about my pleasure? Haven't I tried my best to be the perfect wife, the perfect mother, and all I've gotten in return is crushing loneliness and a quick divorce?

Don't I deserve this? Something impulsive, and hot, and just for me?

Yes, I decide. I deserve it.

And so, I nod. "I want you, Mac. Right now."

He lets out a breath, closing his eyes for a moment as he holds me, then he takes my hand and leads me out of the studio, leaving the shattered vase crunching under our footsteps.

19

TRINA

THERE'S a distant undercurrent of doing something we shouldn't when Mac wraps his large hand around mine and leads me to his house. I mean, we just left Four Cups to come pick up a few boxes of pottery. Everyone will notice if we don't get back. My kids are waiting with my mother. It's not even noon—not that it matters, but the sunlight makes this all feel more scandalous.

We cross the foyer and the living room, walking with purposeful steps toward a hallway to the left of the kitchen. Mac's bedroom is dominated by a huge king-sized bed. The pillows are stacked high, the bed neatly made. Closing the door with his foot, Mac tugs me close and kisses me once more.

Outside this room, the world falls away. My entire attention is caught by the way Mac's hand sweeps down to grip my bottom, the way he groans when he feels me melt into him. There's no one in the world but the two of us.

Heart's Cove doesn't exist. My ex-husband and the mess of our separation definitely don't exist.

"I can't stop thinking about you," Mac says, voice full of gravel. "Every fucking day."

The way the words are torn from his throat makes my body go pliant. He slides my cardigan off my shoulders and tosses it aside—and it's a testament to how far gone I am that I don't protest his mistreatment of my favorite cashmere sweater.

From there, our clothes are ripped off and discarded. I sweep my hands over his chest, over the rasp of the hair sprinkled over his pecs, and I can't resist running my lips over his skin. His palm moves up my spine to cup the back of my neck, and I curl my fingers over his shoulders at the feel of it.

Pop goes the button of my jeans, and Mac's hand is down my pants again.

Oh, I definitely missed *that*. My lids close as my legs go wobbly; the only thing holding me up is the man in front of me.

Why have we held back from each other? I've never met a man who can make me melt like this. I've never felt as completely cherished in someone's arms as I do now. I should have begged him to take me here after ice cream. I should have known from the moment I dragged a finger across the handlebars of his motorcycle that I wanted him to fuck me.

But maybe it's the anticipation over all these weeks that gives his touch an edge. It makes his greedy fingers find every place that makes me shiver. I claw at his pants, pushing them down to his feet while he does the same.

When we're naked together, still standing next to the bed, Mac pulls me close and ducks his head to the crook of my neck, placing soft, hungry kisses down along the line of my pulse. Then with a swift movement, he picks me up and lays me down sideways across the bed, propping his body down on top of mine.

I love the weight of him. The feel of his skin against mine, his leg notched between my own. I love the way his hand slides from my neck, down my chest and over my breast, all the way down to the curve of my hip.

"You're beautiful," he says, and I feel it. I feel beautiful, perfect, worshipped for the first time in far too long.

And when Mac slides down the length of my body and hooks my legs over his shoulders, there's no hesitation or shyness in me left. His lips touch my center, his tongue starts a slow, languorous exploration, and I know there's no turning back.

It's only when my back is arched and my hand is tugging at his hair that consciousness returns to my mind, a brief, fleeting thought that reminds me I've never come this way, with a man's tongue between my legs. I've enjoyed it, sure, but it's never gotten me all the way—

An orgasm washes over me, bright and intense. I gasp Mac's name and he groans in response, but he doesn't lift his head until my grip on his hair weakens. Then, lids heavy, he looks at my boneless body and moves to his bedside cabinet.

Teeth rip the condom wrapper. Strong hands slide it over his hard cock. Then he's back on top of me, kissing his way over my chest and up to my lips.

"You taste good," he growls near my ear while his thighs spread mine wider. "Better than I imagined, and I imagined you'd taste like heaven."

He wondered what I'd taste like. Need splinters through me. I sweep my hands over his shoulders and roll my hips, wanting more. "So do you."

A groan rumbles through his chest, as if he's remembering what we did in his studio in the dark of night. As if that, too—me on my knees in front of him, him thrusting into my mouth—is another thing he spent a long time dreaming about. Then he's nudging at my entrance, lifting his head to look in my eyes, and giving me a slow, steady thrust home.

I'd forgotten what it felt like to have a man inside me. Or maybe—and this is probably more likely—I'd forgotten that it could feel this good. That it could fill me up and stretch me so beautifully.

And with Mac's eyes searching my face with every inch he pushes in, watching, recording every expression I make, I let go. I roll my hips, using my hands to push him, guide him, show him that I want more.

His elbows move above my shoulders to prop against the bed, big body arched over mine, and he gives it to me. Long, hard thrusts that make me see stars. Skin plastered against mine, lips dipping down to taste my kiss. My second orgasm rolls through me without mercy, and I only realize I'm crying out when Mac joins me, calling out my name as his hardness throbs inside me.

My orgasm is so intense, it rips the breath from my lungs. I feel him fill the condom and I wish it was filling me, and another shiver of pleasure ripples through me. This could never be wrong. It could never be anything but utterly perfect.

When we stop moving, still connected and intertwined, I let my hand slide down his sweat-dappled back. He lifts himself up to his elbows and looks down at me, eyes unreadable, then lifts himself off me and moves to the bathroom to wash up and dispose of the condom.

For the few minutes he's gone, I lie in bed and try to make sense of the past few weeks—how quickly I've become addicted to his touch—and I wonder if I should pull back. Protect myself from the hurt he could cause me without even realizing it.

I should be taking things slow.

Then Mac reappears, still buck naked with everything on glorious display, and he climbs into bed, turns me ninety degrees so I'm lying the right way on the bed, and tugs the blankets over both of us. One leg is thrown over both of mine and his arm snakes under my head while the other wraps around my waist, totally ensconcing me in Mac.

It's the middle of the day and the sun is bright as it streams through the half-closed blinds, and being in bed with Mac feels so completely luxurious that I can't help but sink into the warmth and strength of him.

"I was just wondering if you'd want me to leave, but I'm guessing that's a no."

His arm and leg tighten. "It's a no."

A smile tugs at my lips.

"How long can you stay?"

"Don't we have a few boxes of pottery to deliver?"

Mac groans, give me another squeeze, then grunts out a "Fine," before letting me go.

The truth, though?

I'd rather stay in his arms.

20

MAC

WHY HAVE I been denying myself this? Not just sex, but the feeling of Trina in my arms, in my bed. As I pull on my discarded clothes, I'm finding it hard to remember why, exactly, I haven't given Trina everything I have to give. All the years I spent convinced that I was meant to be alone—what was I thinking? What could be better than this?

Trina shakes out her cardigan and pulls it on, moving in front of my mirror to adjust her clothes and hair. I walk up behind her and slide my hands over her hips, placing a kiss where her neck meets her shoulder. "You look perfect."

"I look like I just had sex," she says, meeting my eyes in the mirror.

I grin. "Isn't that what I just said?" I'd like to see her like this—undone, freshly fucked—every day of my life.

After a few last adjustments and some makeup touch-ups from whatever supplies she keeps in her purse, Trina turns to me and nods. "Ready."

"You sure you don't want round two?" I arch my brows and glance at the rumpled bed.

"You're bad," she chides, a smile tugging the corners of her lips.

I kiss the tip of Trina's nose and lead her back out to the studio. After sweeping up the shards of broken pottery from the ground, Trina and I make short work of packing up the rest of the order for Four Cups and loading it into the back of my truck. We ride back to town in silence.

When we pull up to the café, Fiona, Simone, Jen, and Candice are all there. I guess their busy schedules cleared up once Trina and I left. I grin at the thought as Fiona walks out to help us with the boxes, throwing a few curious glances at Trina. Once inside, I help the ladies unpack.

"These pieces are gorgeous, Mac," Candice says, turning one of the new mugs around in her hands. "Good idea, Fiona." She smiles at the other woman. "They fit Four Cups perfectly."

"I appreciate your business," I tell them with a smile. "I should have the second lot to you by the end of October, and the third by the end of the year."

The truth is, the extra money is welcome. The amount of custom pottery they've ordered has been worth well past the five-figure mark, which means I'll be able to do some work on my bike and maybe buy the new pottery wheel I've had my eye on. Not to mention a few things for my classroom over the course of the school year.

So much of my pottery sits on shelves in my studio. It's nice to know that these pieces will be put to good use. As I help the ladies bring the boxes of pottery to the kitchen to wash, I catch Trina's gaze lingering on me. A flush sweeps over her cheeks as she gives me a sweet smile.

In that moment, with midday sun gilding Trina's hair, I think I might forget about my convictions about being alone. *This* is where I'm meant to be. With her.

I understand how my father could move on, how he could be happy. I understand that even after the hell he went through when my mother left, he could look for love again. He could open himself to that kind of hurt. Because isn't it worth the risk, if someone like Trina is the reward?

When I walk back out to my truck and Trina follows, we stand next to the vehicle, unaware of what's going on around. That always seems to happen when I'm around her; nothing else seems to matter as much as memorizing the way she moves, the way the light catches every angle of her face, the way her clothes hug her figure and her eyes search mine.

"So," she says, flicking her eyes up to mine.

"So," I repeat.

"If I keep standing out here with you, I'll never hear the end of it." She throws a glance at the café, and I follow her gaze.

All four of the owners shamelessly grin at us. Simone waves.

Laughing, I turn back to Trina. "I think that ship has sailed."

She bites her lip. "What's the plan?"

I comb my fingers through my hair. "Well…"

The words are on the tip of my tongue. I want to tell her that for the first time in my life, the thought of inviting her into my life doesn't terrify me. Well, that's not exactly true. It does terrify me, but not enough to make me turn my back on her.

Trina is the first woman I've ever met that makes me see a future that isn't lonely. Professing my feelings to this woman feels like an inevitability. The words push against my lips, and all I want to do is tell her that meeting her was an epiphany. How fucking crazy will I sound if I tell her that right now? We barely know each other.

I'm Ted from *How I Met Your Mother*. I need to slow the hell down.

But before I can even attempt to untangle my thoughts, someone walks up to us. "Mac," Belinda says, crossing her arms as she comes to a stop. Ice water sluices through my veins as I look at the woman with thunder on her brow.

"Belinda." I nod, keeping my face carefully blank while my mind whirls with panic.

I don't want to talk to Belinda. The person I was when I slept with her was different from the person I am now. I'm not the guy who will flirt with a mother all through the school year, knowing she'll end up in my bed when it's all over. I'll never do that again. I knew the moment it happened that it was the first and only time, and I should have been clearer with her over the years that followed. I should have told her I wasn't interested, found a way to say it so she wouldn't spread nasty rumors about me.

Trina glances between the two of us, and I know it's rude, but I don't introduce her. I'm hoping Belinda will just move on.

But I'm not so lucky. My ex-fling looks at Trina and arches an eyebrow. "Are you the new one, then?"

"The new one?" Trina says, frowning. She glances at me, then back at Belinda. "Excuse me? I'm not sure I know what you mean."

"The new mom he'll flirt with and fuck, then toss aside when he's done."

Trina's eyes go wide.

"Belinda," I growl. "Do not fucking speak to Trina that way. Do me a favor and walk away, yeah? You know what happened between us was casual, and you have no right to stand here and fling insults at me."

Belinda snorts. "Flirting with me for nearly a year,

sleeping with me, then never speaking to me again? Ignoring me at school events for years? That's what you call casual?"

"Belinda—" I try to cut in, but she doesn't let me speak.

"I only have one thing to say to you, lady," Belinda says to Trina. She leans in, her words sharp as blades. "Don't waste your time."

With one last look at me, the woman snorts and walks away.

I meet Candice's wide eyes through the café window and watch Fiona frown as she leans to ask Simone something. Shit.

Trina's frozen beside me. She watches Belinda turn a corner, then slowly lifts her eyes to mine. "Who was that?"

I gulp, then let out a long breath. "That was... I wouldn't even call her an ex. We slept together once. *Once*, Trina, and it was four years ago."

Her brows lower. "Do you have a thing for single moms, or something? What did she mean, 'the new one?'"

"What? No, I—"

"Everything okay out here?" Lottie stands in the doorway, arms crossed. The expression on her face can only be described as *Mama Bear*.

"Everything's fine, Mom," Trina says, redness rising on her cheeks. "Go back inside."

"It doesn't look fine." Lottie's brows arch as she looks me up and down, this time not as appreciatively as she did in the Grove's parking lot. She looks ready to attack.

"Mom, please. I'll be inside in a minute."

"Fine." Lottie lets the door close, but stands in the doorway staring.

Trina looks at her, then glances at the four other faces in the window, who quickly move away, pretending to look anywhere but at us. She turns back to me, takes a deep

171

breath, and releases it slowly. "I think we need to talk, but I don't want to do it in front of an audience."

I take her hand and squeeze it. "That woman means nothing to me, Trina. We slept together once, and I'll admit I avoided her instead of being straight with her. I was too afraid of pushback and conflict at work." Trina frowns, but before she can speak, I bring her knuckles to my lips. "You mean a hell of a lot more to me than she did. She's a blip from my past, I promise."

She looks in my eyes for a few long moments, and whatever she sees must satisfy her, because she lets out a long breath and nods. "We all have pasts." A weak smile. "My ex-husband is an asshole and I have two kids, so I'm not without baggage."

Tugging her close, I bring her to the other side of my truck for a hint of privacy from our audience and lean my forehead against hers. "What we did today was worth any amount of baggage, I can promise you that."

She rolls her eyes, but a blush sweeps over her cheeks. "You're not really making me feel like much more than a one-night stand with that kind of line, Mac."

"How about this," I say in a low voice, cupping her cheek with my hand as I bring my lips to hers. I kiss her slow and deep, trying to show her all the things I can't say with words yet. All the feelings she's waking up inside me. All the old wounds that are starting to knit back together.

When we pull apart again, Katrina looks a bit dazed. She steps back, shakes her head, and gives me a sexy little grin. "You're too good at kissing. It's dangerous." Lifting a finger, she pokes me in the chest. "But we're not done talking. Don't think you can distract me with sex any time I try to talk about something serious."

"I won't distract you with sex if you promise not to be so sexy and distracting."

Trina huffs, rolling her eyes, but there's a hint of a smile on her lips.

"I'll tell you everything that happened with Belinda. Dinner tomorrow?" I ask. "You can ask me anything you want. I'm an open book." As soon as the words leave my mouth, I realize they're the honest truth. I want Trina to know how I grew up with a single father. I want her to know that I suffered when my mother left, that I never trusted anyone besides my father and my brother to stay by my side. I want to tell her that for the first time in my life, it feels like that might change.

Trina bites her lip, hesitates, but finally nods. "Yeah. I'd like that."

I can't resist the temptation of one last kiss. It's quick, but deep, and I'm hoping it'll hold me over until tomorrow evening. "Pick you up at seven."

"Can you make it seven-thirty so I can get the baths and bedtime routine done?"

"Seven-thirty." Smiling, relieved, I watch her walk back inside to be swarmed by her friends and family, then I get back in my truck and let out a long breath.

If I'm going to tell Trina about Belinda, I'm going to have to tell her about my mother. I'm going to have to face a lot of truths from my past that I've never shared with another woman—but as I drive back home to get ready for the first day of school tomorrow, I know it'll be worth it. Because I know, without a shadow of a doubt, that Katrina Viceroy is worth being vulnerable for.

21

TRINA

THE GIRLS and my mom accept a brief, vague explanation of what happened outside only because Katie and Toby are still in the café. I manage to dodge the hardest questions, grab my kids, and head home. Then there's lunch to make, backpacks to prep for tomorrow, school supplies to label with the kids' names, and all the thousand and one last-minute tasks that need to be done on the Sunday before the start of the school year.

Finally, when the kids are in bed and my mother's reading in her bedroom, I make my way to the kitchen, open the refrigerator, and grab a bottle of white wine that has at least a glass and a half left in it. I pour myself a glass that feels completely indulgent after a day like the one I just had, and I lean against the kitchen counter as I take a sip.

I had sex with Mac Blair.

Holy smokes. My wine tastes dry and a little sour—I probably should have opened a fresh bottle—but it relaxes my shoulders as I replay all the events from last night and this morning in my mind. Mac is dynamite in bed. Explosive. Amazing.

The most incredible thing is I don't feel guilty. In all the years I was married to Kevin, I always felt vaguely bad about doing things for myself, things I enjoyed. It's like my whole existence was structured around making *his* life easier. I took care of the kids all the time and made sure he had time to paint. I dressed up and stood by his side at events, ever the polite wife. I took care of the house and I worked part-time, and it always felt like I was doing those things for *him*.

Last night and this morning, I did things for me, and it feels like a revelation.

Then I think about the woman outside the café. Her words—*she's the next one*. How Mac stiffened beside me when she made that comment about flirting with moms, then the sincerity written across his face when he promised to tell me everything I needed to know tomorrow night, when we had time and space to talk about it.

Maybe I'll tell him about my past. I can tell him about growing up with my mother, about my father dying when I was in my twenties, about my marriage to Kevin and all the layers of suffering that came along with being married to a selfish man like him.

I'll tell him that there's this kernel inside me, this tiny seed that is starting to bud into something bigger. It's like I'm finally scratching the surface of who I am, finding out that yes, I can do this on my own. And hell, maybe I can start a stylist business! Who says I need to be an accessory on an unappreciative man's arm? Why I can't I do something for myself, for my kids?

Tomorrow, things between Mac and me will change, and I'm ready for it.

Quiet footsteps bring my attention to the stairway, where I see Katie's pajama-clad body descending. She pokes her head around the bannister and when she sees me, she freezes. Then, sliding into full view, my daughter bites her lip.

"You okay, Katie?" I put my glass of wine down on the counter and head for the hallway. Katie meets me halfway, wrapping her arms around my body. She buries her head against my stomach, hiding her face from me. "What's wrong, honey?"

"I'm scared," is her quiet reply.

Gently guiding her to the sofa, I sit down and nestle her into my side. "What are you scared of? Did your nightlight go out?"

She shakes her head, her body so small against mine. Katie has a fierce, independent personality, and I sometimes forget just how young she is. She's been running around since she was a toddler, always with mischief written all over her face.

And then there are times like now, when she snuggles up against me and it makes my heart squeeze into a tight ball.

"Tell me," I say, my hand making slow strokes through her hair.

"School," she finally says.

"You're nervous about going to school?"

Katie nods without saying anything.

"But you loved school last year, Katie. This year won't be any different."

"I don't know anyone at *this* school!" She sits up, hazel eyes wide as she stares at me. "What if they're all mean to me? What if my teacher doesn't like me?"

Frowning, I try to keep the hurricane of emotion inside me from showing on my face. Where in the world did this come from? Katie is confident, self-assured, *happy*. Katie makes friends so easily I get headaches trying to keep all their names straight.

"You teacher will love you, honey," I tell her, but my daughter doesn't look convinced. So, I pat her knee and stand up, heading for my phone and the multitude of emails from the school I haven't quite got around to going through. That was going to be tomorrow's job.

Look, I know I'm supposed to be Super Mom. I know I should be all over this stuff and I should know everything about Katie and Toby's new school off the top of my head, but I don't. I'm doing my best not to let the mom guilt eat at me right now, especially when I grab my phone to look for the emails I got from the school when we registered.

"Now," I say, settling in beside Katie, "let's see what we can find about your teacher, *mm*?" I flick through my emails, searching for Heart's Cove Elementary. Half a dozen emails pop up—the most recent one with a welcome pack for both children.

I open the email, click the attachment, and wait for it to load. "It's normal to be nervous, you know," I tell Katie. "I was nervous every year when school started."

"You were?"

"Mm-hmm," I say. "But everything will be okay. You'll make tons of new friends."

Katie bunches her lips to the side, not convinced.

I turn my attention back to the phone, zooming in to the tiny writing on the screen. "Now, here we go. You're going into the second grade—"

"I know *that*," Katie says with a roll of her eyes.

I hide my grin and keep reading. "And your teacher is Mr. Bl—"

I freeze.

That name.

I read it again, and it hasn't changed.

My heart starts thumping so hard I have to gulp down a

breath, but that name still stares at me in big, black writing on my screen.

Blair.

Brows lowering over my eyes, I stare at the name on the screen so hard it starts going fuzzy. *Mr. Blair.* It's still there.

It can't be. It's not him. It's not Mac.

Katie pokes my side. "What's my teacher's name?"

"Mr. Blair," I say quietly.

Katie's feet kick out as she leans back in the sofa, her little hands intertwined over her stomach. She looks just like her father when she slouches like that, and it makes pain rattle through my chest. Snapshots of the marriage I could have had pierce me like a thousand tiny needles scattered over my skin.

But I turn my attention back to the horror on my screen.

It's Hamish, right? Or Lee? It's some relative. It's not Mac.

Even though at the back of my mind, I remember all the things he's told me. He loves kids, "obviously." He gets really busy when the school year starts, but he doesn't have children of his own. He has a lot of prep work to do for tomorrow...*because it's the day before the school year starts.*

Oh. My. God.

I slept with my daughter's second grade teacher this morning. I had oral sex with him yesterday. No, it was so much dirtier than oral sex. I *got on my knees and I sucked his cock.*

Oh no.

The name on the screen stares back at me, taunting. I fucked my daughter's second grade teacher. Holy shit. Oh no, no, no.

But worst of all? I loved it. I wanted to come back every night and do it again and again.

And tomorrow, he'll be teaching my daughter addition and subtraction.

This isn't happening. My chest feels so hot it burns, and not in a good way. It claws up my throat, fuzzing my vision as I try to push the reality aside. I'm jumping to conclusions. Mac isn't a teacher.

"What does he look like?" Katie says, feet still kicking up in a steady rhythm, the fear gone from her face.

"Umm..." I tap on my screen to pull up the school's website with trembling hands, clicking through the pages to find the staff page.

Katie sits up, folding her hands on my shoulder as she peers down at the screen with me.

I scroll through faces, young and old, male and female, praying it's someone else. There must be another Mr. Blair. It's not Mac.

But then I see him, looking nothing like the motorcycle badass, dressed in a smart blue button-down with his hair combed back, a broad smile on his handsome face.

Katie moves closer to the screen and bites her lip. She tilts her head to the side and studies his face for a moment, then sits back. "He looks friendly."

"Uh-huh," I say numbly. "He is."

He was real friendly when he was telling me how good I tasted. When he was telling me how much he loved his cock in my mouth. When he was buried so deep inside me I couldn't breathe.

Super friendly.

I don't really know what happens next. Katie settles down and I put her back to bed. I head downstairs and stare at my forgotten glass of wine, feeling more and more horrified as the seconds tick by.

Then I try to talk myself down.

It's fine. Right?

We screwed around... So what? We're adults. I throw back my glass of wine and dump the rest of the soured wine into it, staring at the golden liquid as I lean against the counter, palms on either side of the glass.

Then I straighten up, because a day ago I was standing in the exact same position, but Mac's hand was down my pants.

I turn away, sliding my hands through my hair and pulling it tight. Okay. Okay, this is fine. It happened before the school year, and it's casual. We can maintain an appropriate relationship while Katie is in his class. Everything is fine. We're adults, we hooked up, and now we need to stop because it's inappropriate.

Then I whirl back around and stare at nothing, because a fresh, horrible thought enters my head:

Did Mac know?

Then it dawns on me. That woman—she said I was "the new one." The new mom he was screwing around with, and he even admitted he slept with her.

Is this what he does? Does he sleep with his students' moms?

Has he been playing me this whole time?

22

MAC

Trina never answered my text messages last night, and as I get ready for my new kids to arrive in class, I try not to dwell on it.

She told me she was busy last night. She's a mother. Sure, we hooked up yesterday morning, and I haven't been able to stop thinking of the way she moaned my name, but we're both busy people. It's normal not to answer every single text. We're going to dinner tonight, I'll tell her about Belinda, and everything will be fine.

That's how I find myself in my classroom on Monday morning, making sure all the kids' name tags are stuck to the appropriate desks, and everything is prepped for the whirl-wind of seven-year-olds that's about to walk through my door.

When I first got into teaching, I thought I wanted to be a high school teacher. I thought I'd prefer having older kids and knowing that I'd had a hand in preparing them for their futures. I even considered teaching art full-time when I discovered I loved pottery.

It didn't take me long to realize I was good with younger

kids. I think it was my second year of college, I was a student teacher doing a placement at a school in a first-grade classroom, and I saw a little girl break down and cry when she was asked to write her name. All the other kids knew how to do it already, and she panicked. I sat with her and coached her through the letters of her name—Laura—then watched her face transform from teary to ecstatic. She then proceeded to write her name on every piece of paper she could find. And the desks. And the walls.

I never quite got over the wonder that young kids have in their eyes. Teaching them makes me feel like I'm actually contributing something to the world.

Movement draws my eye to the door. A little girl points to the list of names I taped to the door and looks over her shoulder, crying excitedly. "It says Katie Paulson! This is my class!" Her eyes move to the classroom, then to me. "Hi, Mr. Blair."

"Hello, Katie," I say with a smile, repeating the name she just called out. I'm pleasantly surprised she already knows my name, and I start looking at the groups of desks for her name tag. I think I put Katie near the front of the class, since she's new at school and I wasn't sure what kind of student she'd be. But before I can confirm, my eyes are drawn to her mother in the doorway, and a ringing starts in my ears.

Katrina is standing there, looking as glamorous and beautiful as ever in her high-waisted blue linen pants and silky white top. Her softly curled hair gets tucked behind her ear as she watches me, her eyes betraying nothing.

She looks gorgeous. My heart seizes. All the words I could have said yesterday come rushing back to me, but they hit the brick wall of my lips.

"Trina," I finally squeeze through my cotton-filled throat. "You…"

"Hi, Mac." She blinks, then puts her hand on Katie's shoulder, who stands frozen between us.

I clear my throat. "You can hang your backpack on a hook, Katie, then find your name tag on the desks. Your classmates should be arriving soon."

Katie frowns, her eyes darting between me and her mother.

Another thing about young kids—they pick up on *everything*.

Shit.

Shit, shit, shit.

"Go on, honey." Trina gives Katie a gentle nudge. "I need to speak to Mr. Blair."

Katie, who had been so excited a moment ago, bites her lip as her brows draw together. "Okay," she drags out, sounding unsure, but she hangs her backpack up on one of the pegs along the wall and starts wandering through the tables looking for her name.

After hesitating for just a moment, I close the distance to Trina. She stands in the doorway, looking ready to bolt. "Now I understand why you never answered my messages yesterday," I say, trying to keep it lighthearted and completely failing.

My chest feels raw, empty. Trina is the first woman I've met who's made me want more. A few minutes ago, I was imagining a future with her. What future can we have now that her kid is in my class?

I can't date Trina. It would be completely inappropriate. Not only that, but if the kids ever found out, they could bully Katie. Parents could think of me differently. It would affect my career.

And when—not if—things between Katrina and me go sour, it'll be awkward for *years*. Just like it was with Belinda.

Which means whatever had been budding between Trina and me...it's over before it ever really began.

Trina clears her throat. "I saw your name on the school papers when I got home after..." She glances away, takes a breath, and looks at me again. "That woman yesterday. She was a mom of one of your students?"

I hate how small her voice sounds. I hate the regret etched into every line of her face. I hate that she feels that way about me.

But most of all, I hate that she's right.

The boulder in my throat makes it impossible to speak, so all I can do is nod. I want to slip my hand in hers and pull her close, but I can't. So I just stand there, across the threshold from her, looking for the right words.

She releases a long breath and closes her eyes. When she speaks, her voice is so quiet I barely make out the words. "Did you know?"

"No," I answer emphatically, my voice finally returning. "I didn't realize until right now. I swear. I thought your last name was Viceroy. I would have recognized the name in the class list..."

"I never took Kevin's name," she finally says, lifting her eyes back up to mine. "Look, Mac—"

A child comes barreling down the hallway, nearly crashing into Trina's legs. "Mr. Blair! Mr. Blair! I'm in your class!" Ricky is a super-smart little boy with white-blond hair. His father, Rick Sr., hangs out at the Grove sometimes. I extend my hand to the father as Rick runs inside and greets Katie, then starts looking for his name on the desks.

"Long time no see," the father says, grinning. His eyes flick to Trina, bald interest written in his gaze. He looks her up and down, and all I want to do is throttle him. I've known this guy for years. I've had countless beers with him. He's a friend—and I want to punch him in the face for daring to look at Trina.

This is bad.

This is so bad, it's not even funny.

I want her, and I can't have her. But I don't want anyone else to have her, either.

Rick, ever the charmer, smiles at Trina. "You look nervous. Sometimes I think the first day of school is harder on us parents than it is on the kids."

Trina lifts her hand to tuck a strand of that elegant hair behind her ear, and I notice the way Rick's eyes flick to her ring finger, noticing the strip of paler skin where her wedding band used to be. His stance shifts instantly, shoulder leaning against the doorway as he flashes a smile at her.

And I want to kill him. In that moment, I know we're not so different from animals, because the primal urge to stake my claim on Trina rises up inside me, almost too strong to resist. I'd pummel him in the face just for the way he's looking at her.

I mean—what the fuck?

A slow, long breath moves into my lungs, then back out. I need to get a fucking grip.

But how am I supposed to make sense of this? The first woman I've ever wanted is officially, completely off-limits.

Bringing my attention back to the two parents, I hear Trina let out a weak laugh that sounds nothing like her. "I know. You're happy they're out of your hair for the school year, but it's still hard to see them walk away." She glances inside the classroom, past me as if I'm not even there, to where Ricky and Katie have their heads bent over the desk, playing with building blocks I'd left out to keep the kids busy until everyone arrives. Trina shakes her head and smiles at Rick. "Especially when it seems so very easy for the kids."

Rick laughs, ever the charmer, then glances at me. When he sees the thunder in my face, his brows twitch together, but he doesn't comment. He glances at Trina. "I was about to get a coffee at the Four Cups Café. Would you like to join?"

That's it. Fuck my career. Fuck my job. I'll fight this man right here in the hallway and throw my future away. I'll piss on all the years I spent building my reputation, because there's no way I'm watching another man ask Trina out right in front of my face. No fucking way.

Not after what happened this weekend. Not after I felt her wrap her arms around me on the back of my bike. Not after I met her ex-husband and saw the hurt in her face. Not after I realized that I want to fix that for her, show her that we could be better together. I want to be the man to make her laugh. I want to be the man by her side.

"Mr. Blair! Ricky said you have a motorcycle." Katie jumps up, eyes wide. "Is that true?"

"It is true, Katie," I say, lingering near the door even though I should go to the students. But my mind is a mess. My palms itch to curl around Trina's body and keep her close. My throat feels raw from holding in all the aggression I want to hurl at Rick.

"I'd better let you go," Trina says to me. "We can continue our discussion at another time." Her voice is...*cold*. Not waiting for me to answer, she squares her shoulders and paints a false smile on her face before glancing at Rick. "My sister is a co-owner of the Four Cups Café. She's expecting me, actually."

Rick grins hungrily, then sweeps his arm down the hallway in an *after you* motion. I watch the two of them walk away together, tasting nothing but ash on my tongue—but there's nothing I can do about it, because Trina is officially off-limits to me until the end of the school year at the earliest.

And judging by my past experience? This is only going to get worse.

Then another child comes to the door, and it's my turn to paint a false smile on my face.

Today is going to be a long day.

23

JEN

HERE'S THE THING. Amanda—Fallon's ex—is really nice. This is the second time she's been in Heart's Cove, and she's super excited about my recipe book. Apart from my friends, she's basically my number one cheerleader.

Take this morning, for example. She came to the café and found me in the kitchen to show me preliminary layouts for the final book. She's lined up food stylists and started talking about media appearances.

She believes in me.

And I feel like a total jerk for resenting her.

I stock up the quickly emptying display cabinet with a fresh batch of croissants, then head back to the kitchen where Amanda is sampling my banana bread.

She looks up when I arrive. "The addition of cardamon is genius, Jen. This is some of the best banana bread I've ever had."

I can't help smiling. People tell me my baking is good, but it's different having an actual professional tell me I'm good *enough*. Good enough to make it in this industry. Good enough to be a real, published pastry chef. Recipes like banana bread are so easy to me that I can whip one up in minutes—but she's made me realize that not everyone has that skill.

"It's a pretty basic recipe." I shrug.

Amanda puts her slice of banana bread down and brushes her fingers off. "You need to stop doing that."

I frown. "Doing what?"

"Knocking yourself down when you speak. You have to get comfortable promoting yourself."

I scrunch my face up, and Amanda laughs.

"Actually, that reminds me. There's a good promotional opportunity happening right here in Heart's Cove next year."

My stomach sinks. I don't have a good feeling about this. "Oh, yeah?"

She stares at me for a beat, as if she's trying to gauge what my reaction will be. She pushes her blond hair over her shoulder and gives me a beaming smile. "There's a TV show filming here next year. A baking competition! And it's for semi-professional and professional bakers."

Anxiety ratchets up inside me. "What?"

"Filming lasts four weeks. You'll be partnered up with a teammate of your choosing, so we just need to find someone to join the competition with you. If your book is out and your social media is set up, it could provide a lot of free publicity. People will absolutely love you. It's perfect, Jen."

"No. Not perfect. I don't want to go on some reality show."

"It's not a reality show. It's very professional. It would give you a huge head start to promote your book."

"I'm not sure, Amanda…" I frown. "I'm not good in front of cameras."

"Look at it as a test run." She smiles. "I just sent the application through to your email to review. I filled it in already."

"Wait—"

"Jen, do you want this book to be a success?"

I huff. "Obviously."

"You have the talent. You have the recipes. We just need to give you the profile." She picks up her tablet and starts ticking things off her list. This book is progressing at lightning-speed. I can hardly keep up with recipe development as she puts everything together.

I watch her sort through a few recipes, double-checking them against my notes and nodding in satisfaction. Even with the thought of being on TV making me want to wet myself, I can already feel my resolve weakening. Amanda's damn good at her job, and even with the whole Fallon thing, I trust her. Maybe she's right. Maybe any publicity is good publicity.

Maybe a baking competition would be...*fun*. I've never won anything in my life! What if I won?

I clear my throat. "So, this competition...is there a prize?"

Amanda lifts her head from her tablet and gives me a beaming smile. "There sure is. A hundred thousand dollars to put toward your own business."

I grip the edge of the table. "And the prize...I'd get to keep it?" Visions of a beautiful little bakery attached to the Four Cups Café flash through my mind. I could make custom cakes. I could expand. I could hire an apprentice baker.

Amanda grins at me. "See, this is the thing I love about you, Jen." When I frown, she puts her tablet down and reaches over to squeeze my arm. "You are so brilliantly confident in your abilities. I mention a competition, and there's not even a question in your mind that you can win it. Now, I just need you to take that confidence and put it into promoting your book."

I frown. "That's different."

"It isn't, but we'll work on that." Amanda winks, and I let out a little snort.

Yeah, I like her. I said it, okay? I like Fallon's ex-girlfriend, even if I can tell she's pining after him. Even if the fact that she still has feelings for him makes it so that I can never get between them. Isn't it better to be pursuing a lifelong dream?

A hundred grand...that could change my life.

For a few brief moments, I just enjoy myself. A few years ago, I was working in an office for a tech company, dreaming of doing something different. After quitting my job and studying to be a pastry chef, I ended up landing a job at a prestigious Michelin-starred restaurant a couple of towns over. It was great experience, but it was grueling. My boss was a decorated French chef who took no bullshit. I learned a lot, but I was glad to strike out on my own with Four Cups.

Now, I could build something even bigger.

I could never have imagined being here, in the town I love, developing recipes that will soon be shared with (hopefully) thousands of people. Maybe tens of thousands. Maybe millions.

"What's this?" Amanda asks.

I look over my shoulder to see her by the fridge, peering inside at the plastic-wrapped cakes I've prepared. "Oh, that's the trial run for Fiona and Grant's wedding cake."

Amanda straightens up, eyes wide. "You're making a wedding cake?"

I nod, returning to the dishes I'd been stacking to put through our industrial dishwasher. "Yeah. They want two flavors, so I'm trying to find a frosting that will work for both."

"Jen." Amanda sounds exasperated, so I glance at her again.

"Yeah?"

"You never once mentioned you were making a wedding cake. You made the chocolate layer cake, but you didn't mention this."

Frowning, I stop what I'm doing. "Okay…" I tilt my head. "Was I supposed to?"

She laughs. "Yes! Yes, you were supposed to. Cakes are a chapter in your book, remember? A tiered cake recipe would be a great inclusion. See? This is what I mean about promoting yourself. You need to *talk* about these things. Normal people don't just whip up practice cakes for their friends' weddings!"

Amanda beams at me and starts talking about photo styling for a wedding cake. She starts telling me we could do a whole series of social media posts, that I could teach people basic cake decorating and refer back to my book. She's brimming with excitement…for me.

And that's when I know I was right to push Fallon away. We kissed *once*. So what?

So what if Amanda is Fallon's ex-girlfriend?

So what if she seems to bat her eyelashes a bit more when he's around?

So what if he invited her to town before he ever showed any interest in me?

Isn't this book more important than some guy who kissed me a single time in a moment of weakness? Shouldn't I be finally, *finally* pursuing something *I* want?

But just as the thought enters my mind, the back door opens and Fallon enters. He'd stepped out when Amanda arrived ten minutes ago, saying something about needing a break. Now he glances at the two of us, eyes lingering on mine for a moment, and gives us a silent nod.

Then he's back at the stove, glancing at the screen as an order for breakfast comes through, and he gets to work prepping some eggs Benedict with the ease of someone who's done it a thousand times.

And even though I only just told myself that I don't care

about him, that he isn't what's important to me...damn it, but my heart does skip a beat whenever he's close.

His presence shouldn't affect me the way it does. That ship has sailed. I made my choice.

Since then, things have changed. We've barely talked, but not in the comfortable, silent way that we used to not talk. Our silence is charged, heavy. He's angry with me. Angry at my cowardice, at my decision not to pursue whatever fleeting thing existed between us.

I steal a glance at Amanda to see her cheeks flushed. She straightens her top and lets her gaze stay on Fallon, and my heart sinks. She walks over to him and leans a hip against the counter, saying soft words I can't hear over the sounds of the kitchen. Her cheeks are flushed, and her hand brushes the top of her shirt in a flirty, sensual movement. Then Fallon says something and she laughs too long and too hard, touching his arm with her hand.

I'm not imagining it. She's still hung up on him.

And that means I need to stay out of their way. No matter how much Fallon swears up and down he doesn't want to be with her, it doesn't matter—because she's the one who can make this book a reality. And if I give in to this attraction to Fallon, I risk losing it all.

I've spent many years on my own. I've lived without a man my entire life, barring three brief years with a boyfriend during college. I've always thought I was better off that way. Haven't I always been independent?

But this feels like I'm giving something up that I didn't even know I wanted.

Needing to leave the kitchen, if only for a moment, I make my way to the front of house to check the display cabinet stock once again. I arrive in time to see Trina entering with a man I don't recognize, who holds the door open for her with a hopeful, flirty smile.

Jesus. Another one. That woman has men trailing after her like lost puppies in need of a good feed. I wonder if she even knows the effect she has on them? From the way she's walking to the counter without paying the man any mind, it doesn't seem like she realizes he even exists.

24

TRINA

I NEED to get out of here. This dad—what was his name again?—is flirting with me nonstop. He drove ahead of me and made sure to wait by the door so he could hold it open. It's sweet, obviously, but I'm just not interested in him. I'm still reeling from seeing Mac dressed like a second grade teacher and not a badass biker babe.

I scan the coffee shop when we enter, looking for my sister, slightly relieved when I don't see her. That means I'll have an excuse to escape. When I get to the counter, I smile at Fiona. "Hey. Have you seen Candice?"

"She's upstairs with Simone," Fiona answers. "The usual?" She nods to the coffee machine.

I nod. "Thanks."

When I reach for my purse, the dad cuts in. "I got it," he says with a grin. "We parents need to stick together."

"Oh, that's okay," I protest, but he's already got his card out and is thrusting it at Fiona.

She arches an eyebrow at me, but thankfully says nothing.

Mac's face when I agreed to come to Four Cups with this

guy was nothing short of thunderous, but what was I supposed to do? *Not* come see my sister? Make some excuse that sounded fake? Linger awkwardly just out of sight until I saw him leave?

Actually—yeah, I probably should have done that.

Sven hands me my usual Americano, his eyes darting to the man beside me as well. No doubt everyone will be questioning me about this little appearance within the hour. Desperate to change the subject, I nod to his fresh pink shirt with the glittery *Heart's Cove Hottie* writing across the chest. "New shirt? This one doesn't have the sleeves ripped off."

"Fiona told me I needed to be professional," he answers.

"Oh please," Fiona quips. "I know how to pick my battles."

Sven just laughs, which gives me the opportunity to turn to...Rick! His name is Rick. Thank goodness. "Rick, it was lovely to meet you, but I really do need to go speak to my sister. She's expecting me."

"Oh, of course. Look, I was hoping I could call—"

"Thank you so much for the coffee. Got to run. Bye!"

I make my escape, feeling foolish and panicked and rude. But honestly, the last thing I need right now is some single dad from my child's class asking me out to more coffee dates. I can just imagine Mac's reaction.

Wait—no. I don't care about Mac's reaction. Mac is my daughter's teacher. I shiver. Just the thought of it feels wrong, wrong, wrong.

Coffee sloshing out of its takeaway cup, I make my way to the bright-red door beside the café and climb the steps to the library above. Wes, Simone's husband, refurbished the space as a gift to her. It's one of the most romantic things I've ever heard. I was in town for their wedding recently, and it was the first time I had actual fun since my separation from Kevin.

Needless to say, the library above the café is a special space. When I push the interior door open, I find Simone tapping away on her laptop near the window and Candice at another desk, frowning at the screen in front of her. She looks up when I enter, relief washing over her. "Thank goodness. If I have to look at this spreadsheet for one more minute, I might explode. I am *not* a bookkeeper. I don't know how you did this for Kevin for years, Trina. I'm going cross-eyed."

Simone snorts. "I told you to leave it for Jen or Fiona. Play to your strengths, Candice."

My sister lets out a sigh, then nods at me. "What's up? You look weird."

I look down at my outfit, frowning. I thought I looked cute this morning. I only agonized over my look for over an hour. There's not exactly a handbook for the appropriate outfit to go see your daughter's teacher who happens to be sex on legs who *also* happens to be the man you had dirty sex with the day before.

"I don't mean your clothes, Trina. I mean your face. Specifically, the expression on it." Candice takes a step toward me. "What's wrong?"

Welp. Here goes nothing. "Mac is Katie's teacher."

Simone stops typing and swivels her head toward me. Candice's face is frozen.

I wipe my sweating palms on my robin's-egg-blue-colored linen pants, then spread my arms wide. "I kind of, maybe, sort of...hooked up with him on Saturday."

The rest of Simone's body swivels to face me. Candice's eyes widen a fraction.

I clear my throat. "And maybe also slept with him yesterday too."

Silence answers back.

Now my hands are wringing together in front of my body. I cringe, glancing at Simone. "Say something."

Without hesitating, Simone answers, "How was it?"

I drop my hands to my sides. "*That's* what you want to know?"

Simone's lips twitch. "Well...yeah?"

Candice clears her throat. "Can we go back to the part about Mac Blair being a *school teacher*? How did we not know this? Did you not ask each other about work?"

"Are you blaming *me* for this?" My voice comes out screechy, and Candice throws her hands up.

"No. No, of course not. I'm just wondering. Did you never ask him what he does for work?"

Helpless, I shrug. "It never came up."

"They were too busy fucking like rabbits," Simone cuts in.

I give her an exasperated glare.

She just grins. "What are you going to do?" Simone leans her elbow on her desk, brows arching high.

"What can I do?" I ask. "I have to break up with him."

"What?" It's Candice's turn to shriek. "Why?"

"Did you miss the part about him being Katie's teacher?" I cross my arms.

"Okay." Simone stands up and heads for the kitchenette. "Let's think about this for a second." She takes a can of diet soda out of the mini fridge and cracks it open, turning around to lean against the counter. "He's teaching Katie, right?"

I nod.

"And does the school have a policy against teachers dating parents?"

"Well..." I frown. "Probably. I don't know, but..." I look at Candice for support. "It just *feels* wrong...right?"

Candice cringes. "It kinda does, Simone."

Simone takes a sip of her drink and lets out a sigh. "I know. But he's just so damn *hot*, you know? And I saw how he looked at you when he was in the café the other day, and how he was ready to rip your asshole ex's head off for speaking to you like that. I just... I just want that for you."

Glancing out the window, I let out a long breath. "I want that for me too."

"Can you just wait until the school year is over?" Candice asks, hopeful. "You can tell him that you're into him, but you're not comfortable dating him while he's teaching Katie?"

I chew my lip, then let it slide out from between my teeth when I think of Mac's eyes darkening whenever I bite my lip in his presence. "I guess so. But I mean, would he even want to wait that long?"

"What, a few months?" Simone snorts. "That'll go by in a flash. I've been in town three years and it feels like I just arrived last week."

I rub my forehead with my fingers, then square my shoulders. "Okay. I'll talk to him tonight. I'll tell him I'm not comfortable dating him while he's teaching Katie, but I'm willing to see if there's still a spark after the school year is over."

"I'm sorry, Trina. I can tell you really like him." Candice walks over to me and wraps her arm around my shoulders. "If he really likes you, he'll understand."

I try to force a smile, but I can't help but wonder if Mac *does* actually like me. What if he was just looking for a hookup? What if he doesn't actually like me enough to wait for me? What if that woman was right, and I was just the new mom he wanted to flirt with? What if I ask him to wait, and it comes off as desperate?

Because that's how I feel right now. Desperate. I feel starved for affection. I feel like my marriage drained me so dry, I need someone to treat me right just so I'll make it through another day.

"What if he's just a rebound?" I find myself saying. "Maybe this is for the best."

Candice and Simone exchange a glance. Simone moves closer, her soda forgotten on the counter. "I mean, maybe, but we all saw how he looked at you. Remember that night at the Grove? Just looking at the two of you made me blush."

"Yeah," I answer, but I'm not convinced.

That night at the Grove feels like it happened in another universe. I was a different person. I wasn't a single mother that night—I was someone who goes out with girlfriends and doesn't have a care in the world. For a few hours, I was unburdened, and that's just not the reality of my life right now.

The door opens, and Fiona bursts through. She holds the doorjamb and looks at me with wide eyes. "Okay, who was *that*? And where do you find these guys? I mean, seriously, Trina, you have a gift for collecting hot men."

My sister frowns at me. "Wait, what? There's another one?"

I groan. "He's just a dad from Katie's class. He kind of, maybe...sort of...asked me out in front of Mac this morning."

There's a beat of silence, then Simone bursts out laughing. "Girl, you're a mess. A walking disaster."

I groan and fall into one of the sofas. "Don't remind me."

"Don't get me wrong," Simone says, taking a seat beside me. "You're a hot mess. I *wish* I was as put-together and glamorous as you when my whole life is falling apart. But"—she whistles—"you're not making it easy on yourself."

I slouch down, throwing an arm over my face. But my lips twitch, and pretty soon, I find myself laughing.

Yeah, I'm a disaster. But even so, I'm happier than I've been in years. My kids took to their new school like ducks to water this morning. Kevin's snide comments aren't being hurled at me daily. Sure, I may be living with my mother, but I'm in a new town with more friends and support than I've had since I was in school myself.

Do I really want to ruin that by dating my daughter's teacher? Do I really want to invite more drama and heartbreak into my life?

I like the guy, but what if there's nothing there? What if he's a rebound, and what we had was a shallow attraction?

I slump down on the sofa, pretty sure that what I *should* do is the exact opposite of what I *want* to do—and what I should do is say goodbye to my romance with Mac. Focus on myself. Focus on my kids.

Move on.

25

MAC

TODAY WAS the longest day of my life. By the time the kids are all picked up, I sink into a chair in my classroom and let out a long sigh.

Katie's a good kid. She was fearless, happy, and already has half a dozen best friends after just one day. I saw so much of her mother in her that it made it hard to focus on my work.

Maybe it wouldn't be so bad to date Trina. Maybe we could make it work...somehow. But if anyone found out and started treating Katie differently, I'd never forgive myself. Not to mention the fact that I could ruin my reputation for good. Letting out a long sigh, I lean back and stare at the ceiling tiles, trying to find some way out of this situation.

The logical thing to do would be to tell Trina it's inappropriate for us to see each other, and to break up. But even *thinking* of doing that makes me feel sick. I haven't met a woman like Trina...ever. Thinking about how she flinched when her ex-husband hurled those insults at her makes me want to drive to her place right now just to make sure she's safe and happy.

I've never wanted to do that. I've never cared about a

woman's happiness, her safety, her *mood* the way I care about Trina's.

And after what happened Saturday in my studio, and Sunday in my bed, I know I want to be the man who gets to lay down beside her every night and wake up beside her in the morning.

But am I really willing to give up my job for that? Am I willing to throw away all the years I've spent building my reputation at this school for a woman who just got out of a relationship? Do I actually *want* a relationship?

I've always told myself I was better off on my own. After Belinda, I vowed to keep even casual sex as far away from my work as possible.

My phone buzzes. I glance at the screen and see a message. Trina wants to talk.

With a sigh, I send her a response. Is it bad that I still want to take her out to dinner? I'm still desperate to see her again. Touch her again.

But Trina refuses dinner. Instead, she tells me she'll meet me at my place once the kids are in bed. So for the next few hours, I find myself tidying my house, changing my clothes half a dozen times, throwing back a beer, and fidgeting constantly—all while trying to come up with some way to get around this situation. Trying to think of *something* that will let me be with Trina.

But it all comes back to what happened with Belinda. The four years of awkwardness that followed our hookup, and all the ways I failed to be honest with her about how I felt.

I respect Trina enough to not make that mistake again.

I respect myself not to throw away the years of hard work that gave me a good name at that school. I can't date parents.

So when she texts me that she's on her way, I find myself walking to the studio just to be somewhere that makes me calm—but then I take one look at the workbench and walk right out. I don't feel calm when I think of what we did in there just a few nights ago. Not even a little bit. So, I head back into the main house and crack open another beer.

I live in a three-bedroom bungalow on an acre plot. It's secluded enough that I can do pottery late in the evening with music playing without disturbing the neighbors, but close enough that my commute during the school year is just twenty-five or thirty minutes. I've lived here for twenty years. Most of the furniture is from local artisans—what little of it there is. Apart from the multitude of hand-thrown pots, plates, and mugs, I'm mostly a minimalist.

Still, I straighten the few cushions on my couch and let out a long sigh, feeling every second trickle by slower than the last.

The sound of a struggling engine tells me Katrina's clunker of a car is near. My heart thumps and I run my hands through my hair once again, pacing my kitchen until I hear the doorbell.

And even though I've had hours to prepare myself, the sight of her standing on my threshold still nearly knocks me back. She's changed into a knee-length black dress that clings to every perfect curve. Thin straps hold it up over her shoulders, with a colorful shawl hanging from her arms. A long silver pendant drops down her front, drawing my eyes to her chest. I close my eyes for a beat, trying to forget what it felt like to touch her perfect tear-shaped breasts, and I step aside to let her enter. She even smells amazing, and I fight the urge to throw all my convictions away just to tug her close and bury my face in her neck.

Fuck the job. Fuck propriety. I'll quit tomorrow if it means I get to stay with her tonight.

As her heels click on my hardwood floors, her hand

hitching her purse higher on her exposed shoulder, I remind myself of all the reasons we can't be together.

It would be unprofessional. Inappropriate. It could hurt Katie—either by upsetting her or opening her up to teasing. Other parents could get mad about preferential treatment. There would be whispers, questions, rumors. I'd never be taken seriously again.

Trina finally takes a deep breath and turns to face me. "I wasn't expecting this to happen."

A dry snort slips through my nose, and I rub the back of my neck just to stop myself from fidgeting. "Me neither."

She bites her lip, and I fight a groan. I've thought of that image of her on her knees in front of me every day since I met her. I barely got any prep work done Sunday night because I couldn't get her out of my mind. My sheets still smell like her. Even now, when everything in my mind is screaming that we can't be together, my cock is swelling with every second spent in her presence.

Trina gulps. "Mac," she starts. "Look. I... It's been really nice getting to know you, but I don't think I'm comfortable seeing you while you teach my daughter."

Even though I agree—even though I've spent the whole day convincing myself of the same thing—her words still hit me in the gut. I hide it with a nod. "Yeah. I agree."

She glances away from me and stares at the wall. "Right." There's tension in Trina's shoulders, in the line of her neck, in the way her hands are clenched together in front of her.

I fucking hate it. I hate seeing her turned away from me. I hate the fact that I can't wrap my arms around her and tell her to forget it all and be with me.

"Listen, Trina..." I take a deep breath. "I like you." *Understatement of the century.* "But..." I grit my teeth, looking for the right words.

"That woman," Trina cuts in. "Was she the only one?" Her eyes lift to mine.

I nod. "Until you."

Trina holds my gaze, then lets out a long breath. "So, what do we do?"

A lump lodges itself in my throat. This is the moment where I tell her that up until Monday morning, I could see a future with her for the first time in my life. I could see myself actually *wanting* to let her in. Opening up. Letting her see all the vulnerable parts of me that have been locked up since I was a child.

But my silence must wear her down, because Trina lets out a bitter huff. "Can we not do this? Can we not dance around it and try to let each other down easy? We've known each other a couple of weeks. We had fun. We hooked up. Now it's over."

I flinch back. She wouldn't even give me a few seconds to think of what I'm trying to say? She won't let me untangle the mess in my mind? Figure out if these feelings are real or not?

She's just like everyone else. More than ready to walk away from me. Using the first excuse to run.

I grit my teeth and nod. "Yeah. I don't date students' parents." My words are hard, brittle. They taste bitter, but they feel good to say. Like I'm wrapping armor around myself, retreating into the safety of solitude.

I don't need Trina. I don't need to open up to anyone. Haven't I made it on my own? Haven't I been perfectly happy up until now?

She's hot, and she was fun to fuck, but that's as far as it goes with me. Always has been, always will be.

So when I cross my arms and meet Trina's gaze, my eyes are hard. All my emotions are tamped down, buried deep where they won't come out to haunt me.

Something flashes in Trina's eyes. Some lingering sadness, a deep kind of hurt. But it's gone as quickly as I see it, and she just lifts her chin. "I understand. I won't waste any more of your time." She gives me a tight smile, then turns to leave.

It's the sight of her back that splinters something in my chest. The feeling of sand slipping through my fingers, of a scent on the wind that I can't quite catch.

I'm losing her.

"Trina," I start, but stop when I realize I don't know what to say.

The truth is, letting her leave is the right thing to do. Is she really worth losing my job over? Is she worth throwing away my reputation? All the years I've spent on my own, building my life just the way I want it—is Trina worth destroying all I've built?

No matter which way I twist the questions around, the only answer is no.

It's not worth the risk. A relationship with Trina would be messy, and it would end in disaster. Just look at how easily she's walking away now.

So even though Trina's eyes are glassy and it fucking kills me to clamp my mouth shut, I know there's no other choice. She glances at me once more, pinches her lips and gives me a nod, then walks out the door and back to her car.

Just like that, it's over before it could really begin.

And the worst part? I was right. She walked away, just like I knew she would.

26

TRINA

WHEN FACED with something that feels suspiciously like a broken heart, I do what any normal, rational woman would do: I pull over to the side of the road to cry, then wipe my cheeks and decide to do something drastic with my hair.

That's how I end up with kitchen scissors in my hand, hacking new bangs into existence across my forehead. Turning the wholly inappropriate and woefully dull scissors upright, I try to snip vertically to blend the bangs in the way I've seen hairdressers do it. Then I spend a while straightening and styling them just to prove to myself that I haven't made a huge mistake.

It's not until the next morning, when I walk downstairs and see my mother's brows arch high, that I start to regret my impulse.

"When did that happen?" she asks, turning back to the cat food bowl as Mr. Fuzzles yowls impatiently.

"What, my hair?"

Mom throws me an amused glance. "Yes, honey. The hair. You haven't hacked your hair off since you were six years old."

"That's not true." I pour myself a mug of black coffee. "I used to cut my hair all the time in college."

"Uh-huh." She refreshes the water bowl but says nothing else.

From there, the morning is swallowed up by kids and breakfast and backpacks and school runs. I drop them at the school gate and watch Katie sprint toward a group of children, already accepted into her new fold. Toby's still in the back seat.

I glance back. "You okay, honey?"

"Why did you and Dad get a divorce?"

Oh, dear. The question catches me off-guard, even though I've known it's been coming. Ever since we moved out here, Toby hasn't been himself. He brightened up when we adopted the cat, but now seems to be slipping back into a funk. The therapist we saw last week, a young, gentle woman named Andrea, told me it was normal, but it still makes my chest ache.

Is *everything* in my life going to end in heartbreak? Can nothing just be easy, for once?

I gulp past the growing lump in my throat and shift my gaze to the school gates. "We..." I pause, looking for the right words. I don't want to lie to him or conceal the truth, but I don't want to turn him against Kevin—no matter my own feelings about my ex. So, with a sigh, I do my best. "We had a grown-up problem, and decided that we didn't want to be married anymore. It had nothing to do with you and Katie. Both your father and I still love you with all our hearts."

Toby's lips pinch into a thin line, and he makes no move to leave the car. "It was Dad's fault, wasn't it? He did something that hurt you. I saw you crying before we moved here."

"I..." Ouch, my heart. I reach back to put my hand on

Toby's leg. "Honey, I'm fine. I was sad because I loved your father very much. But I'm happier now."

"I know." He crosses his arms and juts his chin out at me. "Do I have to spend the weekend with Dad when he comes next time?"

Another sigh slips through my lips, and I give my son a small nod. "Yeah, Toby. I'm sorry, but the courts said he gets the two of you for one weekend every month. If I keep you, I might get in trouble, no matter how much I might want to."

"What about what *I* want?"

I squeeze my son's thigh and give him a soft smile. "Let's just give your father a chance, okay? And we can ask Andrea about it on Wednesday."

"Dad said therapy was useless."

"When did he say that?" My voice goes screechy. That *dick*!

"When I told him about it on the phone last night." Toby unlatches his seatbelt. "But I still want to go. Andrea's nice."

The school bell rings, so Toby opens his door. To my surprise, instead of running off the way Katie did, Toby knocks on my window. I roll it down, and he reaches in to give me a hug through the opening. Then he says, "I like your new hair," before flashing me a little grin and scampering off to school.

All in all, I'm pretty proud of myself. I only cry for about twenty minutes when I get home.

FROM THERE, routine sweeps me away. I start looking for work, sending out half a dozen applications every week. At the back of my mind, I wonder about the whole stylist business idea. But I can't do that. I'm good at it, sure, but I can't start my own business. No one would hire me. I'm not good enough. No way.

So, I send application after application out, and get crickets back. The kids get signed up for all kinds of activities —soccer and karate for Toby, soccer and piano lessons for Katie—which require pick-ups and drop-offs. There are groceries to buy, rooms to clean, meals to prepare.

I avoid going to Katie's classroom, and she's all too happy to leave me at the school gate. Toby goes to see the therapist, Andrea, even though his father gives both of us snide comments for it. I'm proud of my son for not caving to his father's pressure.

Mac and I don't talk, and it's for the best. That's what I tell myself, anyway. And any time I feel weak and I want to pick up my phone, dial his number, and hear his deep, warm voice in my ear, I just remind myself of what he told me.

He doesn't date students' parents.

No softening the blow, no explanation, no indication that he ever had feelings for me. Just eyes that were hard and cold, and the latch of his door closing behind me.

I try not to think of all the other mothers I've met at drop-offs who point to his motorcycle and talk about how sexy he is. I try to just be a mother to my children and forget about men altogether.

Men are too much work, anyway. It's not worth the pain.

Even though some nights, when sleep evades me, I think of the way it felt to be on the back of Mac's bike, flying over the asphalt with not a care in the world. I think of his kiss, the brand his hands left on my body...and I miss him.

A few weeks pass. My existence becomes split into a series of upcoming milestones, because it's easier to think about the future than it is to be present with my life the way it is. There are holidays to plan for, kids' sporting events to train for, Kevin's visits to brace for.

His next visit is the last weekend of September. My ex-husband picks the kids up on the Saturday morning, and I hate to say it, but he looks good. He stands on the doorstep while the kids put their shoes on and gives me one of the smiles I fell in love with. "Don't miss the kids too much while I've got them."

"Impossible."

Kevin's eyes crinkle. "You always were a great mother."

Um, what? Is that...a compliment? Is he being nice to me right now? I frown, trying to figure out what his angle is.

Kevin sees my expression and lets out a quiet sigh. "I mean it, Katrina. I couldn't have done it without you."

Gratitude? What alternate universe have I stepped into now?

"Ready!" Katie cries, throwing her arms around my waist. "Bye, Mommy!"

"Be good." I give her a kiss, then reach for Toby. He gives his father a suspicious look, then accepts a hug from me. Then I watch my kids leave with my ex-husband, close the door, and wonder what the hell I'm doing with my life. I do a deep-clean of the house just to fight the feeling of emptiness. When my mother finds me scrubbing a toilet like my life depends on it, she takes the toilet brush from my hand and shoves me toward the tub with stern instructions to shower and get the hell out of the house.

That's how I find myself entering the Four Cups Café an hour later.

Kevin's there with the kids. Wonderful.

I make to leave, but my ex-husband calls out my name. When I turn, he's jogging toward me. He's wearing one of those linen shirts he likes so much, and there's a little splatter of paint on the sleeve. His jeans hang on his long, skinny legs, a rumpled sort of masculinity. He doesn't have the brawn or the sheer sex appeal that Mac does, but I still know why I fell for him. It's because of looks like he's giving me now, when his whole, undivided attention is on me. When I just *know* he's wondering how he'd paint me in this moment.

Kevin blinks, and his eyes seem to focus on me. "Toby told me he has a big soccer game next week. The school's main rivals, he said."

"He does," I answer slowly. My eyes dart to the counter, where Fiona's standing with her head angled toward us.

"Well, I was wondering if you'd have any problem with me coming."

I frown. "You want to come to Toby's soccer game?" Who is this man? "You've never gone to any of the kids' activities."

Something like shame tugs Kevin's lips down. "Maybe I'm realizing what a mistake that was." He arches his brows. "So? Would you mind if I came? And maybe I could have the kids for a night next weekend to celebrate after the game?"

I bite my lip. According to our custody agreement, no, he absolutely can't have the kids one single night outside our agreed times. But what about my whole speech about effective co-parenting? What about giving Kevin a chance to be a good father to Toby when that's what Toby needs most?

I hate the suspicion in my son's eyes whenever Kevin's around. Wouldn't something like this be exactly what Toby needs?

So, letting out a sigh, I nod. "Of course, Kevin. Toby will love that."

When my ex-husband smiles at me, something weird happens to my chest. It's like an echo of how I felt before. A physical memory of the layers and layers of feelings I had for Kevin. *Have* for Kevin, maybe?

No. God, everyone knows my ex is an asshole. Even I know that.

I'm just an emotional mess right now, and I'm not used to being on my own. Maybe breaking up with Mac was a good thing. I need to get used to standing on my own two feet.

Kevin leans toward me as if he's going to hug me, then stops himself with a rueful smile. "Sorry. I just— Thanks." He nods, then heads back to the kids.

Fiona appears at my elbow with a coffee. "On the house, girl. Figured you probably wouldn't want to stick around."

"Was it that obvious?" I take a sip of coffee and let my eyes dart back to my ex-husband and kids. He's got Katie on his lap, and Toby's laughing at something.

A snapshot of a perfect family.

I shake my head and lift my cup. "Thanks, Fi."

And with one last look at the family I could have had, I walk out of the café, wandering until my coffee is cold just to try to clear my head.

It doesn't work.

27

TRINA

Toby's soccer game is at the elementary school on Friday afternoon after school, so I make my way there at the end of the school day. I pick Katie up from her after-school care group and hold her hand while we go back outside. My heeled boots click on the asphalt as I make my way around the building to the field at the side of the school. Katie darts off toward the playground, and my stomach knots when I see Kevin on the sidelines of the field. I walk up to my ex-husband and give him a nod. "You made it."

"You sound surprised." His eyes soften. "But I probably deserve that."

Self-awareness? Did he just say something that sounded like...regret?

Okay. This needs to stop.

What is going on? Where's the asshole who marched into the Four Cups Café and called me a whore? *He* was easy to hate. He made it clear that I was making the right decision. This Kevin—the one who reminds me of the man I fell in love with—makes me remember things I'd rather forget, like how happy I was when we first married.

"Daddy!" Katie comes sprinting from the playground. My daughter crashes into his legs and wraps hers arms around them, beaming up at him.

"Hey, little monster." Kevin smiles as he hauls her up for a hug and spins her in a circle.

Emotion clogs my throat, and I turn my back to the two of them. Was it really less than a year ago that we were all together? A seemingly happy, well-adjusted family? How is it possible that my life has imploded so quickly and so thoroughly in such a short amount of time?

As I angle my body away from Kevin and Katie's, my eyes lift to see a man push open the school doors and jog toward the field.

Oh no.

Mac is wearing athletic shorts, white socks pulled high up his hard calves, and has a big mesh bag full of soccer balls slung over his shoulder. If this were a movie, it would be some weird *Baywatch* remake, but instead of beach babes in tight swimsuits, there's only Mac running in slow motion toward me wearing a soccer coach's uniform.

I see the exact moment Mac spots me. It happens to be the same time he has to jump over a little lip in the pavement, and his toe catches the edge of it while his eyes grow wide. This time, instead of crashing into a table and spilling beer everywhere, Mac recovers with a quick stumble, his eyes still on me for a moment before he changes trajectory to make his way to the team.

"Mr. Blair!" Katie shrieks at top volume. Kevin sets her down as she thrusts her arm toward her teacher. "Daddy, that's Mr. Blair!"

Mac gives her a wave and a smile, but doesn't come any nearer. He drops the mesh bag of balls on the ground and opens it up while the other coach instructs the boys to start warming up. Toby starts dribbling one of the balls through a line of cones, not even throwing a glance our way.

My eyes drift to Mac again, then dart to Kevin.

My ex-husband is frowning as he stares at Mac, his hand still around Katie's shoulders. "He looks familiar," Kevin says.

I close my eyes. Please, *please* let him not recognize him from the café.

"That's because his picture is online," Katie informs her father. "Mommy showed me before the first day of school."

"You're probably right, kiddo," Kevin says, but he throws Mac one last questioning glance before shifting his gaze to Toby. "Your brother is good."

"He's the best on the team," Katie announces. "He scored three goals last week."

My daughter's voice fades into the background. Mac jogs onto the field and starts coaching the boys, clapping his hands and directing them into lines, calling for sprints and drills for their warm-up. The group moves closer, and I watch Mac take a ball to demonstrate the next drill.

Of course he can play soccer. Is there anything the man can't do?

"Trina," someone calls out behind me. I turn to see Rick, the dad from Katie's class. He smiles warmly at me, then shifts his gaze to Katie and Kevin, and his steps slow. His son Ricky is at his side, eyes on the field where the older boys are playing.

"Hi, Rick," I say pleasantly, while on the inside, I scream. Why the hell is he here? Why the hell is Mac here? Why couldn't they both show up *last* game, when Kevin was safely in another city? I shift my gaze to the field and hunt through my panicking brain for something to say. "Which one is yours?"

"Number twelve," Rick answers, pointing. "Nate." He

scrubs his son Ricky's head and points to a stray soccer ball. "Go kick a ball around."

Ricky glances at my daughter. "Wanna come play, Katie?"

"Can I, Mom?" She looks at me.

"Of course."

The two kids dash off, and I'm left with my ex-husband on one side of me, the man who wanted a coffee date with me on the other, and my daughter's second grade teacher—who I slept with a few weeks ago—jogging off the field toward the team bench.

Wonderful.

"I haven't seen you at any of the other games," I tell Rick, keeping a pleasant smile on my face.

"Nate's mom usually handles the extracurricular activities, since I work late most nights. Had the evening off, so I figured I owed it to Nate to come support him."

"How nice." I smile. Just *great*. Must be the theme of the weekend.

Mac jogs closer, and my stomach tightens. He looks really good in shorts, I notice. Defined calves, strong thighs. Legs made to be shown off. Standing about twenty feet away and facing me, Mac instructs the boys to start jogging as he delivers balls to them in some sort of give-and-go drill. His eyes flick to me, and I look away.

Kevin clears his throat.

Ah, right.

"I'm Katrina's husband," Kevin tells Rick while extending his hand, and I nearly have an aneurysm.

"*Ex*-husband," I correct, giving him a death glare, which he completely ignores. The two men shake hands in front of me. Some weird male stare-off happens for a few seconds while I stand awkwardly between them.

I breathe in through my nose and out through my mouth,

fighting to keep my hands still and not fidget. Everything is fine. Everything is perfectly, wonderfully fine. We're just a bunch of parents watching our kids play a sport. A totally normal interaction. Nothing to worry about.

I glance back at Mac and make eye contact again.

Damn it.

Just one short hour. That's how long I need to last. One hour till Toby's done with his game, then I can give my kids a kiss and send them off to their dad's for the night and run far, far away from here. Hopefully without ever having to speak to Mac.

Mac kicks a ball toward the kid in front of me—hard. The kid catches it and brings it down under control with his foot, and Mac claps. "Good work, Nate."

I'm staring at Mac's thighs again. The way the muscles contract when he moves. How he lunges, and the shorts hike higher to show off the paler skin, the sparse, coarse hair of his upper thighs. I saw those legs completely bare just a few weeks ago. I saw what the shorts are hiding too.

I need to stop staring. Just—look away. Look away *now*.

Oh, Kevin's frowning at me. Wonderful. Did he see me ogling my kid's soccer coach?

Side note—why is Mac even here? He wasn't coaching any of the other games! So I have to ask: Why me? Why today? Why now?

And why does he have to look so damn good all the freaking time?

I clear my throat and glance at Rick, then ask him what he does for work. I'm too busy thinking about Mac's legs to actually hear his answer, though. That's why I don't see the soccer ball come flying at my face until it's too late to dodge it.

Mac shouts a warning that I hear a split second too late.

The projectile smacks me right in the middle of the face,

and I fall flat on my ass, smacking my head on the ground behind me. Pain explodes through my nose and my eyes immediately start watering. That's when I hear shouts and noises, and see my ex-husband's face appear above my head on one side, Rick's face on the other.

"You okay, Trina?" Kevin says, something like real concern on his face. Huh. How about that.

"Yeah." I try to sit up, but my head is killing me from the fall and as soon as I move, blood starts gushing out of my nose.

That's when Mac shoves aside the small crowd of parents that has gathered around me, his eyes wide as he crouches beside me and wraps and arm around my shoulders. Before I can stop him, he shifts his weight, tears his T-shirt off, and shoves it under my nose to catch the blood.

It smells like him. Oh, God. Mac is shirtless beside me, keeping one arm around my shoulders and holding the shirt against my nose with the other hand. It's only been a few weeks, but I missed his touch. His scent. His voice. I missed how safe I feel in his arms. I close my eyes for a moment, then I hear Kevin's voice.

"She's fine," he says, annoyed. "Back off, buddy."

"Where does it hurt?" Mac says, ignoring my ex-husband.

"Mostly my pride," I answer, muffled by the tee bunched up near my nose, because did I mention Mac is shirtless?

He gives me one of those sexy half-grins, and my core spasms.

"Lie down." That comes from Kevin. He's stripping *his* shirt off now too. Why? Why would he be doing that? He unbuttons it and bunches it behind my head, now wearing nothing but a thin undershirt. He glares at Mac. "What the hell was that kick for? Were you *trying* to hurt her?"

"Fuck off," Mac grits out.

Mac's arm moves from my shoulders, and Kevin helpfully replaces it with his own. There is way, *way* too much testosterone here right now.

Kevin tightens his arm around my shoulders, pulling me into his body. Mac's jaw tightens at the movement, but he stares into my eyes, concerned.

"I'm fine," I say, tasting blood. "Really."

"You hit your head on the way down. I need to check you for a concussion." Mac ignores my ex-husband's soft stroking of my shoulder and pulls his shirt away from my nose to prod at my aching face.

I wince, and Kevin gets in Mac's face. "You've done enough. Back. The fuck. Off."

"Guys, there are kids around," I say. "Stop swearing so much."

A whistle blows, and Mac glances up. "Shit."

"Go," I tell him. "I'm fine."

Mac hesitates, then glances at Kevin's hand on my thigh, his other arm braced across my back. He flinches back, eyes going cloudy. Then he nods. "I sent one of the supervisors to get the first aid kit. Just...let me know if you need anything else. Please." Then he's up, grabbing a zip-up hoodie from the sidelines and covering up his gloriously bare torso to the great displeasure of all the moms in attendance.

I shrug out of Kevin's hold. "Stop fussing."

"How many fingers am I holding up?" He holds up two fingers, and I roll my eyes.

"Two." I hold up my middle finger. "How about me?"

Surprisingly, Kevin cracks a smile. "There's the woman I married."

Uh, *what*? I hold Kevin's gaze until Katie comes into view, her little brows drawn together. "Are you okay, Mommy?"

"I'm fine, honey."

She gives me a kiss, then burrows into Kevin's arms. He picks her up as she wraps her arms and legs around him, and my heart gives another stutter.

Was I wrong to divorce him? Did I act too quickly? I've denied the kids the chance to grow up with their family together, and for what? People forgive each other for infidelity all the time. Maybe I should have tried harder to get marriage counseling, to keep us together.

Doubt worms through my heart as I watch the father of my children be, well...a *father*.

Then I glance at Mac, and I know that no matter how great and caring and sexy he is, he'll never be Katie and Toby's dad. He must sense my gaze, because he glances over his shoulder. I'm still holding his bloodied T-shirt, and his eyes flick to the red stain on the fabric. Then he looks at Kevin, his lips pinch, and he looks away.

Well. That's that, then.

He made it clear how he felt about me. A soccer ball to the face obviously hasn't changed his mind.

28

MAC

THE ONLY REASON I'm driving to Katrina's house is because I want to make sure her face is okay. It's purely medical. I'm the one who kicked that ball; I'm the one who should be checking on her.

It's not because my stomach has been writhing like a pit of snakes since I saw her ex-husband with his arm around her. It's not because she dismissed me and stayed with him on the sidelines.

I was being a fucking idiot when I kicked that ball. I'd seen her hungry gaze on me every few seconds since I ran out of the school, and like a hormonal, idiotic teenager, I wanted to show off. I kept hitting the soccer balls harder and harder in the warm-up drills, until that one hit my cleat wrong.

The sound of that ball hitting her face has been echoing in my head ever since.

So, when I pull up outside her house and cut the engine to my truck, I look at the yellow light spilling from the curtained windows and I let out a deep breath. Grabbing the flowers I bought at the grocery store from the passenger seat, I run my fingers through my hair and push the car door open.

One thing I realized today, when I watched Shitstain Kevin be the one to comfort her, is that Trina *is* worth it. I need to get over myself, get over my fears, and tell her how I feel. Who cares that she's a parent of one of my students? Who gives a fuck?

Not me, that's who.

Okay, so it might not be a purely medical visit.

These flowers might not be saying, "I'm sorry I hit you in the face with a soccer ball," but instead they mean, "I'm sorry I pushed you away because I think I might actually be in love with you."

I freeze halfway up the path as that thought clangs through me.

Am I... Am I falling in love with Trina?

I stare at the colorful bunch of flowers in my hand, smelling the sweet scent of them as the world whirls around me.

I am. I'm in love with Trina. What other explanation could there be for these feelings? For the abject misery I've felt since she showed up in my classroom wearing those pale-blue pants? For the complete disinterest I've had in every other woman? For the near-obsession I feel every morning, hoping she'll show up at my classroom door with Katie even though I know she won't?

What other feeling could be so great and also so damn horrible? It has to be love.

Before I can talk myself out of it, I'm hurrying up the last few steps to the door and pressing the doorbell. I hear girly laughter and a little squeal—Katie—as my heart bangs against its cage. Because my ribs feel like a cage right now, like they're the only thing preventing my heart from jumping right out of my chest and into Katrina's hands.

Then the door opens, a halo of golden light around her

head, and I'm breathless. She's so fucking beautiful it hurts, with those wide, hazel eyes and her perfect rosebud mouth.

There's a bruise forming around her eye—from the soccer ball, no doubt—and I hate that I'm the one who put it there.

"Mac." Her brows jump as she takes me in, then glances at the flowers.

I thrust them toward her. "For you." Nothing else comes out.

Tentatively, she wraps a delicate hand around the stems, then glances at me again. "Thank you." Those lips I miss kissing curl into a smile. "Is this because you kicked a ball in my face?"

I angle my face away and rub the back of my neck. "Look, I—"

"It's fine." She laughs, and my heart nearly breaks at how good it sounds. "Although I'm going to have a nasty black eye thanks to you. Concealer works wonders, but even I'm not sure it'll be able to cover this up."

"I hate that I did that to you."

"Stop it." She lifts the flowers to her nose and smiles as she inhales. "Thank you for the flowers."

There's a pause, and I know this is my chance. This is when I open my coward mouth and tell her how I feel. This is when I say that I'm sorry for pushing her away, that she's nothing like Belinda, that I don't give a shit about propriety and professionalism.

This is when I tell her that I'm falling for her, even if it freaks her out, because I don't think I can keep those words held in.

But just as the words are about to tumble out of me in a rush of emotion, a man's voice calls out behind her. "Trina?"

Trina stiffens in the doorway. "I'll be right there," she calls over her shoulder.

"Who's at the door?"

Trina glances at me, and the short, sharp inhale she takes tells me everything I need to know. Then I catch a glimpse of a tall, familiar man walking across the living room windows, and it feels like a slap in the face.

Her ex-husband is inside with her.

She took her ex-husband home with her tonight. The man who called her a whore just a few weeks ago. The man she was so comfortable cuddling with on the sidelines when she needed comforting.

"I have to go," she tells me, and I notice that she never told Shitstain Kevin it was me at the door.

"Trina, wait."

"Thanks for the flowers. I... I can't talk right now. Goodbye."

Then the door closes.

I stand there, stunned, listening to the lock flick shut as Trina goes back to her ex-husband and her kids, and I'm left outside in the cold. I stare at my hands, which had just been holding a bunch of flowers that I wasn't even sure she'd accept. They're trembling.

I don't even realize I get in my truck and drive to the Grove until I'm pushing open the heavy timber doors and stumbling inside. My brother looks up from the bar and frowns as I slide onto the closest stool.

"Drink," I gasp. "I need a drink."

Lee doesn't get me a drink. He leans his broad palms against the worn wood of the bar and stares at me. "What the hell happened to you?"

"Get me a fucking drink, Lee," I bite off.

"No. Not when you're like this. You've never used alcohol to cope. Tell me what the fuck's the matter."

"She's with *him*," I hiss. "She went back to him. I pushed her away, and she's back with her ex." I tug at my hair, trying to make sense of it. "And I fucking love her. I'm *in* love with her. I can't stop thinking of her and dreaming of her and remembering what it felt like to bury my face in her hair and *she's with him.* That's what the fuck's the matter."

Lee pushes off the bar and, without another word, gets me that drink. He makes it a double.

I LIED TO KEVIN. I told him it was the school who brought the flowers over on a welfare check to make sure I was okay after the incident at the soccer game.

Well, I guess it's not *exactly* a lie—except I'm pretty sure Mac wasn't there on behalf of the school.

I let out a long sigh and glance across the room at the vase full of flowers. Blushing pink roses, a few white lilies, frilly carnations, and enough greenery to make the bouquet look full and bursting with life.

When Kevin saw the bouquet, his lips did that pinching, downturning thing he used to do when he was upset with me. It made a sour taste coat my tongue as I busied myself putting the flowers in water. Then Kevin told me—didn't *ask*, mind you—that he would be showing a few pieces at the pop-up gallery opening in Heart's Cove in January. He said his agent recommended it, since there are so many artists who live here, and the town has a reputation for fantastic art. But isn't it great, he said, that he'd be able to spend an extra weekend with the kids?

And when he said it, I wondered—is this healthy co-parenting, or is he stomping on my boundaries? Is he inserting himself in my life where he shouldn't, or is he just trying to be a more present father than he was before? Should I refuse to give him more than the court-ordered time? Is that spiteful and vindictive on my part? What's best for the kids?

I don't know the answer to any of those questions.

Now, after he's taken the kids to his rental for the night and I slump down on the sofa with Mr. Fuzzles curled next to me, I can't stop thinking about the look on Mac's face when he heard Kevin's voice. I wanted to explain that Kevin just came over to make sure I was okay and get the kids' stuff for the night, but I also didn't want to be standing there so long Kevin would come investigate and see Mac on my doorstep.

I still don't think Kevin's put two and two together. He still doesn't know Mac is the motorcycle man from the coffee shop, and that's how I want to keep it. Especially since Mac made it abundantly clear that he never wants to be with me.

Except, tonight, there was a moment...some look in his eyes when I first opened the door that made me think he wasn't just here to apologize.

Then there was the other look. The one he gave me when he heard Kevin's voice, and when I started closing the door to keep him out. A look of pure, intense hurt. Anger. Shock.

Mr. Fuzzles's fur is silky-soft as I run my hand along his body in smooth, even strokes. I lean back on the sofa, trying to dispel the image of Mac on my doorstep.

How did I get here? How did I end up caught between these two men when I'm supposed to be divorced and living my best life?

In an interview, goddess and legendary singer Cher once said that men are like dessert. "I adore dessert; I love men," she said. "But you don't really need them to live."

Why am I ping-ponging between these two men like it's my job? Why am I worried about the look on Kevin's face when I brought flowers into *my* house? Why do I feel guilty about the look on Mac's face when he realized the father of *my* children was inside *my* house?

I don't need these men to live. I've been fine without Kevin. Even though he's recently reminded me of all the reasons I first fell in love with him, I still viscerally remember how it felt to have to carry our family on my shoulders when we were married.

And I don't need Mac. As wonderful as he makes me feel, I don't need him to push me away, then steal lingering glances at me whenever I'm close. I don't need some weird, awkward flirtation with my daughter's second grade teacher.

What I *need* is to stand on my own two feet. I need to be a mother to my children and a woman they'll be proud of when they grow up.

Pushing myself up from the couch, I give those flowers one last glance and march to the door. I stuff my feet in the first shoes I see—a pair of sneakers that are usually reserved for yardwork—and grab the keys from the bowl by the door. Then I'm in my car (a hunk of junk, sure, but a car I bought *on my own*, without a man, and negotiated it down from the dealer's first offer by fifteen percent, by the way!) and I'm driving toward the center of Heart's Cove.

The lights are on in the library above Four Cups. I park the car and jump out, kick the door closed, lock it, then take the steps two at a time. When I burst through the door, my sister and her three friends are lounging on the sofas around the room, drinking tea and laughing. As usual.

They all stare at me in the doorway.

"I don't need men in my life," I announce. "Not Mac, and definitely not Kevin. I can do this on my own."

"Hear, hear!" Jen lifts her mug. "They're more trouble than they're worth."

Candice sits up, studying my face. "Although I admire your strength, I'm wondering where it's coming from. And— is that a black eye forming on your face?"

Everyone stiffens.

I wave a hand. "Mac kicked a soccer ball in my face. My nose isn't broken. It's fine."

"He did *what*?" Simone screeches.

"When? How?" Fiona frowns as she stares at me.

"Forget about that! I just had an epiphany. I've been running around after men for years and *I don't need them*. They're just dessert!"

Simone grins. "Cher. Classic."

I take a deep breath, open my mouth, and start talking without even knowing what I'm going to say. All I know is I need to *do something*. I need to be someone I'm proud of. I need to push all thoughts of Mac to the deepest, darkest part of my mind and lock him there, or maybe just let them fly free. I need to acknowledge that Kevin has some good qualities, but he's not the man for me.

I need to focus on the main course. Me.

But what comes out of my mouth startles me. "I'm starting a personal styling business," I announce, then clamp my mouth shut because, well, *where the hell did that come from*?

Four surprised faces look back at me, but they're soon jumping up to offer me all kinds of congratulations and encouragements. Simone offers to help me with a website and social media. Fiona volunteers herself as my first customer. They tell me I can put flyers on the café counter if I want to.

I giggle, then clamp my hand over my mouth, then give my sister a big hug.

I said it. I'm going to try it. I'm going to start my own business, and even if I crash and burn, at least I'll know I had the guts to give it a go.

A mug of tea appears in front of me, along with a plate full of fudgy brownies that Jen tells me are still in development. I sit down at a table and let Simone sketch out website ideas, my mind reeling.

I don't know what I expected when I ran up here and announced that I was swearing off men. But maybe this idea has been taking root in my mind for weeks, months. And it fills me with a bright, effervescent sort of excitement.

I mean, yes, I've always wanted to do it. But starting my own business? Going out on my own? When I was married to Kevin, it never seemed possible. I was The Mom. I was the person who took care of everything at home, of dentist appointments and doctors' visits. I bought presents for every family event—Kevin's and mine—and dealt with schools and daycares and almost everything child-related.

I couldn't have started a business even if I tried.

So why does this feel like it's actually possible now? Why does it feel like if I *don't* try, I'll regret it forever?

The memory of Mac's face looms in my mind, but I just ignore it and think about fashion.

By the time my tea is down to the dregs and the brownies are reduced to a few crumbs and chocolate smears on the plate, Simone has a sketch for the website branding and logo design, and I've started talking about intake forms and consultation prices with Fiona.

And, best of all, I'm not thinking about Mac, or Kevin, or the kids, or my mother, or any other of the thousand things that have taken up the top of my to-do list for years.

I'm thinking about *me*.

It's only when Jen and Candice are at the kitchenette, and Simone is at her computer to come up with some rough ideas for my branding, that Fiona reaches across the sofa cushion separating us and squeezes my hand. "You okay?"

I force a smile. "Yeah. I've always wanted to do this."

Fiona lets out a snort. "Not the stylist thing, Trina. We all know you could do that in your sleep. I mean are *you* okay. It kind of seems like you're throwing yourself into this project right now because you're trying not to think about something...some*one*...else. I mean, you did just burst in here and announce that you were done with men after one of them accidentally gave you a black eye."

I snort out a laugh. "I did, didn't I?"

"You okay?"

I release a sigh and give her a tentative smile. "I think... yeah. I think I am. I saw both Mac and Kevin today, and you know, when they were both stripping down and giving me their shirts—"

"Wait, what?"

"—I was just sitting there thinking, how did this happen? How are they both trying so hard right now? Where was Kevin for the past *nine years* of our relationship, ever since Toby was born and he checked out? Where was Mac's affection when he was telling me that he could never be with me because of some silly rule he has for himself?"

Fiona hums. "You realized you were letting them rock the boat in your life. They were in control of your feelings when they had no right to be."

"Yes!" I sit up and lean my elbows on my knees. "Why do *they* get to make me feel out of sorts? They don't get to just march into my life and make me feel like I'm missing out, when I know for a fact that I'm not."

"Maybe you just need to be single for a while," Fiona muses.

I glance sideways and give her a grin. "Are you sure you weren't a therapist in a past life?"

She snorts. "Simone has been my best friend since college. I've seen it all."

"Rude!" Simone spins around in her office chair to mock-glare at us. "But true." Then she turns right back around to tap away on her laptop.

"Well, I think it's great." Candice drops down in the armchair to my right and gives me a decisive nod. "You deserve to have your own thing, Trina. I can talk to Blake about it too. He might have some Hollywood people who need a stylist."

My eyes widen, and nerves immediately start twisting in my belly. "Maybe I should start smaller than a literal Hollywood movie star."

Candice grins. "Why? Why keep making yourself smaller? Rise up, Trina."

Those words whirl in my mind for many hours after that, when I've said goodbye to the girls and gone home, when I've had some leftovers for dinner, when I'm lying in bed thinking about what I've just committed to tonight.

Rise up.

It's a challenge. A gauntlet. Why wouldn't I be able to pursue my passion and be damn good at it?

As I lie in bed and think about the two men in my life— the sour expressions on both their faces when they realized I wasn't acting how *they* wanted me to act—I realize that yeah, this is the right decision. No matter how much I might like the company of a man, I can't keep running after them.

I'm going to take care of me, for once. And it's going to be awesome.

30

TRINA

"I HEARD YOU DO FASHION." Agnes stands next to my table at the café, arms crossed, eyes hard.

I look up from my laptop, where I'm trying to untangle all the back-end website dashboards that I need to figure out how to use, and give the older woman a nod. "Yeah."

"You fixed Fiona's closet."

"Well, I don't know if I'd say 'fixed,' but I helped her, yes."

Agnes studies me for a moment, face unreadable. It's only been a week since I announced I'd start trying to strike out as my own stylist. I've had a logo made, a simple, one-page website built, and I've started all-new social media business pages. I had no idea how good Simone was at her job until I started working with her. She's coached me on all types of social media strategies, and even created a framework of a business plan for me to fill out.

I've started doing a series of videos on my social media pages where I break down celebrity street-style outfits that work and don't work, and my following has already grown to a thousand people on all platforms. It's crazy.

And...I'm having fun. It's the first thing I've done that's

been entirely for me—well, that's if you don't count my short tryst with Mac Blair, of course.

But styling—that's my thing. It's not related to mom duties, it has nothing to do with art or my ex-husband, and it's unashamedly girly. Like me. Plus, I get to use my business brain. I remember when Kevin was starting out and I was helping him with bookkeeping and managerial duties. I loved it. It felt like we were building something together.

And now...I get to build something for me.

So when Agnes tilts her head to the side and tells me she wants to hire me, it comes as a shock and a delight all at once.

"I have short, stumpy legs, and I'm sick of looking frumpy," she tells me.

"Have a seat." I smile at her, and even though the grumpy older woman doesn't smile back, her expression softens.

Clothing has the ability to make people feel powerful, confident, or vulnerable and self-conscious. A woman like Agnes, who's usually hard as nails on the exterior, is exactly the type of client I'd love to help.

I take her through my new intake questionnaire, ask her questions about budget and style, and plan to meet her to go through her closet in a few days. When she gets up to leave, there's a buzzing in my blood, an excitement I haven't felt in a long, long time.

I'm doing it. I'm *freaking doing it*! I have my second client already!

So when Agnes exits the café, I have a broad smile on my face, and it doesn't even completely fade when my phone rings with Kevin's name on the screen. Taking a deep breath, I swipe to answer. "Yes?"

"I want to come see another one of Toby's soccer games, and Katie told me she had a piano recital coming up," my ex-husband says without preamble. "Can you send me their schedules? If I can make it the same weekend as my gallery opening, even better."

Let me just get right on that, Mr. Demanding. I'm sure my children's activities will be happy to reschedule around you.

"One sec. I'm on my laptop right now." With a few clicks, I've got the schedule sent. Then I pause, letting my frustration ebb as I try to find the right words. "The kids will appreciate you showing up again, Kevin."

What I really want to say is, *I'm proud of you for trying.* But is that really something that needs praise? For a father to have the slightest bit of interest in his kids' activities?

Not to mention he's trying to make it coincide with his *own event.* So is that even really something that needs to be praised?

He lets out a breath. "Yeah. Okay, well, I'll let you know when I'm in town. We might need to juggle my weekend around."

Then he hangs up before I can answer, and I send out a silent thank you that I'm not still married to that man. Life is a lot easier when I don't have to be his assistant, his mother, and his maid.

Sure, he might have some redeeming qualities, but some other woman can appreciate them from now on.

It's like a switch flicked in my mind that night of the soccer game. I saw these two men who demanded so much from me, and I realized I didn't want to carry them on my shoulders. Now, I feel lighter than ever.

Fiona walks into the café in one of her new outfits. It's nearly November now, and there's a definite chill in the air. She's wearing a cropped bomber jacket with a silky scarf, jeans, and cute suede booties. She sheds her jacket to reveal a simple, elegant cardigan-cami combo. I grin when I see the way she tucked the cami just like I showed her.

Seeing me across the café, she spreads her arms and gives me a twirl. "What do you think?"

"Two thumbs up," I tell her.

Fiona smiles at me, all confidence and swagger, and moves to the till to order her coffee and talk to Sven.

I shut down my computer, pack up, and say goodbye to the girls. And I realize as I'm hugging Fiona goodbye that I no longer think of her as my sister's friend—she's *my* friend too now.

My steps are light as I walk outside, inhaling the crisp scent of autumn, then my heart jags at the sound of a motorcycle.

Damn it.

I wish my body didn't react that way. I wish I could hear a loud engine and not think of Mac. I wish I didn't still miss him.

I'm not supposed to miss him. I'm supposed to be a strong, independent woman who don't need no man. I'm supposed to be avoiding dessert for a while. I'm on a no-man diet. Main course only.

Hamish comes into view with Margaret on the back of his bike. She waves at me as they come to a stop in front of the café, and I hike my laptop bag strap higher on my shoulder before giving her a quick hug.

"You look like you belong on that thing, Margaret." I nod to the bike.

Hamish gives a grunt of approval. "She's a natural."

Margaret laughs, smooths down her helmet hair, and gives Hamish a kiss on the cheek. "Thanks for the ride." She winks, then heads inside the café.

Hamish, still seated on his bike, shakes his head. "That woman makes me feel young again."

"You guys are good together," I say, and I mean it. Smiling

and inhaling to say my goodbyes, I stop when Hamish speaks first.

"You haven't been spending any time with Mac."

It's not a question, so I wait for a beat, then finally shake my head. "No."

"He was happier when he was with you."

Damn it. My heart gives a sharp tug, and it's hard to hide the pain in my face.

But it's the same story all over again, isn't it? *He* was happier. I should change my life around because it was better for *Mac*. When is it my turn to be happier? When do my needs start taking priority?

I let out a sigh and give Hamish my best smile. "Maybe, but it wasn't meant to be. See you later."

The old man says nothing as I walk away, and I'm grateful.

31

MAC

I'D BE LYING if I said I didn't count the days until the first parent-teacher interview I have with Trina. The first one is a couple of weeks after the soccer ball incident, and I spend the minutes before our scheduled time together combing back my hair, fidgeting with my shirt, pacing my classroom.

I haven't seen her since the day I hit her in the face with a soccer ball—since the evening she made it clear she saw me as nothing more than a rebound, and might even be getting back with her ex.

Then Trina walks in, and all the breath leaves my lungs.

For weeks since the start of the school year, I've thought of the way she felt to kiss, to touch. It's been one long cycle of torturing myself with thoughts of her, then torturing myself with guilt for it. Weeks and weeks of my dreams offering up visions of Trina naked and splayed for me, waking up with my cock a steel bar begging to be attended to. And after the attending was done, self-flagellation for being weak, for giving in. Two long months of trying to remember the taste of her, wishing I'd had more than two stolen moments with her.

And the past two weeks?

They've been even worse, because I know I lost my chance. When it comes down to it, Trina doesn't want me. She made that abundantly clear last time we saw each other.

She's wearing painted-on jeans, a tight white top with a lacy neckline, and a deep-blue blazer. I want to peel those clothes off her body, one item at a time, and kiss every inch of creamy skin that I reveal. I want to lock the door and take my time with her. I want to throw out every conviction I've ever had about propriety and professionalism.

Even after the soccer ball incident, I can't help the way my body reacts to her.

But she walked away. First she came to my house, told me our hook-ups were fun, but that she didn't want to see me again. Then when I was ready to throw all my inhibitions away, she'd already chosen her ex-husband.

I gesture to the two adult-sized chairs I've placed near a too-small desk. "Hi, Trina. Come in."

She smiles at me, and it's like the sun breaking through the clouds after a long, grey winter. My heart seizes, and I stumble over a wrinkle in the carpet. Catching myself before I fall, I take a seat and shuffle the papers I've prepared on Katie.

Trina has sexy, heeled, ankle-high boots on, and she sways those perfect hips over to her chair. She's all grace and control as she sits down, folding her hands over her lap like she was bred to sit at expensive fundraisers talking to senators and CEOs. She lets out a little huff and shakes her head. "I always get nervous at these things. I feel like I'm in trouble." She nods to the door and gives me a little smile. "My son's teacher just told me that he's 'extremely bright but struggles with being disruptive.' Hearing that felt like *I* was doing something wrong." She laughs nervously, tucking a strand of hair behind her ear.

"Well, I have only good things to say about Katie."

"Oh, good." Trina lets out a sigh of relief, color sweeping over her cheeks.

I can't help but smile, even though the sight of her makes my chest ache fiercely. For the first time since the soccer game, the tension in my body unwinds in her presence. I've been keyed up, stressed. Like a piece of me has been missing. Or maybe I've just been crazy with need for her, and being in her presence is like a single drop of water on my parched tongue. Gaze lingering on hers, I hold back a groan when she catches those beautiful lips between her teeth. I drop my gaze to my papers and clear my throat.

"Katie's a joy to teach. She's very advanced in math, and she's been a leader in the classroom. I've assigned her as class helper six times so far, and she's always carried out cleanup duties very efficiently." I glance up and grin. "She's extremely good at delegating."

Trina laughs. "You know, just yesterday she somehow convinced me that it was my turn to do Mr. Fuzzles's litter box when I know for a fact she hasn't done it in a week and a half."

"Executive management in the making." I grin.

Trina leans back in her chair, her shoulders dropping a bit.

This is easy. It's always been easy with Trina. But today... there's something different in the set of her shoulders, the way she carries herself. I half-expected this meeting to be awkward, but Katrina is completely at ease with herself, with me.

It's fucking hot, to tell the truth. And it makes me feel like an asshole for expecting the worst from her.

And I can't help myself. I veer off the parent-teacher

conference plan and hear myself asking, "How have you been?"

"I've been good," she says, meeting my gaze over the child-sized table. "I, um, started a new business—well, I don't know if you can call it a business yet, but I've started a project that feels like it could be a business." She gives me a wry grin. "Still driving my old car, though, so some things haven't been upgraded yet."

I clench my hand in a fist to fight the urge to reach over and touch her. "That's good. I'm really happy for you." I clear my throat. "You never mentioned this project before, did you?"

A blush sweeps over her cheeks. "Actually, I didn't really consider seriously pursuing it until that night after the soccer game."

I tilt my head. "The night I came over?" *And you were with your ex.*

She laughs. "Truth be told, I was pissed that you came over and made me feel like I'd done something wrong. Then I was pissed at my ex for making me feel the same way when I was gracious enough to let him cross the threshold in the first place. So I guess I have to thank you for giving me the push I needed." She blinks and shifts her gaze to meet mine.

My heart clenches, and something bittersweet buds somewhere deep and hidden inside me. So...she wasn't with her ex that night?

Still, it feels like she's moved on. Like I lost my chance. So, all I can say is the truth. "I'm sorry." I clear my throat. "I shouldn't even have gone over to your house that night, and I definitely shouldn't have made you feel bad about yourself, or about...us...or about anything. Especially considering I kicked a ball in your face."

Trina just grins at me. "Yeah. Especially considering that."

Her eyes sparkle, and I want her. I want her so bad it hurts. "Why were you coaching that day, anyway? I hadn't seen you before or since."

"The other coach had a family emergency," I explain. "I was filling in. Just the once."

"Ah." She nods, and is it just me, or did it sound a bit like disappointment?

This isn't how it felt with Belinda. We'd flirt over the course of the school year, every single interaction sexually charged. It was all out in the open. She knew she wanted me, she knew I wanted her, and we were both all too happy to make bad decisions together.

Being with Trina feels different. Somehow, I know that a drunken fuck on the last day of school wouldn't be enough to get my fill of her. She's burrowed her way under my skin. I want to listen to her talk about her kids. I want to hear her laugh. I want to wake up beside her and wrap my arms around her body, feel her melt into me like she knows she belongs there.

I want to hear about this new project and support her however I can. I want her to be the entrepreneur she wants to be, because I know she'll accomplish anything she sets her mind to. Anyone with a brain could see that she's capable of big things.

But there's a wedge between us. There's this job. There's the fact that she was so quick to tell me I wasn't worth it. There's her divorce, her baggage. *My* baggage.

There's the fact that our conversation right now is friendly, but sterile. It feels a lot like Trina has moved on.

"Do you ride your motorcycle all through the winter?" she asks. When I arch my brows, Trina smiles. "I saw it parked outside and was surprised. We've gotten quite a bit of rain lately. Seems like it'd be unsafe."

"You worried about me?"

Her blush deepens, and a spark of hope fires in my chest. Maybe she hasn't moved on?

She shrugs. "Just curious."

I chuckle, ignoring the curl of heat deep in my gut. We can't be together. We decided. We're being polite, appropriate. Things are how they should be. I bet she's not imagining her body bent over my desk right now the way I am. "I'll probably only get another week or two of riding before I have to keep it in the garage for the winter. Apart from being unsafe, riding in the rain isn't very fun."

She smiles, and another spear of warmth pierces my chest and moves lower. "Between the pottery, the motorcycle, and teaching seven-year-olds, you don't seem to be the type of man who would mind getting wet and dirty."

As soon as the words leave her lips, Trina's eyes widen and her cheeks turn bright red. Heat builds at the base of my spine, and the flush of her cheeks makes me want to reach over and tug her onto my lap to show her just how wet and dirty I'd like to get. I grip the edges of my chair and try to school my face into a placid expression.

I fail. I know I fail when Trina flicks her eyes up to mine, and I hear a sharp intake of breath at the look on my face. Her blush deepens, and the air between us grows charged.

She stands abruptly. "I should go."

"Yeah." I stand as well, keeping the papers clutched in my hand to hide my growing erection. I hand her the summary report on Katie's performance in class so far, making sure that my fingers don't touch hers.

"Thanks." Her eyes slide away from mine, shoulders tense.

The wedge between us hammers us just a little further

apart. Another reminder of all the reasons we can't be together.

WHEN I GET HOME that evening, I find myself heading for the studio. I put some music on a bit too loud to drown out the memory of Trina's voice, and I focus on the spinning of the pottery wheel to dispel the image of her sitting across from me, and especially the image of her jumping to her feet and angling for the door.

32

TRINA

I SLUMP into a chair at my sister's house. My kids are playing in the living room in the open-plan space while my mother reads a book beside them. Allie, Candice's teenage daughter, is in her room, so I find myself sitting at the kitchen table with Candice, Blake, and a large glass of wine.

I might need the whole bottle after that parent-teacher conference. "Honestly, Blake, you might be the famous actor and all, but I think I deserve an Oscar for what just happened."

Candice laughs. "That bad, huh?"

I drop my head in my hands, peeking out through my fingers at my kids. Those little sponges are listening to every word, even if they look totally engrossed in their game. I look at Candice again and shake my head.

She knows where I was just now. She knows it's the first time since the soccer ball incident that I've seen Mac. She knows I still think about him far too much.

These past weeks have been a strange kind of twilight zone. The days are somehow slow and lightning-quick all at once. Now that I've decided on a direction in my life, it's like I can't wait to get started, but time just flies by without me being able to grasp it.

I remember when Kevin and I first married, it felt like a beginning. Like the start of something big, the true start to my life. I knew for sure I was doing the right thing. Maybe that's why now, even though I feel so excited about my new business, about my kids loving their school, about all the good things in my life, I still feel slightly apprehensive. Like it might all come crashing down.

"I still don't get why you can't date him," Blake says, topping up Candice's glass.

"Shh," I say, glancing toward my kids.

Candice just laughs and shakes her head. "She's in denial, Blake."

"So it runs in the family, huh." He arches a brow at my sister, who swats his arm.

"I wasn't that bad." Candice takes a sip of wine before sticking her tongue out at him.

"I came into the café every day for *weeks* before you admitted to yourself you wanted me." Blake rests his arm across the back of her chair, and Candice can't help but laugh.

"Fine. Maybe a *touch* of denial. But Trina's situation is different."

Blake waves a hand. "Just go for it, Trina. So he's your kid's"—he drops his voice—"teacher." A shrug as his voice returns to normal volume. "Life's too short to worry about that kind of shit."

"Blake said shit!" Katie shouts without taking her eyes off her game.

Yep. Little sponges listening to everything. I glance at my daughter, then shift my gaze to Candice, who gives me a knowing smile.

"Katie, just because an adult says a bad word doesn't mean you can say it too."

She looks up, frowning. "*I* wasn't saying it, Mommy. I was just quoting *him*."

Damn that infallible seven-year-old logic. I give her my best stern look, and my daughter replies with an impish grin. Toby looks at his sister, then at me, and smiles wide. And I'm probably being a bad mother for not chastising the both of them, but the sight of those two smiles hits me right in the chest. I wouldn't be able to discipline them if I tried.

I take that as my cue to stand up, drain the dregs of wine left in my glass, and usher my kids toward the door. Mom offers to drive, which is great, because I feel all out of sorts. We still only have my old clunker car, which I swear I'll upgrade once I have a bit more stability. Whenever that happens.

By the time the evening routine is finished and the kids are down for the count, I find myself in my bedroom, lying on the bed as I stare at the ceiling.

This is good. Life is marching on, and I'm finally doing something. Moving forward.

So what if Mac looked like pure, off-limits sex in his smart button-down and combed hair? So what if I sat across the tiny table from him and wondered how he'd react if I walked over and straddled him? My heart thumped the whole meeting, and I could hardly stand to be so close to him without squirming.

I squeeze my eyes shut.

That's done. I don't need him. He's dessert.

With a sigh, I force myself to think of something else—and the next thing on my long list of engagements and to-dos is Fiona's wedding.

When we worked on her closet, she asked me to help with

the reception. She offered a generous payment for me to style the whole wedding party, which I of course tried to refuse. She and the rest of the girls have done so, so much for me over the past months. When Fiona insisted on paying me, I told her my services would be her wedding present. So now I've got Agnes's closet and Fiona's wedding to focus on, which will hopefully keep my mind off whatever happened at that parent-teacher conference.

The look in Mac's eyes when I made that stupid, *stupid* comment about being wet and dirty. The way my whole body tightened and heated. The way that even though I tell myself I've moved on, that I'm happy with my new projects and my kids and my independent life, I still remember how it felt to be in Mac's bed.

If I just keep myself this busy and don't think about motorcycles, pottery, soccer balls, or elementary teachers, then I can get through this school year unscathed.

Hopefully.

33

FIONA

WHEN GRANT first proposed to me, I never envisaged a big wedding. I thought the second time around for me should be low-key. But over the past months, that has changed. The invitation list has grown to include most of Heart's Cove, and Grant himself insisted on making an event of it.

So that's how I've ended up with an ivory, tea-length dress with a Bardot neckline, my hair tied in a complicated updo with a veil nestled in the bun at the back of my neck. Looking in the mirror in the dressing room of the old cannery-turned-wedding venue, I let out a deep breath and turn to the girls. "What do you think?"

"Gorgeous," Simone says with tears in her eyes. "Just beautiful."

"Congratulations, Fiona," Candice says, just as teary as Simone.

Jen adjusts the hem of my dress, then squeezes my arm.

Trina stands off to the side, as if she doesn't feel like she belongs. What she doesn't understand (yet) is that she's one of us. She gives me a smile and a nod. "You look incredible, Fiona."

"Thank you for helping with everyone's outfit, Trina. We wouldn't look half as good as we do without you." I smile at her, then glance at everyone's outfits. I didn't want to make them buy bridesmaids dresses they'd never wear again, so I just told them to wear something with green in it. It's festive, but still classic. Trina knocked it out of the park.

Simone is wearing a fitted, deep-forest-green dress with matching heels. The tailoring on the dress is exquisite, with each seam hugging her curves like it was made for her. A square neckline gives it a sophisticated air, and Trina added a delicate gold chain to set off the look. Simone's red hair looks insanely vibrant against the color of the dress, swept up in a mess of curls with tendrils framing her face.

Jen looks *ah*-mazing. She's wearing a dark-green skirt-and-top set. The crewneck, short-sleeved top fits her perfectly, and the skirt is high-waisted and hits her mid-calf. She looks like a 1950's queen.

Candice opted for a fluttery dress with a nipped waist and a plunging neckline.

Trina was surprised when I told her I wanted her in green as well. She went with straight, wide-leg pants in a rich, emerald color, combined with that fitted white bodysuit with the low back. She's wearing green earrings, and her bangs, which have grown out to frame her face really beautifully, look awesome. The woman could put on a paper bag and look like she just walked off a runway.

Finally, I let my eyes land on Clancy. My soon-to-be step-daughter is wearing a dress cut similarly to mine, hitting her mid-calf with the same Bardot neckline, but hers is cut in green silk. She looks so beautiful it makes my heart hurt. I've been so lucky to be able to spend the last couple of years with her, and I spread my arms for a hug.

Clancy's lip wobbles as she wraps her arms around me,

squeezing me tight before pulling away and readjusting my veil. "I'm happy you'll officially be my stepmom, Fiona."

"Me too." My voice is choked with emotion, and I accept a tissue from Jen to dab at my eyes before I ruin my makeup.

Looking over my closest friends, I let out a little squeal and spread my arms. I'm marrying the man of my dreams. I'm living my dream, and Clancy will officially be my step-daughter by the end of the afternoon.

But this matters too. My girlfriends—the women who built me back up and gave me a purpose in Heart's Cove with the Four Cups Café and everything that goes along with it.

"I'm ready," I announce.

"I'll let them know," Jen says, leaning over to tick some-thing off on her tablet. Without me asking, she took over the organization of the day, applying the military precision she uses in baking to making sure everything went off without a hitch.

I love these women.

The venue is mostly exposed brick, with rich oak flooring throughout. The main ceremony will happen in a room just off the reception hall, with chairs set up in neat rows and an organza archway to serve as the altar. I stand just outside of it, breathing hard, with a sudden explosion of butterflies in my stomach. I smile as Simone gives me one last hug, then heads into the room.

When I asked Simone if she'd consider being our wedding officiant, seeing as she's the one who brought me to Heart's Cove and pushed me to stay with Grant, she burst into tears, then immediately went online to figure out how to apply for her license.

Jen gets our attention as Grant's groomsmen appear—Wes, Fallon, and even Mr. Cheswick, the man who first intro-duced him to woodworking many years ago—and lines everyone up, then thrusts a bouquet of flowers in my hands. Then, the most beautiful minutes of my life pass as I walk down the aisle toward Grant, more than ready to be his wife.

The thing is, it feels like the first time. I know I've been married and divorced already, but this feels so right that everything that came before pales in comparison. As our procession walks down the aisle, I can't keep my eyes off Grant. The man looks like he was born to wear a tux. He stands tall next to Simone as tears fill his eyes and a smile spreads wide across his face.

We take our places, and in a short, sweet ceremony, my best friend marries me to the man of my dreams in front of all the people who matter most to me.

When Simone gives us the go-ahead to kiss, Grant bands a strong arm across my back and tugs me close. "I love you so much, Fiona," he says in a gravelly voice, then kisses me like no one is watching.

When the shrieks and hollers get too much, we fall apart, head next door to the reception hall, and start to party.

I feel so incredibly lucky. The food is divine—overseen by a hawk-eyed Jen—and every single speech leaves me a sobbing mess. Especially Clancy's. When she showed up on Grant's doorstep, I never thought we'd end up here. I know step-relationships can be tough, but the two of us have carved out a perfect relationship that's as close to mother-daughter as it could be.

And when Grant takes my hand and leads me to the dance floor for our first dance, I rest my head on his shoulder and let all my happiness buoy me. Grant chose our song, and as we sway, I listen to the words of "I Found You" by Alabama Shakes and feel love permeate every bit of me. It's bluesy, soulful, and it makes me cry.

Then we break apart, and Simone, Candice, Jen, Clancy,

and Trina are there to hug and dance and cheer with me. I cry so much I must look like a mess, but I don't care. I'm married to the man of my dreams, my wedding has been perfect, and all the people I care about most are here to celebrate.

After speeches and dinner, there's cake. Jen made a delicious three-tiered cake with alternating chocolate and vanilla layers, chocolate ganache and raspberry fillings, and the most delicate sugar work I've ever seen to decorate it. It's the perfect cake for a beautiful wedding.

I've never been happier.

34

TRINA

I CAN TELL by the look on Katie's face that's she's tired and on the verge of dipping into Tantrum Land. So, weaving through the multitude of wedding guests to a table near the front of the room, I find Fiona and Grant and offer them one last congratulations, then gather my kids up and head for the door.

I feel...light. Seeing Fiona and Grant together, Candice and Blake, Simone and Wes—it made me think about myself, and how there could be hope for me too. It made me feel like divorcing Kevin was absolutely the right decision, since there's no way he's in the same league as the men in this room.

I try not to think of Mac. He was just a rebound, and I need to focus on myself. I *have* been focusing on myself, and I've been happier than ever.

On my way out of the room, I pass Margaret and her plus one, Hamish, arm in arm on the dance floor. Margaret gives me a smile while Hamish winks, and I try to ignore the squeezing in my chest at the sight of them. I haven't been back to the Cedar Grove since our girls' night, and I have no plan to go back any time soon. My future as a pool shark is unfortunately dead in the water.

Loading up the kids into the back of my old car, I give Katie a kiss on the forehead and glance over to make sure Toby has his seatbelt on. He's latched in and already leaning against the window, fast asleep. Maybe I should have left earlier, but I have to admit, I was having fun.

Fiona's wedding was laid-back, but so beautiful it made more than a few eyes in the room teary. With the past month being one long marathon of after-school activities and Mom Duties, not to mention the exhilaration of actually pursuing a career as a stylist, today was a welcome relief. It was more than a wedding, really. It was everyone coming together in a celebration of love and friendship. It made me realize just how easily I've been accepted into this little community.

And I hadn't realized how much I needed that. I hadn't realized how isolated I'd felt with Kevin, and how difficult the decision to leave had been. It felt like I was walking out into the void, with no idea if there was even a floor under my next step.

I've discovered more than a floor. Divorcing Kevin and moving to this town has been like stepping into a whole new world full of friendship and light and laughter.

So things with Mac didn't work out. That's okay—or at least that's what I keep telling myself. It was too soon for me to be with a man, anyway. I need to work on myself, focus on my kids.

The engine struggles to turn over a few times, but finally my car starts. I use the window wipers to clear a few fat snowflakes off the windscreen and blast the heat. The wedding venue is about a half hour drive out of town, and seeing as I live on the opposite side, I should be home in forty minutes. I turn onto the road and flick my lights on in the darkness, settling in for the drive.

The kids are asleep in the back, and I let out a long sigh.

I can do this.

The thought zings through me, and for the first time, I actually believe myself. I can raise my kids. I can navigate the complicated relationship I have with Kevin. I can make sure Toby and Katie end up as happy and well-adjusted as possible.

And I can be a stylist. I can pursue things *I* want.

Just when a smile starts curling my lips, headlights illuminating a triangle of pavement in the dark of the winding road, my car starts to clunk. A rattling noise soon joins it and, frowning, I glance down to see the check-engine light flashing angrily at me.

Uh-oh.

I'm only about halfway home, in the middle of the woods, with two exhausted kids in the back seat. I'm not even sure anywhere would be safe to stop. Squeezing the steering wheel, I will my car to make it back to town.

It doesn't work.

After another mile, the clunking gets louder and louder until it finally stops...along with the rest of the engine. Biting back a curse, I navigate the car onto the shoulder and turn on my hazard lights, checking the mirror for traffic behind me.

I'm stuck in a gentle bend in the road with dark forest all around, with no traffic lights and limited visibility. The snow is still falling—melting when it hits the pavement, but how long till it starts to stick? This isn't safe. Visions of a semi-truck smashing into the back of my car fill my head, until I take a deep breath and try the ignition again.

Nothing. My car is completely dead.

Pawing my purse in the passenger seat, I find my phone

and unlock it, heart pounding. Do I call a taxi? A tow truck? My mother?

With a deep breath, I close my eyes and try to relax.

I can do this. Wasn't it just a few minutes ago that I felt sure I could take on the world? This is nothing. This is a hiccup. A blip.

"Why are we stopped, Mommy?" Katie's sleepy voice comes from the back seat.

"Everything's okay, honey," I tell her. "I just need some help with the car."

"Is it broken?"

"It's no problem, Katie. Close your eyes. I'm getting us help. You can go back to sleep."

Katie, of course, doesn't go to sleep. She sits up and pokes her brother until he blinks awake in confusion. "Where are we?"

"We're nearly home," I tell him. "I just need to make a phone call."

When I step outside, there's a definite bite to the air. I face the direction we came, trying to dispel the fear of someone crashing into us.

No, it's fine. We're well off the shoulder, I've got my hazards on, and everything will be fine. I've stopped in as safe a place as I can manage. I take a deep breath and tamp down the panic rising inside me.

This is fine. I'm capable. I'm a strong woman. Accidents and crises will be thrown at me for the rest of my life, and I made a decision to face them alone. It's a broken-down car, that's all. Everything will be okay.

Glancing at my phone, I make a decision. I pull up my web browser and send a silent thank you to whatever cell phone provider made sure this particular patch of land had service. Then I look up a tow truck company. I wipe a little dot of water from a melted snowflake off my screen and find the phone number.

My plan is to get the car towed and call a taxi after, so I can take the kids straight home. I'll deal with the car tomorrow.

The closest result for a tow truck company is familiar—it's Remy's garage, the man who fixed up my tire and serviced my car back in August. I briefly consider calling someone else, but my kids are more important than my pride. So what if Mac hears about this? Who cares?

"Remy," comes the gruff voice on the phone after one short ring.

"Um, yes, hello," I start, pacing back and forth on the gravel shoulder. "I need a tow truck. Or maybe just a jump or something, I'm not sure. My car broke down while driving and now it won't start."

There's shuffling on the phone, and a noise in the background goes silent. "Where are you?"

"I'm just outside Heart's Cove, on Seaview Drive. About... twenty minutes from the cannery? I'm in the woods."

Remy grunts. "All right. I can be there in fifteen. Name?"

"My name is Trina. Katrina Viceroy."

"That hunk of junk finally gave out on you, huh," comes Remy's reply, followed by a soft chuckle. "Don't worry. I'll be there soon."

I let out a long breath and close my eyes for a moment. "Thank you."

"You on your own?"

"My two kids are here."

He grunts. "Hang tight. I'll organize a ride for the three of you back to town."

"Thank you," I repeat in a low whisper. I don't know why it's such a relief to not have to organize a taxi. It would be simple—one more phone call—but having it taken off my plate feels like a weight off my shoulders. Yes, I'm strong and capable, but I'm also stretched thin.

We hang up, and I slide back into the car.

"What's going on?" Toby asks, his hand reaching to rest on the edge of my seat.

"The tow truck will be here soon."

"A tow truck?" Toby asks, straightening. When I nod, a smile tugs at his lips. "Cool."

Chuckling, I lean my head against the headrest and ask my kids if they enjoyed the wedding. Katie tells me about all her favorite dresses (Jen and Simone's) and how she saw Grant crying when he spotted Fiona. Toby regales us, in great detail, with his thoughts on the food. We've barely been talking ten minutes when I see two sets of headlights coming from the direction of Heart's Cove. The front car gives two little honks, and I smile when I see the tow truck drive past. Thank goodness.

The car behind it is a pickup truck, but I don't get a chance to have a good look at it. The two vehicles pass us, then reappear a few minutes later heading in the same direction as us, having turned around somewhere safe down the road. When the tow truck pulls up in front of my car, I smile at the kids and tell Toby to open his door and step out.

"Katie, you go out on Toby's side. I don't want you walking out on the road."

She shuffles across the back seat without protest, and pretty soon the three of us are standing beside the car as Remy exits the tow truck and calls out a hello. "Bad place to break down," he says, heading for the back of the tow truck. The snow has changed to a misty, wet drizzle, the cold seeping in through my jacket.

"Tell me about it," I answer, then put my hand on Toby's shoulder. "Give Remy some space to work, honey."

"But I want to watch!"

"Listen to your mother," comes a different voice from behind me.

My eyes widen at the sound of it, and I freeze—but Katie doesn't.

"Mr. Blair!" she cries. "What are you doing here? Our car isn't working. It stopped right here in the middle of the road and Mommy called for the tow truck."

Spinning slowly, I try to stop my heart from giving out.

Mac is striding toward us, a soft smile on his lips pointed at Katie. "I heard. I'm here to take you home."

"You are?" Katie's head tilts to the side, and she glances at me. "Why is Mr. Blair taking us home?"

My throat is drier than it's ever been. I still have one hand on Toby's shoulder, who's busy watching Remy hitch the car up to the back of the tow truck. Katie's hand is in mine, but she's tugging at it to get my attention.

"Did you call Mr. Blair, Mommy?"

I shake my head. "No. He's Remy's friend. He's doing us a favor." Finally, I let my eyes climb up to meet Mac's.

It's been nearly three weeks since that parent-teacher conference, and I thought I was over him. I'd been so busy with the kids and school and the business that I convinced myself he was a rebound, and whatever happened between us was casual. Fleeting.

Well, it feels like the furthest thing from fleeting right now. It feels like my whole body has turned electric.

"You okay?" Mac asks softly, and I can hardly take it. That voice, when it's sweet and caring, undoes something that I've always tried to lock in the depths of my heart.

Unable to make my voice work, I just nod. Then I clear my throat. "You didn't have to come here."

"I was at Remy's place when you called," he explains. "I wasn't going to leave you stranded."

"All done," Remy says. "You got everything you need from the car?"

"Um..." I glance in the windows, then open the door to grab my purse. The back seat is empty, so I close the door and nod to Remy. "All good."

"Come on, Katie," Mac says, gesturing to his pickup. "Let's get you home."

"Do you have a tow truck too, Mr. Blair?"

Mac chuckles as I slip my arm around Toby's shoulders to guide him to the waiting truck. "No," he says. "I'm just helping someone I care about."

"You care about Mr. Remy?"

Mac opens the door to his truck and helps Katie up. "Yeah. Him too." He glances over at me, eyes lingering on mine before dropping to Toby. "Come on, buddy. Let's get you home."

In that moment, I decide to ignore his comment. If I think about the fact that he essentially just admitted he cares about me, even though we haven't so much as spoken in weeks, I'll never get my head straight.

I've been good. Really good. The last thing I need is sexy, sweet Mac scrambling my brain again.

With the kids safely clicked into the back seat of the huge four-door cab, Mac opens the passenger door for me and nods to the departing tow truck. "You need a new car."

I snort. "Yeah, well, if you direct me to the car fairy, I'll ask her to drop one off for me."

Mac's lips tilt, his broad hand still curled over the top of the passenger door, effectively stopping me from entering. I watch his hands clench for a moment. "You been okay?"

It's funny how a simple question can hold so much weight. It's the same thing he asked me at the parent-teacher conference. I've been asked if I'm okay a thousand times in my life, but when Mac says it, standing on the side of the road looking at me like he cares about the answer, it makes my throat close up.

"Yeah," I answer softly. "Busy. Good. You know how it is."

He watches me for a moment, the light from the cab of the truck illuminating his masculine, angular face, and it feels almost painful to be this close to him without being able to touch him.

Mac is the type of man who came to my rescue without even being asked. Who dropped everything to drive me and the kids home when he could have just as easily stayed in town, and I never would have known any different. He's the type of man who's reliable, dependable—even when sex is off the table.

We agreed that we can't be together, but he's still here.

I don't know why that affects me so much, why it makes it so hard to look him in the eyes, why it makes my heart feel like it's trying to break through my chest.

He's doing what any decent person would do and helping out a single mother in a bind. But how many decent people really exist? How many decent *men* have ever done something like this for me?

And how fucking unlucky am I that he's the one man I can't have? The one man I shouldn't want?

Throat thick with emotion, I give him a quick nod. "I should get the kids to bed."

He snaps out of whatever stupor he'd been stuck in and drops his hand from the door, but he doesn't immediately move to the driver's side. He waits until I've climbed into the cab of his truck, then he closes the door for me before striding around the front of the vehicle to get in the other side.

I glance behind me and see the kids quiet, their seatbelts fastened and their eyes wide and alert, then watch Mac enter the truck with his usual grace and confidence. Finally, I settle back in my seat and let him take me home.

And I realize that I'm glad it was Mac who showed up with Remy, because from the moment I heard his voice, I felt nothing but relief. I felt safe. I knew for sure that everything would be okay.

35

MAC

I WALK Trina and her kids to the door, giving Katie a smile and a wave before she disappears up the steps behind her mother. Then my eyes shift to the woman standing before me.

The weeks haven't dulled any of my feelings. Ever since the last parent-teacher conference, I haven't been able to tamp down the tiny kernel of hope that's taken root inside me.

She didn't choose her ex-husband. She wasn't with him that night.

That means the two of us could have a chance...right?

Trina leans her shoulder on the doorjamb and gives me a soft, reserved smile. "Thanks again, Mac."

I nearly groan at the sound of my name on her lips. I've spent the last three months trying to convince myself she was just like any other woman. Is she, though? I can't stop thinking about her. Dreaming of her. Reading and re-reading the employee handbook to make sure I wouldn't get fired if we were together.

It was never about the rules, though, was it? It was about

my reputation. About awkwardness at school for myself, for Trina, for Katie. It was the fact that I've built my career over years and years, and I didn't want anyone to think differently of me for getting involved with a parent.

But it's been torture to know that Trina is here, that she's thriving on her own, and I gave up the right to be part of that when I pushed her away.

It was my own dumb pride, wasn't it? I've been so caught up in the conviction that I should be alone, that no woman could ever be right for me. It was the scars from my childhood that clouded my decisions.

But the truth?

The truth is I've known I loved Trina since she stepped into the doorway of my classroom wearing those pale-blue pants, regal and elegant and unattainable.

"I've missed you," I blurt.

Trina stiffens. "Mac..."

I shake my head. "I'm sorry. I just had to say it. I was wrong to push you away and I was wrong to tell you we couldn't be together. It kills me that I hurt you. I just want you to know I'm sorry."

Trina swallows, her eyes steady on mine as her hands smooth down her shirt. She takes a deep breath. "Nothing has changed, though, has it?"

I let my eyes slide away, staring at the paved stones beneath my feet. "It feels like everything has changed."

"You're still Katie's teacher."

"I'll wait. The school year will end."

I know I sound desperate, but I can't quite bring myself to care. I've let my pride stand in my way for three months now, avoiding Trina, teaching Katie every day and wishing I was standing by her mother's side. I've dreamed of Trina's body, sure, but what I've missed most is her smile. The way it feels to have her in my arms. The way she laughs when she's at the pottery wheel and the way her breath catches when she feels my touch.

I've missed *her*. I've missed the way she carries herself with her back straight and her head held high. She's emerged from her divorce with grace and strength, and I love her. I love her so much it hurts—physically, I mean. It hurts my heart to be in her presence and not be allowed to touch her, to tell her.

Trina releases a sigh, closes her eyes, and that resolve I admire so much straightens her shoulders. She looks at me and gives me a sad smile. "I'm doing really well right now, Mac. I've got a new business and my kids to take care of. I've got a lot on my plate. I just don't have the time or energy to put into a relationship—especially when I know that anything with you would be intense and all-consuming." She reaches over to put her hand on my shoulder, and the weight of it feels like an anchor. "I just got out of a marriage that I'm still reeling from. It wouldn't be fair to you or me if I jumped into something new."

"You sound sure," I answer with a strangled voice.

She holds my gaze for a moment and squeezes my shoulder. "I am."

"So you won't even try?"

When she drops her hand from my shoulder, it feels like losing a limb. Katrina shakes her head. "I'm sorry, Mac. I need to focus on myself and my kids. I can't give you what you're asking for."

My throat is tight, and all I can do is nod. When she closes the door, I stand on the doorstep and let a long breath slide through my lips.

As I walk back to my truck, I sit in my cab for a few moments and glance at her house. This doesn't feel the same way it did when she came over to my place after the first day of school. That day, I was closed off and so sure that I was making the right decision.

It doesn't even feel like the last time I was here, flowers in hand and hope budding in my heart. I left angry and hurt, and I ran to my father's bar to lick my wounds.

No—this time, I feel determined.

I know Katrina is the woman I want. If she says it's not the right time, then I'll wait. I'll make damn sure that when the right time comes, I'll be standing there with my arms open.

When I roll the doors to my studio open and flick the lights on, I turn on the space heater and let my lips curl into a smile. I still have a few pieces to finish for the Four Cups order, but that's not what I'm going to work on. Tonight, I'm going to create something that reminds me of Katrina. Something I can show at that stupid gallery opening in January that will mean something only to me.

And if I'm lucky, it'll mean something to her.

36

TRINA

FOR THE NEXT WEEK, I replay that conversation with Mac in my head. No matter which way I turn it over, it always feels like I made the right decision.

I'm better on my own. Ever since I decided to pursue this business, focus on myself and my children, things have fallen into place. I can talk to Kevin without needing an hour to recover afterward. I can arrange hand-offs with the kids and even think rationally about the fact that he'll have them for Christmas this year since I had them for Thanksgiving, which had previously been something that broke my heart.

The first thing I do is buy a new car—well, a new used car. No more fear of running out of money. Things will work out, and I need to have a reliable vehicle. Then, in that new car, I take the kids Christmas tree shopping with my mother, and we end up decorating it the second weekend of December. I promise them that Santa Claus knows they'll be with their dad, and promise we'll do a mini-Christmas here before they fly up to see Kevin in Seattle.

It's a new life that feels unfamiliar, but good. Yes, I can

have family time with my kids and they can have time with their father, and it'll be okay.

I'm stepping into my life with my eyes wide open. There's no more void beneath my next step, no fear of what comes next. I don't think too closely about that corner of my heart that still aches when I look at that misshapen bowl in my cupboard, or the fact that maybe I did meet a good man so soon after my divorce—then lost my chance.

It ends up taking me a week to find my third client. I do about a dozen free styling consultations that turn into a dozen rejections, but number thirteen ends up being lucky, for once. It's a woman in her late twenties who's starting her first corporate job after the holidays. She needs a professional wardrobe that still has personality, and our sessions together end up being a blast.

It's more affirmation that I'm doing the right thing. When the young woman sends me photos of her planned outfits for her first week of work, my heart feels so light I might burst.

I've never felt like this, ever. Like I have gifts that are worth something. I can make money and serve other women and make them feel *good*. I can be as girly as I want, and it's not sneered at.

In the days before the kids leave for Seattle, Katie comes into my room on a Saturday morning and climbs into bed with me. I wrap her in my arms and kiss her silky hair, loving the way she nestles against me.

With her head on my shoulder, my daughter grabs my hand and looks at my nails. "You need a manicure," she announces.

I look at the regrowth on my shellac. "You're right."

Katie lifts her head and looks at me. "Can I come too? I want red and green nails." She wiggles her fingers and beams at me, hopeful.

I don't know why that fills me with joy. It's just my daughter wanting to do something with me, but it's more than that. She's not ashamed of liking pretty things. She's not looking down on me for wanting to do something girly. So, I smile and nod, and take her to a nail salon in town for a mani-pedi. We only give her normal polish, obviously, since anything else would require upkeep and could damage her nails, but my daughter is wide-eyed and giggly the whole time.

"Look, Mommy!" She thrusts her hand at me, and I see the red and green alternating nails with tiny snowflakes dotted on each finger. She brings her hand up to her face and beams. "So pretty!"

My heart is overflowing. When we're done, Katie walks with her nails fanned out as she struts down the street. When we meet my mother and Toby at the café, Katie runs up to the counter and shows Sven, Fiona, and Candice, who all *ooh* and *aah* over her hands.

"She's her mother's daughter." Candice winks.

I grin. Six months ago, if Kevin had said that to me, I wonder if I would've taken it as a compliment.

Things are good. Really, really good.

Then Mac walks through the door with a box of pottery, and my heart nearly bursts out of my chest. His eyes zero in on me, sweeping from head to toe. I immediately combust.

Hmm.

Maybe things could be better.

"Mr. Blair!" Katie sprints toward him. "Look at my nails!"

Mac puts the box down on a table and crouches down, inspecting Katie's hands and nodding appreciatively. "Wow. Did you do that yourself? It's very good. I love the snowflakes."

Katie rolls her eyes. "No, of course not." She flicks her hair over her shoulder. "Mommy and I went to the nail salon." She wiggles her fingers, then prances back to her table.

I bite back a smile as Mac glances at me, laughter dancing in his eyes.

Fiona comes around the counter and shakes his hand, and they both peer into the box.

"That's everything you've ordered," Mac says. "I've included the final invoice in the box. If there's anything you're not happy with, just let me know."

"It looks lovely," Fiona says, unwrapping a large plate. It's the same peach-and-gold of the rest of the order, and as I drift closer, I can't help the tightening of my chest. Fiona hums. "We've gotten so many compliments on our mugs, Mac. You should leave some business cards, or even put a few pieces on display here. We'd love to help you sell them."

Mac's gaze is on me, those honey-colored eyes hungry as they roam over my face. "Sounds good," he tells Fiona without looking at her. Then, with a shake of his head, he says a few quick goodbyes and walks out of the café.

I feel like I just ran a marathon.

Candice catches my eyes, arching a brow. "Still sure about that decision of yours?"

She's being vague because my little sponges are sitting at a table beside me. She means my decision to push Mac away, to focus on myself.

I let out a breath and nod. "Yeah," I say, "I'm still sure."

SAYING goodbye to the kids is awful. They're greeted by flight staff and given badges that say "Unaccompanied Minor" before being led off toward the gate. My chest feels so tight it hurts, and all I can think about is how I'd love for Mac to be beside me, for his arms to be wrapped around me, for his lips to be near my ear while he whispers comforting words to me.

I want to feel the way I felt when I heard his voice after my car broke down. Safe, secure, and absolutely sure that everything will be okay.

But I made the decision to do this alone, and I have to trust in that.

I mostly spend the holidays at Candice's house. I cook a lot, eat even more, and exchange presents with my family. I video call Toby and Katie as much as they'll tolerate. I laugh and I do have fun, but I still miss my kids something fierce. It's not the same without them.

You know who I end up buying the most presents for? Mr. Fuzzles. I fill that void in my chest with toys and catnip, and I'm pretty sure even the cat knows I'm trying to bribe him for affection.

So, when it comes time for Toby and Katie to fly back a week later, I get to the airport well early of their arrival, and as the two of them walk out toward me, I take my first full breath in a long time. I hug them both and kiss them all over until Toby scrunches his face and pulls away.

"Gross, Mom, stop!"

I laugh, then take them both by the hand and lead them to the exit. When I look down, Katie's nails are bare.

I frown. "What happened to your manicure, honey?"

Katie blushes and looks down at her feet. She tugs her hand away from mine and curls her hands into fists. "Daddy said I was too young to have my nails painted. He took it off."

Heat spears through my chest as anger explodes inside me. It takes every single ounce of self-control to keep my features under control. "He did what?"

Katie bites her lip. "It's okay. I didn't even like my nails painted." A blatant lie. Katie was preening for days. She looks up at me, brows high, and shrugs. "It's just something stupid girls do, anyway."

I'm going to kill him. Kevin must have a death wish, because he really went and put those thoughts in my sweet, brilliant daughter's head. I'm going to fly up to Seattle and throttle him right now. Sucking a breath in through my nose, I count to ten and try to get my rioting emotions under control. My vision is blanketed in red, and I feel about ready to explode.

Some last, barbed hook buried deep under my breast-bone works itself loose. For the first time in a decade and a half, I can see clearly.

Kevin will not get one minute outside his court-ordered time with the kids. He will not ever step into my house again. He won't fill my kids' heads with garbage, and he sure as hell won't make Katie feel small. He can show up a day early and watch me close the door on his face. He can come to soccer games, he can try to blot my bloody nose, he can sweet-talk me as much as he likes, but it won't change a thing.

We are *done*. My boundaries will be cast in stone. My tone will be frigid. From this moment on, I will not *ever* let him cross a line I set. So long as my kids are with me, I'll keep them safe from his toxic, insidious, *bullshit* opinions.

I'll make damn sure Katie paints her nails whenever and however she wants.

But before I can find the words to tell Katie that her father is a piece of shit, Toby puts his arm around his sister. "I don't think nail polish is stupid," he announces.

Katie frowns at her brother. "You don't?"

Toby shakes his head. "No. I want to paint *my* nails. I think it's cool."

Her brow wrinkles. "But you're a boy."

"So?" Toby holds his sister's gaze until a hint of a smile tugs at her lips.

"What color do you want?" she asks in a small voice.

"What color should I get?" Toby looks at his hands.

"Something glittery because it's going to be New Year's soon," Katie says with a nod. Then she looks at me. "Can we paint our nails when we get home?"

Tears well in my eyes. I nod. "Yeah. We'll do it together."

Katie slips her hand back into mine, and my anger vanishes. Toby, instead of moving to my other side, takes his sister's free hand. I meet his gaze over her head and quickly brush a tear from my eye. Toby just gives me a cheeky little smile, and we head out to the car.

An hour later, we all have glittery nails.

WHEN I GET to work the first Monday of the new year, the first thing I see is Fiona's face. She's standing behind the counter at Four Cups, and she looks stricken.

There's a piece of paper in her hands.

When she lifts her gaze to meet mine, her brows draw together.

"What?" I frown. "What is it?"

She clears her throat, staring at the paper again. "Fallon just put in his notice. His last day is in two weeks."

"His—" I stop, frowning. My heart thumps. "Fallon quit?"

Fiona lets out a long sigh. "He said he had another talented chef lined up to take his place. A young guy who worked with him before who's not happy at his current job. He said he could stay on for an extra week to show him the ropes if we needed him."

I don't give a shit about the new chef, but I don't say that. I just feel my throat constrict as I glance toward the kitchen. "Fallon quit his job?" I repeat.

"Oh, Jen, I'm so sorry." Fiona puts the paper down and

comes around the counter, and I endure a hug from her for a few moments before pulling away.

"I should get to work," I say. "Amanda will be here soon. She has the proof copy of my book to show me."

I'd hoped to show Fallon the fruits of all my hard work. I wanted his feedback. I wanted him to be happy for me.

But when I walk into the kitchen and see his broad back standing at the prep station, all I feel is dread.

"You're quitting?" I say, my voice coming out strangely.

Fallon pauses as he chops chives, putting his knife down on the board. He turns slowly, his dark, dark eyes lifting inch by inch to meet mine. He gives me a slow nod. "It's time for me to move on."

"But..." I trail off. "But, why? I thought you loved it here."

"I did," he answers quietly, and I don't miss the fact that he used the past tense. He lets out a long sigh. "There's nothing for me here, Jen. I'm stagnant. My life is in a holding pattern, and I need to move on."

There's a sharp, pulsing pain in my chest.

Somewhere, deep in the recesses of my mind, I thought he'd always be here. I thought I could push him away, but I'd still get to see him. I thought, maybe, in time, we could pick up where we left off.

I'm so, so stupid.

"Hello-oo!" a singsong voice calls out. Amanda steps into the kitchen, brandishing a bag. "I've got a late Christmas present for you." Her smile fades when she sees my face. "What's wrong? What happened?" Her eyes flick to the other side of the kitchen, and her face does that softening gaga thing it does whenever Fallon's around. "Hey, Fallon."

"Amanda." He nods, then turns back to his prep work.

Amanda slides up to me and reaches into the bag. She

pulls out a gorgeous, glossy book featuring a perfect, beautiful picture of my salted caramel brownies. My name is right there on the front. Jennifer Newbank.

"You don't look happy."

I glance up to see Amanda frowning at me, so I try to force my lips to curl up. "I am," I lie. I flip the book open as I set it down on the counter, running my fingers over all my best recipes, finally in print. "I can't believe it's done."

Amanda puts a hand on my forearm, and I look up to see a soft, kind smile on her face. "You worked hard, Jen. You deserve it. It's normal to be overwhelmed."

I nod, throat tight. "Yeah. I'll have a look through this tonight and let you know if I see anything that needs to be changed."

"There's already buzz around this book, Jen. It's going to be huge." She puts her hands out. "Huge."

That does put a real smile on my face. I nod, run my hands over the book I poured my heart and soul into, and try to ignore the fact that soon, everything will change.

Fallon appears on my other side, his arm brushing mine as he reaches to flip the book over to look at the front. His fingers slide over my name, and I finally gather the courage to look at him. His eyes are impossible to read. Guarded.

"Congrats, Jen," he says in that deep, rumbly voice. "I'm happy for you."

I just nod, sadness sinking deep into my gut. He's leaving. He'll be gone soon. "Thanks."

Suddenly I can't take it anymore. I have to say it out loud. "Fallon quit," I tell Amanda, jabbing my thumb toward his chest. Then I clamp my mouth shut and turn to look at him.

"You quit?" Amanda says, her voice quiet, subdued. "Do you have another job lined up?"

Fallon looks at her over my head, and I just want to shrink down to nothing. He sweeps a broad palm over his jaw and releases a sigh. "I've got things I need to do."

Amanda frowns. "Things?"

Fallon looks at me, then looks at Amanda, and nods to the back door. "Can I talk to you?"

They're gone for a few long minutes. Amanda comes back first, her face drawn. She grabs her bag from the counter beside me and gives me a curt nod. "Let me know what you think. I'll see you tomorrow."

"Is everything okay?"

She pinches her lips, then drops her shoulders. "I broke up with Fallon five years ago, and I thought it was the right decision. Then I came here, and it felt like a mistake. I missed him. Who wouldn't?" She huffs and glances at the back door before sliding her eyes back to mine. "It was stupid of me to hold on to the past. I know it never would have worked between us. We're too different." She slaps a hand on her forehead and squeezes her eyes shut. "I think I just need to get laid. Badly."

I stand completely, utterly still. I'm not sure if I'm uncomfortable or happy or upset.

Her eyes open and land on me. "Anyway, it's over now. Really over."

Happy. I'm happy. Does that make me an awful person?

"And...how do you feel about it being over between the two of you?"

Amanda releases a sigh and gives me a tight smile. "I'll live." She hooks her bag over her shoulder and looks at me strangely. "How do *you* feel about Fallon leaving?"

"Terrible," I tell her honestly.

She snorts. "I like you, Jen. I'll call you later about your comments on the book." Then she's turning around and walking out to the front of house, her heels clicking on the floors with every step.

A gust of air tells me Fallon is back. Our eyes meet for a moment, and I'm the first to look away.

TRINA

"I'M NOT GOING TO GO," I tell Candice.

She whirls to face me, mascara wand in hand. "Excuse me?" She's got one eye done as she shoves the wand back in its tube and points it at me. "What did you just say?"

I snap my blush shut. "I'm not going to the gallery. Why would I? Kevin's only showing pieces in Heart's Cove because he wants to get to me. He wants to weasel his way back into my life. If I don't go, he can't do that. He won't win." I glance at the door, intending to walk downstairs to tell Allie I don't need her to babysit the kids after all.

"No, if you don't go, he *will* win." Fiona steps out of the en-suite bathroom, a curling iron in hand. "If you go, look at his stupid paintings, and show him that you don't care what he does, he'll know that this is *your* town. If you stay away, you're telling him he can stomp all over your turf."

"Plus, Mac is showing some pieces too." Simone walks in with a fresh bottle of wine.

"I don't see how that's relevant," I answer.

Everyone rolls their eyes. Even Jen, who's the designated driver and therefore not full of wine like the rest of us.

"Don't be ridiculous," Fiona says, thrusting her glass out for a refill.

"Guys, I already told Mac I didn't want anything with him. He said he missed me and I told him I wasn't interested. It's done. As in, finished."

"So?" Simone gives me the sassiest eyebrow arch I've ever seen.

"This is stupid," I say, but I flip my blush compact back open. "Going there tonight is a bad idea."

"Going there tonight is a *great* idea," Candice says. "You'll look like a bombshell, you'll fangirl over Mac's pottery while totally ignoring Kevin's dumb, pretentious paintings, and then you'll catwalk out of there without even giving that asshole the time of day."

I have to admit, when my sister says it like that, it does sound pretty good. So that's how, an hour later, I end up in front of a previously vacant store which has been transformed into a bright gallery with all-white walls. When we pile out of Jen's car and stand outside, the door bursts open.

My mother stumbles out. "It's terrible in there. Not worth it." She points to the car. "We should go."

I frown. "What?"

Candice's eyes are narrowed as she meets my mother's wide-eyed gaze. "What are you talking about, Mom?"

"Terrible exhibit. Terrible art. Waste of time." She turns me around and pushes me toward the car.

"Mom, stop." I shake her off. "What's gotten into you? If it's terrible, won't it be more entertaining?"

"No. Awful. Waste of time." She spins me around again and I sidestep her, only to see Dorothy and Margaret in the doorway.

They both shake their heads. "It's a bust, ladies. Let's go to the Cedar Grove for a drink."

I exchange a glance with the girls and plant my hands on my hips. "What the hell is going on here?"

My mother wrings her hands. Let me repeat that: my mother, Lottie Viceroy, the woman who has never been unsure of anything in her life, *wrings her hands*. "I really think it's best if you don't go in there, honey," she tells me. "It's…it's Kevin's stuff. It's bad."

"Bad, how?" I ask, a pit opening up in my stomach.

"Just…*bad*." She jerks her head to the car. "Please, sweetheart?"

I stare at my mother, and finally shake my head. "Nothing he can do is that bad, Mom. I just spent two hours getting ready while I let these girls convince me this was a good idea. I'm going in there."

Dorothy sucks in a breath and looks at Margaret, and they finally step aside for me to walk into the gallery.

The first thing I see is Mac's work. Three vases are displayed on their own white, knee-high pedestals, each of them more gorgeous than the last. They're huge—almost as tall as me—all sweeping curves and fluted openings. The first reminds me of the vase I broke, but it's about three times the size. It's painted in deep purple and navy blues, with splatters of a starry night sky. There's some sort of metallic glaze in the starry splatter, making the whole thing twinkle like a true night sky. The middle vase is all bright yellow and orange and vibrant green, like a midsummer's day. It has two big, gracefully curved handles. The third vase is breathtaking. It's tall and thin with a rolled top, glazed to look like a sunrise—or maybe a sunset.

I stop short, breathless.

I had no idea he was capable of this. The pieces he made for Four Cups are simplistic compared to these three vases.

There's no other way to describe them but pure, soul-shattering beauty—made by his own strong hands.

"Wow," Simone says beside me.

"I know," I whisper.

"Oh, that *ass*," Candice mumbles from the other side, and, frowning, I follow her gaze to the far wall.

And my stomach bottoms out.

Four massive canvases are displayed on the back wall of the gallery, and I know Kevin's work the moment I see it. Oil paint, all vibrant colors and hyper-realism.

He painted me.

The first canvas is me in bed, wearing my favorite pajamas, a silky, olive-green cami-and-short set that used to cling to my body in a way I liked. He's painted me lying on my side, all soft curves, my clothes hiked up high over my hips and my breasts nearly spilling out of my top. It's...vulgar. My nipples are poking through the fabric, the straps falling off my shoulders. My hair is spread over the pillow in a wild halo. I stare at it, heart thumping, feeling oddly, horribly violated. He took a moment of vulnerability—when I was literally asleep in his bed—and presented it to the world. He put me on display.

The second canvas is me, crying with slashes of red and black behind me. Mascara is streaked down my face, red lipstick smudged. I look like a fucking mess.

The third painting is a depiction of me walking away, Katie held over my hip as Toby walks beside me with his hand in mine. There are suitcases beside us, and I'm looking over my shoulder, through the canvas, the picture of an angry, venomous woman.

And the fourth canvas is a self-portrait of Kevin, head in hand, tears spilling down his cheeks, hair disheveled. Pathetic and sad and in need of sympathy.

Together, they tell a story, and the story is: She was

perfect when she was meek, quiet, *asleep*, until she blew up and took my kids away, leaving me on my own.

"He's literally painted himself as the victim," I say, stunned. My voice is muted, far away. Somehow, my feet have carried me closer to the canvases, and I laugh when I see the price tags. "He wants twenty-five hundred dollars for each of these." I turn to Candice, who's standing beside me with her hand over her mouth.

My sister meets my gaze, horrified. And that's when I realize the room has gone silent. Dozens of pairs of eyes are on me as I turn my back to the paintings and watch each and every person in the room make the connection.

My heart thumps. I want the ground to swallow me up, because this is the most humiliating moment of my life. My ex-husband, the decorated, genius artist, has painted a story that in no way reflects reality. The people staring at me whisper behind raised hands, and I can hear what they're saying.

That's her. That's the woman who took his kids and left him.

I want to scream. Where's the painting that shows him cheating on me? Where's the painting that shows me raising our kids? Where's the painting of me giving him thirteen years of my life? Where's the painting of every snide comment he made to cut me down?

I'm shaking. I can barely stand. I grip my sister's arm so hard she winces, but I can't let go or I'll fall. I can't... I don't...

What the fuck?

Kevin appears in my line of vision, a smug smile on his lips. He spreads his arms. "What do you think, Katrina? Some of my best work, no?"

"No," I answer.

Kevin chuckles and joins me, looking up at his paintings.

"I think I captured the essence of the past year quite well, actually."

"You had no right to paint me," I hiss.

"The muse strikes at the oddest times," he replies, eyes on the painting of me in bed.

I feel sick. I need a shower. I need to scrub my body raw just to get rid of this slimy feeling on my skin.

I want to rip it up. I want to take a knife and tear through that canvas until it's reduced to ribbons. I want to burn it from my memory, from everyone else's mind. I want to erase this from existence, *forever*.

A woman in all black hurries toward us. She leans toward Kevin, her face pulled tight with excitement. "Mr. Paulson, we've just had an offer on all four pieces."

Kevin's eyes dart to me, triumph written in his gaze. "All four of them to the same buyer?"

I'm going to puke.

"There's just one condition," the woman says quietly. "They ask to take possession of the paintings immediately."

Kevin's eyes leave mine as he frowns, looking at the gallery manager. "Immediately? So they wouldn't be displayed beyond tonight?" He glances around the room. "There aren't even fifty people in the room, and they're all from around here." His voice goes up. "No one has seen these yet! No one important, anyway."

The woman spreads her palms. "It's your choice, of course, but it's a very generous offer." She drops her voice. "The buyer said that he would double the purchase price to take possession immediately. He was quite taken with them."

"Double—" Kevin chokes on the word, then he can't agree fast enough. "Yeah, of course. Sure. He's got great taste." He smiles, eyes flicking back to me. "The buyer was quite *taken* with these, Trina, so I guess I have you to thank."

The woman produces a paper from a black folder held under her arm, and with a few quick strokes of his pen, Kevin makes the deal in front of me.

Twenty thousand dollars. Someone paid twenty grand to buy these four paintings right now because they loved my pain so much. What kind of sick fuck would—

Mac walks out from a side room and nods to the gallery manager, then strides to the first painting—the one of me in bed. He tears it off the wall and tosses it facedown on the floor. It lands with a loud slap on the hardwood. Everyone jumps.

I look at the wooden frame, the canvas stapled around the edges, then back at Mac.

He's already got the second canvas in hand and is tossing it down on top of the first. It clatters down, then slides off the first one, landing at an angle.

The crowd gasps. I look up to see my mother on the other side of the room, both hands held to her mouth.

The third canvas lands on top of the other two, and I finally snap out of my stupor.

I look at Mac—really *look* at him—for the first time. He's dressed in black jeans and a perfectly fitted white tee, his leather jacket unzipped and hanging open. His hair is mussed, face covered in scruff and jaw set in a tight line.

He reaches for the last painting, the self-portrait of Kevin crying, then pauses. Ignoring Kevin, he turns to me. "I think this one should stay up. What about you?"

"I..." I gulp. "Mac, what are you... I'm... I don't..."

"I'll give you a moment to decide." He walks to the paintings tossed on the floor and picks them up under an arm. They're so big they brush the ground as he carries them toward the back door.

I follow him, mute, as someone opens the door for him to step through.

In the back alley, a big green dumpster looms. Mac slings the three canvases over the lip and brushes imaginary dust off his hands, then turns to me. "That fourth one. You want it in here with the others, or you want everyone to see an accurate representation of the kind of man your ex really is?"

Oh. My. God.

I gulp, trying to find my voice. "Leave it up," I finally croak.

Mac nods, his face remaining grim. Determined. He pats the pockets of his jeans, front and back, then his jacket, and finally reaches into his breast pocket to pull out a silver Zippo lighter. He flicks it open and lights it. It flickers in the gentle breeze, and his eyes return to mine. "Your choice, babe. Say the word, and those pieces of trash are going up in flames."

"Trash!" Kevin splutters behind me. "You can't do this. You can't ruin them. That's *my* art! I haven't even had time to have these recorded and photographed for my *catalogue raisonné*. If you burn them, it's like they don't even exist. That's my best work!"

The gallery owner clears her throat. "Mr. Paulson, you signed the papers, which means—"

"He *can't* do this!" Kevin marches out, red-faced, hurrying to the side of the dumpster.

Mac's eyes are still on me, and I feel something beautiful and warm spread through my body. This is the feeling I had when he showed up to take me home when my car broke down after Fiona's wedding. This is what I was missing at the airport, when I had to say goodbye to my kids.

It's someone in my corner. Someone who stands up for me. Someone who isn't afraid to fight for me.

I know I'm able to stand on my own. I know I can navigate this world without anyone by my side...but do I have to? Do I have to make my own way when there's someone who could be my strength when I feel weak? There's power in being alone, but being with someone else doesn't mean I have to give that up. I can be in a relationship without abandoning my sense of self.

I know myself now, probably better than ever. And I know that Mac is nothing like Kevin. He's willing to burn fifteen thousand dollars' worth of art—for me. He's willing to erase these pieces from existence—for me.

Tears welling in my eyes, I give Mac a watery smile, and I nod. "Burn them."

He tosses the lighter, and Kevin shrieks. "There's still time—they're flame-resistant! We can still get them out."

The fire whooshes, and the smell of burning garbage fills the alley.

Mac closes the distance between us and hooks an arm around my waist. He tugs me close, his eyes never leaving mine. When he speaks, his voice is a low growl. "I'm in love with you, Trina. If you want to wait until Katie's out of my class, I'll wait, but I just need you to know that as soon as that last bell rings, I'll be heading straight for you."

Tears are flowing freely now, and I barely even hear Kevin's pathetic wails. All I see is Mac, the firelight from the burning dumpster flickering over his face, the soft leather of his jacket stretched over his broad shoulders, his tousled hair, and the expression on his face that tells me he's telling the absolute truth.

He'll wait for me. He loves me. He's *in* love with me.

"I don't want to wait," I tell him.

Then Mac Blair, master potter and motorcycle enthusiast —teacher, lover, protector—kisses me like his life depends on it. I lose myself to him, in him, and I finally let myself fall.

"*You*," Kevin says, marching close to us. "You're the soccer coach. You're the biker. *You're Katie's teacher.*" He rears back, staring at me. "You fucking whore." He whirls on Mac. "I'll have you fired. I'll place a complaint."

"I don't give a fuck," Mac tells him, then slides his arm around my shoulders and pulls me close. "Now if you'll excuse me, my woman and I have somewhere to be."

"*No!*" Kevin screeches again. "I'm calling the police! This is assault."

"Let's go, babe," Mac says, his lips close to my ear, and my lips twitch.

When I glance at the crowd spilling out of the gallery's back door, it only takes me a moment to find my new girl gang, my mother, the ladies from the hotel, and my face splits into a smile.

All of them throw their hands up and scream in delight, which causes Kevin to wail louder.

I laugh, hook my arm around Mac's waist, and let him walk me down the alley and onto the street. His motorcycle is parked near the curb, and I arch my brows. "I thought you put this thing away for the winter."

"Weather's been nice, and I needed to ride tonight, especially since I knew there was a chance I'd see you. I was planning on the fact that I'd need to clear my head."

My eyes flick up to his, and I find myself reaching up to brush my fingers over his cheek. "I'm sorry I pushed you away."

He turns his head and kisses my palm, then speaks against it. "I'm glad you did," he says, turning back to face me while I run my palm over his jaw. "It made me realize how much I care about you. If you hadn't pushed me away, I probably would have sabotaged what we had and hated myself for it. I think I needed the time apart to reflect."

I blink back tears. "Me too," I whisper.

Mac smiles, then produces a brand-new, robin's-egg-blue helmet from one of the bike's saddle bags.

I let out a happy little squeal. "I love this color. I have pants exactly this shade."

"I know," Mac says, slinging his leg over the seat and lifting the kickstand. "You wore them the first day of school."

I meet his gaze, heart thumping. "You remember what I wore that day?"

"You looked beautiful. The moment I saw you in my doorway, deep down, I knew I loved you." He says it matter-of-factly, as if telling me he loves me for the second time ever isn't completely earth-shattering.

Then I glance down at the helmet. "You must have been awful sure that I'd come back to you when you bought this."

Mac gives me a half grin, eyes glimmering. "A man can dream, can't he?" When I plant my hands on my hips, helmet still in hand, Mac jerks his head. "Woman, strap your helmet on, get behind me, and wrap those arms around my waist. I'm taking you home."

So, lips twitching, I strap my helmet on, get behind him, wrap my arms around his waist, and I let him take me home.

EPILOGUE
TRINA

THAT EVENING, Mac and I make up for lost time. We're barely through the door and clawing at each other, frantic. We have sex right there on the living room floor. Then again in his bed. Then a third time in the shower.

I'm going to be sore tomorrow.

When I'm sprawled on top of Mac's chest, my mind flits back to those gorgeous vases. After I ask Mac about his inspiration, he hums, fingers sifting through my hair. "Originally, I was only going to do the night sky."

"Like the one I broke," I cut in.

Mac chuckles. "Like the one you broke." His fingers keep moving through my hair as he inhales. "But the evening after I dropped you off at your place when you needed a tow, I started thinking about our time together. The sunset we watched when we had ice cream. The daylight streaming through the windows when we—you know."

"Hooked up?"

"Yeah." I can hear the smile in his voice.

"You were inspired by...me?" The question comes out small.

Mac's arms tighten around me. He curls a finger under my chin to tilt my head up, his eyes soft. "Every damn day, Trina."

I didn't think I had it in me, but we end up going for round four.

As much as I want to stay the night, when I get out of the shower and wrap a towel around myself, I let out a long sigh. "I need to go home to my kids. My mother is there, but I have to be there when they wake up."

I'm sitting on the edge of the bed, and Mac sits next to me. He places a kiss on my neck. "I'll get dressed; we can take the truck."

WE DECIDE to take things slow for the next six months. He's still Katie's teacher, and we still need to be discreet. I need to make sure my kids won't freak out about me dating anyone, and the last thing I want to do is have men in and out of their lives.

But when we pull up outside the house and Mac gives me a sweet, lingering kiss, I know in my heart he's here to stay.

"We'll have one weekend a month to ourselves," I tell him. "Is that enough?"

"Every single night with you wouldn't be enough, Trina, but I'll take what I can get."

I put a hand to my chest, because my heart just exploded. Then we kiss some more, until I tear myself away and sneak back into my own house, a big smile painted across my face.

KEVIN DOES, in fact, complain to the school, but since there's no rules against Mac and me dating, and we agree to keep things discreet until the end of the year, there's nothing that can be done. I have a feeling that if it came down to it, Mac would quit before breaking up with me, and that is truly an amazing feeling.

Not that I'd want him to lose his job, but just knowing that he'd actually put me first. He'd value our relationship more than anything else.

So, we spend a few torturous months stealing moments together, spending weekends alone when Kevin has the kids, and trying to do our best to keep our hands off each other when we need to. It's hard, but it also feels a bit scandalous and hot.

I focus on my business, and by the time a few more months have passed, I'm making a pretty steady income. Not much, but enough to make ends meet. The business is growing, though, and I pour my heart into it. I love being my own boss. I love helping other women feel better about themselves. And most of all, I love that *I* did this.

From January till June, I feel like I'm going to burst— but the time is welcome, and it lets me broach the subject of me and Mac with the kids. It gives me time to make sure they're okay with me dating, they're adjusting well, and they won't freak out when Mac does start showing up at home.

On the last day of school, Toby and Katie come home high on life, happy to be done with another year, and I ask them if they'd be okay with a friend of mine coming to dinner.

We're in the living room as Katie greets Mr. Fuzzles. Toby flops down on the sofa and frowns. "What kind of friend?"

I take a deep breath. "A special friend."

"Your boyfriend?" Katie asks, eyes wide. Mr. Fuzzles hops onto her lap, curling into a ball on top of her.

My heart thumps. I've spent months getting ready for this

conversation, but it still feels so, so difficult. I nod at my daughter. "Yeah. My boyfriend."

She exchanges a glance with her brother, then looks at me. "What's his name?"

"Well, that's the thing." I bite my lip and let out a little awkward laugh. "It's Mr. Blair. Mac."

Katie's brows draw close together, that wrinkle in her nose on full display. "Your boyfriend is my teacher?" She glances at her brother, then bursts out laughing. She picks up Mr. Fuzzles and lifts him up so the cat's face is in line with hers. "Did you hear that, kitty? Mommy and Mr. Blair are dating."

Mr. Fuzzles flicks his tail, and Katie glances at me. "He says it's okay with him."

Toby snorts and rolls his eyes.

I sit next to him. "If you don't want him to come over for dinner, it's okay, honey. He doesn't have to." The words are hard to say, because all I want is for my kids to spend time with Mac. After all these months, I want him to be part of my life—part of *all* of it. Not just weekends alone, or a few hours when Mom is watching the kids. I want him to be welcome here, and hopefully, eventually, sleep over.

Toby just pushes himself up and gives me a little grin. "It's fine, Mom. Just don't like, kiss him or anything gross like that."

I let out a little laugh. "I'll try not to."

"I like Mr. Blair. I'm glad he's coming over," Katie announces, putting the cat down and standing up. She looks at me. "I'm hungry."

Heart brimming, I stand up. "Let's get you some food then."

A few hours later, after coaxing my mother to spend the evening with her girlfriends, the doorbell rings. Toby changed into a button-down shirt and combed his hair. Katie put a dress on. Neither of them was asked to do this, and seeing them peer down the hallway toward the door makes my lips curl into a smile.

I open the door to see Mac on the doorstep, all jeans, motorcycle boots, and leather, and everything inside me softens.

"Hey," he says, a question in his eyes.

"Hi," I answer, then open the door wider so he can step through. "Come in."

His shoulders drop, and a smile tilts his lips. "The kids were okay with me coming over, then?"

"Hi Mr. Blair!" Katie screams from down the hall. She comes tearing around the corner. "Mommy and I made cookies for you just now. They're in the oven."

"Is that your motorcycle?" Toby says, eyes wide. "Can I ride it?"

"Absolutely not," I answer, while Mac says, "Sure, as long as your legs can reach the foot pegs."

I glare at him, and Mac laughs. He looks at Toby. "We might have to work on your mom for a bit before she says yes."

"Work on me, huh," I say, closing the door behind him. Suddenly this dinner doesn't seem like such a great idea.

Mac grins as he kicks off his motorcycle boots, and my heart seizes at the sight of them next to all our shoes. They belong there, I realize. Just like he belongs here. With me —with us.

"I can think of a few ways to change your mind," Mac says, slinging an arm over my shoulder and pulling me close. "If it's safe enough for Dorothy and Margaret to ride with me, it's safe enough for a ten-year-old boy."

"I'm not following that particular line of logic," I grumble, but my lips betray me with a twitch.

Toby sees it, and his eyes sparkle. He glances at Mac. "It's working."

Mac just grins, and I roll my eyes.

But the truth?

Yeah, it's working. And by the time we sit down at the table for dinner together and I see my kids settle into comfortable conversation with Mac, I know I'll do anything to make sure this is how we stay for the rest of time.

Together. Happy.

A family.

JEN

THIS WAS A TERRIBLE IDEA.

I lock my apartment door and let out a sigh.

I should not be doing this.

Tossing a duffel bag into the back of my car, I lean against the back door and look up at the clear blue sky. In a few short minutes, I'll be driving across town to the set of the hottest new televised baking competition. I'll compete against five other teams for the chance at winning a hundred thousand dollars, some free publicity, and a bigger "profile" that Amanda insists I need.

I still don't know how she convinced me to sign up for this. She said she had a young apprentice pastry chef lined up to be my partner, and laid out some pretty logical arguments about promotion, social media, and book sales. Not to mention a hundred grand to start my own bakery if I win.

But actually signing up for this crazy thing? I blame Fallon leaving. I was reeling, shocked, and I ended up hitting "submit" on the application for the TV show before I could talk myself out of it. Then I had six months to agonize over the decision to compete while I missed Fallon day after day after day.

He left a hole in the kitchen at Four Cups, and it's my own fault for pushing him away.

The drive is short, so I delay by taking the long way through town. When I turn onto Cove Boulevard, I frown at the sight of a familiar Jeep parked in front of the Four Cups Café.

That looks a lot like Fallon's car. It's black, just like his, and has that dent in the front bumper he never got fixed. I wish I remembered his license plate so I could check.

Is he back? After six months of radio silence, he's at Four Cups right now?

Frowning, I slow as I look in the café windows, trying to spot a familiar hulking shape of the man who left half a year ago. Then, seeing no one, I shake my head and turn my face forward.

There are thousands of Jeeps around. Lots of people have dented bumpers.

Fallon left, and he never looked back. He told me he needed to do something bigger and better with his life, and can I really blame him? I'm here doing the same thing.

I check the rearview mirror and glance at that Jeep again. I could have sworn...

My turn comes up, so I take it, and the black Jeep disappears from view. It's not him. Fallon left. He told me he wasn't coming back. He had that tortured, sad look on his face, and he said the words, "There's nothing left for me here."

That includes me.

I wasn't enough to hold him here. He wasn't enough to risk the book.

Fair's fair.

We kissed once over a year ago. Why do I even care?

Fallon's gone, and I'm about to be on television with a co-competitor I've never even met.

It's going to be a total shitshow.

Jen's story continues in Book 5: Dirty Little Midlife Debacle!

EXTENDED EPILOGUE

TRINA

I've ridden Mac's motorcycles a good few times in the past eleven months. Still, as I stand next to it in my blue helmet, there's a hint of trepidation in me.

"We should get going," he says, a hand sliding across the back of my brand-new motorcycle jacket. "If we make good time today, we can make it to Santa Monica by midafternoon."

"I'm nervous," I blurt.

Mac pauses beside his bike, then turns to look at me. He tilts his head. "About riding?"

"The longest we've ridden is an hour or so. We're about to do two full weeks, Mac. What if my butt hurts?"

"I'll massage out the aches." A wicked smile.

I put my hands on my hips. "I'm serious."

"Babe." He moves closer, tugging my hand to bring me nearer so he can wrap his arms around me. He nuzzles his nose against mine, then pulls back to look at my face. "You'll be fine. I thought you liked the idea of seeing part of Route 66."

"I do. In theory." I bite my lip.

His eyes grow intent. "You don't want to do this?"

I squeeze my eyes shut and take a deep breath. I do want to do this. Really. Kevin has the kids for two weeks, and Mac and I decided we didn't want to stay in an empty house doing nothing. *I* was the one who suggested we ride along Route 66. I went down a deep, deep rabbit hole of all the attractions we could see along the way, even if we can only make it partway and back in the time we have.

I think of the wind whipping past my face, Mac's body warm at my front, and I release a long breath. "Of course I want to do this. I'm just being dumb."

"You're never dumb," he replies, then drops a sweet kiss on my lips. Winking, he slings his leg over his bike and jerks his head. "Now get on. We're going on a road trip."

Glancing back at the house, I wave at my mother in the doorway and sling my leg over the seat. I nestle close to Mac, giving him a squeeze with my thighs that earns me a rewarding groan, and then the engine roars, and we're off.

It takes us nearly eight hours to get to Santa Monica. I know Mac is driving slower than he would if he were alone, and I appreciate it. He points out the terminus of Route 66, where we'll start our ride tomorrow. Then, he turns off and heads toward the ocean.

When we pull up in front of a massive hotel, my brows jump. We dismount, and Mac packs our helmets away before grabbing the two small bags we packed this morning. A sly gleam in his eyes tells me he's planning something.

"I thought we'd start this trip with a bit of luxury," he says, shifting the bags so they're both held in one grip so he can take my hand with the other.

"Mac," I say softly as we step through the sliding glass doors into pure luxury. The hotel lobby is all gleaming marble, huge chandeliers, with a view straight through to a sandy white beach beyond. When we check in, the receptionist calls him Mr. Blair and mentions something about a suite.

Then we're escorted up to the top floor, and my eyes widen at the word *Penthouse* on the door to our room.

He slides a tip into our escort's hand, pulls me in the door, and kicks it closed behind him. Then the bags are dropped at his side and he's picking me up to sling me over his shoulder.

I squeal. "Mac! I'm nearly fifty, put me down."

"Quiet, woman." He smacks my ass and start walking across the room. From my perch, I crane my neck to see an incredible view through floor-to-ceiling windows. There are plush couches arranged around a coffee table, a full bar setup, and a massive television on the wall.

He opens a pair of double doors, and I'm soon tossed on a rose-petal-covered bed.

I laugh, running my hands over the petals before glancing at Mac. "This is not the seedy motel you promised."

His lips quirk. "Trina, as long as I live, I will never put you and seedy in the same sentence." He's stripping that leather jacket off and placing it on the back of a chair. Then he grabs his tee from the back of his neck and tugs it off in one strong, masculine movement.

My core spasms.

It happens every time I see him naked. Or any time he touches me, or whispers something naughty in my ear.

"Take off your clothes," he growls, kicking his boots off before reaching for my own shoes.

Breathless, I do as he says. My new jacket disappears along with the rest of my clothes, until I'm lying on the bed in a matching pair of lacy navy underthings.

Yes, I've replaced almost all my underwear in the past

year, and it feels amazing—especially when Mac's eyes go lazy at the sight of me.

I've never felt sexier than when he's looking at me. He makes me feel young and hot and free. And when those sinful hands sweep up my sides and he dips his head down to suck one nipple through the lacy fabric? I feel like I'm on fire.

My hands tangle into his hair, and I let go of a long breath.

Mac growls in response as he lays a hundred kisses down my stomach and across my hips. He pushes my knees apart, using one wicked finger to tug my panties aside, then he gives a lot more kisses in a very special place.

Side note: I've had many, *many* orgasms like this in the past year.

When Mac finally kneels between my legs and thrusts inside me, I can't help the smile that spreads across my face.

"Two weeks of this, Trina," he growls, dipping his lips behind my ear. "Two weeks of just me and you. I can do all the dirty, depraved things I've been dreaming of for months."

As he fills me with another hard thrust, I spread my palms over his back and hook my legs over his hips. I arch into his movements and let out an answering moan.

Two weeks isn't enough, but it'll have to do.

We make the most of our time in the penthouse. A couple orgasms to start the evening off, then a long soak in the over-sized tub, then a few more orgasms in bed before we finally collapse on the pillows, exhausted.

Mac slides his hand through my hair and places a kiss on my temple, and I've known him long enough to know he wants to say something.

"What's on your mind?"

Mac's hand pauses on my head, then he lets out a low chuckle. "How can you always tell?"

"I just know you, Mac."

His other arm gives me a squeeze, and then he pulls away to look down at me. "I want to move in together."

I freeze.

"Don't panic, Trina."

My heart thumps, but I manage to make words. "I'm not panicking."

He chuckles. "I know your moods too, Trina, so there's no point lying."

"Okay, I'm panicking a little."

"You don't want to overwhelm the kids."

"Yeah."

He gives me a soft smile. "Me neither. I don't mean right away, babe, and we can take as much time as the kids need. But I'm getting real sick of spending my nights alone."

My heart squeezes. "Me too," I say, and it's the truth.

"You're my woman, and I want us to be a family."

Okay, now my heart just turns to goo right there in my chest. "A family?"

"Yeah. A family, Trina. The kids don't have to call me Dad or anything." He pauses. "I mean, unless they want to," he adds quietly before giving me another kiss. "I don't want to step on your ex's toes, but I want to be there for them. I want to make pancakes on a Sunday morning, and I want to watch them grow up with you. I want to make you coffee and take out your trash—"

"You want to take out my trash?"

"—and eat dinner with the three of you every night. I'll wait as long as it takes, Trina, but I'm just telling you that's what I want."

I mull over his words for a few moments, trying to tamp down the budding excitement in my chest. Then I turn my head and sit up, letting my fingers drift over his cheekbones. "Okay."

He searches my face. "Okay?"

"I'll do some research, talk to the therapist, figure out the best way to do this."

His eyes soften. "Yeah?"

"Yeah." It comes out as a croak, because holy *shit* I just agreed to move in with my new man. But my lips tug, and then a laugh falls out of my mouth, and then Mac is rolling me onto my back and kissing me hard.

I push his shoulders back, panting. "My mother lives with me."

"We'll find her her own apartment."

I grin. "Not interested in living with Lottie, I take it?"

"I love your mother, but no. I'm sure she'll understand."

"It might take a while to figure everything out."

"We've got time, Trina," he says, body braced over mine. "We've got the whole rest of our lives."

"I like the sound of that," I whisper, then pull him down for another long, hot kiss.

ALSO BY LILIAN MONROE

For all books, visit:

www.lilianmonroe.com

Forty and fabulous

Dirty Little Midlife Crisis

Dirty Little Midlife Mess

Dirty Little Midlife Mistake

Dirty Little Midlife Disaster

Dirty Little Midlife Debacle

Brother's Best Friend Romance

Shouldn't Want You

Can't Have You

Don't Need You

Won't Miss You

Military Romance

His Vow

His Oath

His Word

The Complete Protector Series

Enemies to Lovers Romance

Hate at First Sight

Loathe at First Sight

Despise at First Sight

The Complete Love/Hate Series

Secret Baby/Accidental Pregnancy Romance:

Knocked Up by the CEO

Knocked Up by the Single Dad

Knocked Up...Again!

Knocked Up by the Billionaire's Son

The Complete Unexpected Series

Yours for Christmas

Bad Prince

Heartless Prince

Cruel Prince

Broken Prince

Wicked Prince

Wrong Prince

Lone Prince

Ice Queen

Rogue Prince

Fake Engagement/ Fake Marriage Romance:

Engaged to Mr. Right

Engaged to Mr. Wrong

Engaged to Mr. Perfect

Mr Right: The Complete Fake Engagement Series

Mountain Man Romance:

Lie to Me

Swear to Me

Run to Me

The Complete Clarke Brothers Series

Sexy Doctors:

Doctor O

Doctor D

Doctor L

The Complete Doctor's Orders Series

Time Travel Romance:

The Cause

A little something different:

Second Chance: A Rockstar Romance in North Korea

Made in the USA
Las Vegas, NV
09 September 2021

29898033R00185